THE MISSIONARY

BY JACK WILDER

THE MISSIONARY

ISBN: 978-0-9891044-7-0
Copyright © 2013 by Jack Wilder

Cover art by Sarah Hansen of Okay Creations. Cover art © 2013 by Sarah Hansen.

Interior book design by Indie Author Services.

To my wife, for always believing in me.

1

—Now—

THE STENCH WOKE HER. A thick miasma of rot and garbage and death, laced with something acrid and almost sweet. The next thing she noticed was the heat. And then the pain. Everything hurt.

Something with too many legs skittered over her foot.

She couldn't open her eyes; either that, or she was in a darkened room. Memory was a foggy thing at best. Thought was difficult, her brain sluggish.

What's my name?

Where am I?

She couldn't summon the answers to those questions. The pain made it too hard to think. The pain, and the smell. And the heat. She tried to open her eyes again, and this time, she felt like she was successful. She was blinking, her lashes shuttering against her cheek. She turned her head, or tried to. Something went *skritch* under her scalp, and she felt the tug of her hair catching, so she knew she'd achieved some kind of motion.

Her fingers wiggled behind her back, pinned underneath her body. She tried to bring them around in front of her, but she couldn't. She strained, pulled: pain sliced into her wrists. She was bound. Tied by sharp, thin wires of some kind. She scissored her legs, discovering that only her hands were bound. Blink again, strain against the darkness. Nothing. Was she blind?

She focused on her physical senses: sight, smell, taste, touch, and sound. She could see nothing, not even shadows within shadows. Smell...the stink around her was so clotted she could taste it. Touch? The surface beneath her was uneven and gritty. Dirt perhaps. There were sounds, now that she focused. The distant caw of a seagull, the faint, amorphous din of a city: horns honking, the rumbling of a diesel engine, voices speaking rapidly somewhere above her. She couldn't understand what was being said, but one voice sounded angry.

Then there was a sixth sense. Or perhaps it was emotion, or memory.

Fear.

Not just the simple too-fast thumping of her heart and clenching of her stomach. No, this was deeper, powerful beyond comprehension. This was pure, unadulterated terror. She couldn't summon the reason for the terror, but it was there, tainting everything. It was why she didn't call out, ask for help. She was tied up in the darkness, in pain, and some instinct told her to stay quiet. Avoid attention.

Don't be noticed.

Don't let him know you're awake.

Him?

She wasn't sure who *him* was, but the terror increased to a hammering, nauseating level at even the nebulous idea of *him* knowing she was awake, seeing her, coming back. He'd caused the pain, she knew that much.

Then, a flash of memory.

A hard palm across her mouth, another around her throat, cutting off her ability to breathe, much less make a sound. Being dragged backward, away from her friends. Away from the street. Away from the light, into an alley. She thrashed and fought and tried to scream, to kick, to elbow and bite. Something hard bashed into her skull, skittering stars across her vision. Words rasped harshly in her ear. Not English, but the meaning was clear: SHUT UP. *She thrashed harder, and then something sharp jabbed into her bicep. A needle.*

NO.

She fought it, the coldness snaking like ice through her blood. But fighting was futile. She seemed at once heavy yet light, her body drowsing and drowning until she felt weighted down by irons at her arms, while her mind floated up and away, swirling and skirling and twisting.

She noticed, dully, absently, as the cracks of blue sky visible through the corrugated roof were replaced by a low ceiling. A door closed, its sliding slam signifying something—a van? She was floating, weightless, unable to move. Unable to want to move.

A face hovered over her, round features, narrow eyes. Hard, cruel. He grinned, showing cracked and rotten teeth. He spoke, and the sound was distorted. "Not so tup now, American?"

Not so tup? What did that mean?

Tough. Not so tough.

He pushed her face to one side, almost an affectionate nudge to see if she would respond. She couldn't. She wanted to. She didn't like him. She didn't like his touch. She summoned willpower, and when he touched her again, she snapped her teeth at him, trying to bite. It was all she could do, but she missed. He laughed, said something in his language—her hazy, muddy, sludgy brain supplied an answer: Filipino—and then slapped her across the face so hard it rocked her entire body to one side. She couldn't cry or whimper, but a tear trickled down her cheek.

Then he hit her again, this time with a closed fist, and all went dark.

Her mind felt as thick as treacle, but she knew something had happened to her. She'd been kidnapped.

A surge of panic cut through her like a knife, giving her terrified clarity:

Wren. Her name was Wren.

She needed to speak, to say it, to remember. "My name…is…Wren." Her voice was sandpapery and rough from disuse and thirst. "My name is Wren Morgan."

A voice shouted from above, spitting out rapid-fire Filipino. Hinges creaked, and a square of light emerged over her head, illuminating a hard-packed dirt floor, concrete walls. Feet clomped on wooden stairs, dirty feet in green plastic flip-flops. The face from her memory appeared in front of her, smiling.

"Need more?" He held up a syringe filled with clear liquid. "Yes, I tink you need more."

"No…" She tried to scramble away from him, but only managed to kick at the floor with her feet. "Please, no more."

He laughed and crouched beside her. She drew deep and forced her body to roll over, nearly dislocating her shoulder in the process. He grabbed her by the hair and jerked her back. He was thin and wiry, but brutally strong. She struggled, knowing what was coming. Fear cleared her mind, and she suddenly remembered everything.

The mission trip. Manila. Getting lost. Doug and Aaron and Emily. Hands on her, cutting off her scream before it could erupt.

She fought and fought. But someone else came, held her right forearm in a vise grip, slid the needle into her vein. The plunger went down slowly, inevitably, flushing the euphoric high through her, making her heavy and weightless and warm, making her forget all over again.

The drug didn't mask the pain when he kicked her in the ribs.

Green plastic-sandaled feet tromped up the stairs, and the square of light vanished, leaving Wren lost and alone in the darkness, beyond terrified but unable to remember what she was afraid of.

2

—One month earlier—

STONE PRESSFIELD DIDN'T CONSIDER himself a musician. Not even close. He knew enough guitar to play simple chord progressions without screwing up, and he had a pretty decent singing voice—deep and smooth—but that was the best that could be said.

He'd only really ended up on the stage leading the eighty or so college students in worship because he was the sole staff member with even a modicum of musical skills. To be truthful, he hated leading worship. He hated the attention, all the eyes on him. It wasn't in his nature. He would have preferred to be in the back of the small, overcrowded sanctuary, running the sound and projector equipment, and the PowerPoint presentation Pastor Nick would use during his message. But Nick was Stone's buddy from way back, so when the previous worship leader got a paid, full-time offer at a bigger church, he asked Stone to fill in and there was no way to say no. Nick couldn't carry a tune to save his life.

LifeBridge, the college-age ministry of Charlottesville Nondenominational Christian Church, was new, and had next to zero staff to speak of. Just Nick, who ran the program, doing the message, picking out the worship songs, and about 80% of everything else. Nick's wife, Amy, organized the activities and outreach, while Jimmy, a recent college graduate, did the sound and helped stack the chairs at the end of the meeting. And then there was Stone. Four staff members and eighty students. A tad unbalanced, but it was better than having no staff, or no students.

The kids were there every Sunday night, and they brought friends. They soaked up Nick's messages and sang with energy. They were eager and honest and passionate, and that was good enough for Stone.

Letting the last note hang in the air, he offered the students a small smile. This was where he was supposed to say something to them, something wise and Jesus-y and inspiring, the kind of platitudes that came to Nick as easy as breathing did.

Stone unslung the guitar and stared out at them, his throat clogged with nerves. He could sing without getting nervous, for some reason, but ask him to talk? Yeah…no.

He had to try, though. "Um. I—"

Nick stepped up beside him and clapped him on the shoulder. "Our God really is an awesome God, isn't He?" The students cheered noisily, and Nick joined their applause.

Stone breathed a sigh of relief as Nick saved him from embarrassing himself. He stepped off the stage and put his guitar back in its hard black case.

It wasn't that he didn't believe, it was just that he always felt stupid when he tried to say things about God. Nick sounded so natural, so right—his words always came out smooth, with a readymade segue into his message.

When Stone thought about saying stuff like that, he felt like a hypocrite. Like the students would look at him and know he was a fake.

He wasn't a fake. He just…sometimes he felt like one. He wasn't good and holy and whatever, not like Nick. He didn't have Jimmy's earnest, eager personality. Nor even Amy's kind, nurturing nature. He was quiet, stoic. Words didn't come easily to him. They never had, and they never would.

Stone Pressfield was a soldier. A warrior. He'd graduated from high school at 17, gotten permission from his dad, and applied for the Navy SEALs. He'd passed the physical screening test with flying colors, aced the ASVAB, earned a SEAL Challenge Contract, and within months of graduation was mucking in the mud in boot camp. By the time he was 21, he was a hardened combat veteran.

He'd seen and done things no one in the sanctuary could ever comprehend. That was what made him feel like a fake when he was up there leading worship. He wasn't a worship leader. He wasn't a pastor. He wasn't a good Christian. He was a soldier, and he believed because he'd seen the truth. He'd experienced death and felt the presence of God. He'd witnessed miracles. Bullets that should have taken his life, missing without any explanation. Grenades landing at his feet and not exploding. He'd seen the worst in humanity and dealt death to the scum of the earth. He'd also seen true heroism and courage, seen sacrifice and the power of faith. He'd seen the Gospel change lives. He'd seen acts of kindness transform entire villages.

So yeah, he believed.

But his was the kind of faith grounded in gritty reality, and it was tempered by an awareness of what went on in the world beyond the narrow field that these kids experienced.

Kids.

Most of them were only a few years younger than him. Some, like Jimmy the sound guy, were basically his peers, within two or three years of his age. But

Jimmy, at twenty-three, was still a kid. He'd never left Virginia. He'd attended the private Christian school connected to the church where he now volunteered. He'd gone to a Christian college, graduated with a Christian degree. He was so innocent and well intentioned and naïve that Stone almost couldn't stand him for it. He was a good kid, a great kid. But Jimmy wasn't even on the same planet as Stone, it sometimes seemed.

With a sigh, Stone rested his spine against the back wall of the sanctuary, near the doors that led out into the foyer. He crossed his arms over his chest and listened to Nick's message about being genuine in a world where falsity was king.

When the message was over, Nick dismissed the students, and they gathered in the foyer and the sanctuary to socialize. Stone watched them, listening in to conversations, and wondering what it was like to be so innocent. He'd never been like that, even as a kid. Not growing up with the parents he did.

There was one student who always caught his eye. Stone had to make himself think of her as a student, because that was safest. He kept his back to the wall and watched her laugh with her friends, and he had to work hard to keep his thoughts pure.

Wren Morgan. Short and curvy, thick hair cascading in a loose cloud of raven wing black down her back, dark, happy eyes, tan skin. Wren was a joyful person. She exuded sheer happiness, no matter the situation, and she always, always had a brilliant smile for everyone.

Wren was the girl who would sit in the back with the awkward new kid and make them feel at home. She would befriend the lonely ones, and she would do it with the kind of easy grace that made it seem like she was the one benefitting. She would volunteer to do the things no one else wanted to, stayed late to help out, showed up early.

Stone never let himself get too close to her, talk to her too much. It wasn't smart, or ethical. He was staff, she was a student. Sure, she was only a few years younger than him. Twenty-two, he was pretty sure, to his twenty-six.

It wasn't easy, but he kept his distance.

His phone buzzed in his pocket and he checked it, answering the text from his buddy Sam, who was a Recon on leave in DC. When he shoved the phone back in his jeans pocket, she was approaching him with that delicious sway to her hips.

Knock it off, Stone. He forced his eyes to her face, and fixed a polite smile on his lips. "Hey, Wren. What's up?"

She graced him with a smile so genuine and bright that he couldn't help smiling wider at her.

"Hi Stone! I was wondering if you'd help me figure out the chord progression for 'Mighty to Save.' I just can't get it right."

A few months ago, Wren had asked him to teach her to play guitar, so every Wednesday night they'd sit on the stage together and he'd teach her. She'd grown proficient enough that he couldn't teach her much else, but every once in awhile she'd still get stuck and ask for his help.

"Sure. Show me what you've got." He set his case on the floor between them and lifted out his beat-up old Taylor, handed it to her and crossed his arms over his chest again.

He didn't miss the way her eyes followed his arms, watched his chest as it flexed. He had to resist the urge to flex again for her. He did his best to keep his gaze where it belonged, on her fingers as she worked the simple guitar chords of the song she was trying to learn. Within minutes he'd identified her problem.

"Hold up," he said. "You've got the chords right, but your rhythm is wrong. Here, lemme show you." Bending toward her and taking the guitar, he couldn't stop his eyes from traveling down the front of her V-neck shirt as she leaned over to hand it to him. He averted his gaze, mentally chewing himself out. She had on a small silver cross necklace, a delicate piece of jewelry with a tiny diamond in the center of the cross. It fell free from her shirt as she leaned forward, and she immediately slipped it back in between her breasts.

Forcing his attention to the guitar on his lap, Stone showed Wren the correct rhythm, then watched as she played it through a few times.

"Looks like you've got it," he said. "I should go, though." He had to get away from her before temptation had him looking at places he had no business looking.

Wren's smile faltered for a moment as she tucked the guitar away and locked the clasps. "A bunch of us are going to grab some dessert," she said, glancing up at him. "You should come. Jimmy will be there, and…you should come."

Her eyes held his, and he knew he should say no. But dammit, he didn't want to. And then he chastised himself for swearing. "I need to hit the gym," he said. He'd already worked out that day, but it was a good enough excuse. And he'd go again, just so it wasn't a lie.

"Oh, come on. It's not like you're gonna get any less buff if you skip *one* workout," she teased.

Or, at least, her tone was teasing. Her eyes were clearly appreciative though, and Stone found himself reaching behind his head to scratch his shoulder in such a way as to flex his arm. It was stupid, he knew, but he couldn't help it.

"I really should just go home," he said, telling himself as much as her.

"You never hang out with us," Wren said, pretending to pout. "Don't you like milkshakes?"

He tried not to laugh. "No, I like milkshakes just fine."

"Then come have a milkshake with us."

He glanced at the now-empty sanctuary, where Jimmy was stacking chairs and rearranging them for the prayer meeting on Wednesday. Nick was gathering his notes and chatting to his wife in low tones, then leaving with Amy holding onto his elbow. The foyer was mostly empty too, as most of the students had either gone home or out with their various groups of friends. A cluster of six cars sat idling with their headlights on. Waiting for Wren, obviously.

"Fine, I'll come," he said. "But I've gotta help Jimmy first."

"Yay!" Wren stood up, clapping her hands. "I'll help, that way we can go sooner."

With three people, the work went quickly. Stone couldn't help watching Wren stack the chairs, couldn't help admiring her curves. He also noticed Jimmy ogling her rather openly, and that put a damper on his emotions. Jimmy was better for Wren. He was nearer her age. He was like her, too, from her world.

Stone resolved to step back and let Jimmy have his shot, and even adjusted his pattern in stacking chairs so Jimmy and Wren would end up next to each other. Except, Wren never even seemed to see Jimmy. Every time she looked up from the line of chairs, her gaze locked on Stone.

And this didn't escape Jimmy's notice. He waved at Stone halfheartedly, then cast one last wistful glance at Wren, who waved cheerfully—cheerfully, but platonically. When the last chairs were stacked and the remainder rearranged in the requisite semi-circle, Wren shut off the lights, leaving them in the middle of the sanctuary, bathed in darkness lightened only by moonglow from the windows.

Wren slipped her hand around his. "Come on. Let's go get milkshakes."

Stone let her pull him out into the parking lot, and they each got into their own cars. At the diner, he retreated by sitting back in the booth and listening. Wren would draw him into conversations every once in a while, but since he was several spots away from her—intentionally—it wasn't hard to keep his hands busy with shredding napkins and sipping his black coffee.

It was well past midnight when the group broke up. Stone pretended not to watch Wren discussing something with her best friend Emily and glancing at him every so often. He paid for his coffee and milkshake at the register, surreptitiously adding Wren's to his tab, then waved to her as he pushed through the two sets of doors.

It had been heaven to spend so much time near her, listening to her talk and watching her laugh. It had been heaven, yet also an exquisite form of torture, and he was suddenly exhausted. He was about to start the engine of his '83 Monte Carlo SS, which he'd been restoring himself over the last year. The tranny needed replacing, and the exhaust manifold left something to be desired, but it was a work in progress, and one of the few hobbies he enjoyed.

And then the passenger door opened and Wren slid in, shutting the door. "You don't mind giving me a ride home, do you?"

Stone was flustered. His ride was his sanctuary, the one place he could be himself. He twisted slightly to face her. "Um. What about your car?"

"Emily wanted to stay for a while," Wren said with a too-innocent shrug. "She's got that thing going on with Brett, you know. So I figured she could drive my Honda home and you could give me a ride. It's not out of your way, is it?"

"Well…I mean—sure. Why not." He couldn't say no, not with those deep brown eyes fixed on him. "Where do you live?"

"Not too far. UV apartments."

Stone suppressed a groan. The University of Virginia student apartments were on the complete opposite end of Charlottesville from his loft.

He *wanted* to spend time with Wren. She made him feel...alive and present in reality, which was a huge improvement over most of the time, when he felt like he was drifting and disconnected. Ever since his discharge from the SEALs, he'd been at loose ends. Being around Wren grounded him.

Yet, he shouldn't spend time with her. He wasn't the right man for her. He was too messed up. He had too much blood on his conscience.

He shook his head and started the Monte Carlo with a throaty rumble. The 350 small block idled with a powerful grumble until Stone backed out of the parking spot and headed towards the university.

The silence was awkward. Now that he was alone with her, he had no idea what to say. He glanced at Wren, who was clearly trying not to stare at him, and barely containing a grin.

"This is a cool car," she remarked. "What kind is it?"

"1983 Monte Carlo."

"So is it a muscle car?"

Stone's lips quirked involuntarily. "Yeah, I guess so." Another long, awkward silence. Then Wren laughed, shaking her head. "What's funny?" he asked.

She rolled her window down, slid lower in the seat, and rested bare feet on the side-view mirror. "Just you. You're funny."

Stone frowned. "Why? What'd I do?"

She glanced at him, holding her loose hair in place with one hand. "Nothing. That's the point. You've got the whole strong-and-silent act down to a science."

Stone rubbed his forehead with a knuckle. "It's not an act. I mean, I'm not trying—" He cut himself off, not sure what he was even saying. "I'm just not good at conversation."

Wren giggled. "No kidding. Getting more than four or five words out of you at a time is like pulling teeth." She shoved at his bicep playfully. "I'm pretty good at talking, so maybe I can teach you."

Stone lifted an eyebrow. "You're gonna teach me how to be a better conversationalist?"

She raised one brow back at him. "Yep. You definitely need help. So. Here's how this works. I say something, and you say something back. But you can't just answer the most basic part of what I said. You have to leave room for more...I don't know, more stuff to be said. You can't just grunt yes or no answers, you know? You have to keep things open for us to have a conversation. And...you could always try something really daring, like asking me questions about myself. That's how we get to know each other."

Stone did sigh then. "Wren, I didn't say I didn't know how to have a conversation. Just that I'm not very good at it."

"Well, the only way to get better is to practice. So, give it a try."

"Give what a try?"

"Conversating with me."

"Is that even a word? And, isn't that what we're doing?"

"Conversating is a word if I say it is. And I say it is." She dug in her purse and brought out a ponytail holder, tied her hair back in a tight bun, then stuck her hand out the window and adjusted the plane of her palm so the rushing wind lifted and lowered her arm. "This is where you ask me something about myself. I'm an open book, so ask anything."

"What am I supposed to ask you about?"

Wren gave him a wry glance. "Whatever you want to know about. Duh."

The problem, Stone reflected, was that he wanted to know everything. "Fine, I'll play along. Um… what's your major?"

"Well that's kind of a boring conversational gambit, but you're new at this, so I'll let it go for now."

Her warm smile made something in his belly shiver. "I'm majoring in elementary education."

"So you're gonna be a teacher? Which grade?"

"Third, ideally." She shrugged. "But they'll put you where they need you, and as long as I'm teaching, I don't really care too much. Now it's my turn to ask a question. Ready?"

"As ready as I can be." Stone tried to ignore the squirming nerves, knowing she was going to ask a question that didn't have an easy answer.

"What do you do besides lead worship on Sunday nights?"

"Um. Well, I work on this car. I work out. I do some personal security jobs."

Wren gave him a look that told him she knew he was omitting some information. "But what do you *do*? For a career, I mean."

Stone sighed. "That's complicated."

"Meaning you don't want to talk about it."

"Pretty much." He watched Wren out of the corner of his eye, and felt a niggling sense of unease. She looked disappointed in his reticence, perhaps hurt that he wasn't willing to share the truth with her. "Look, Wren. It's just…it's complicated, okay? I don't really have a career anymore."

She pulled her feet in and twisted in the seat to face him. "What's that mean?"

Stone rubbed at his face with his palm. "Where am I going, anyway?"

Wren just waved vaguely. "Why can't we just drive around a little bit? I live on campus."

Stone turned the car onto a narrow dirt road, away from the city, away from the university, out into the countryside. "I used to be a Navy SEAL."

"But now you're not?"

He shrugged. "Nope."

Wren rolled her eyes. "See, now we're back to one-word answers. What happened?"

"Disability discharge." He didn't want to have to explain, but he was going to. She was persistent, and had a way of drawing answers from him.

"And that means?"

"It means…disability discharge is when you're no longer fit for active duty."

"Well that explains it all, doesn't it?" Stone watched her thinking through it. "So something happened that made you have to stop being a SEAL?"

"Pretty much."

"So what happened?"

Stone cursed under his breath, then sighed in frustration. "It's a long story, and not one I really want to tell. It's…not a good memory."

Wren nodded, but he could see the disappointment on her features. It made him feel cowardly and guilty, but he also knew it wasn't a story a sweet girl like her should hear. Just no, on so many levels, just no.

That didn't stop Wren from giving him a look akin to silent pleading.

"Stop looking at me like that, Wren. Here's the short version, and it's all you're gonna get. I was wounded in combat. My leg got fu—messed up so bad I'm not fit enough for the SEALs anymore."

"You don't limp, though."

"Yeah, well, that took a lot of PT. SEALs are like olympic athletes. We're the best of the best. So I might have been able to stay in the Navy, but I'll never be a SEAL again. So I chose retirement."

Wren gave him a long, considering stare. "You were wounded in combat? So do you have one of those Purple Hearts?" Stone just laughed, and Wren frowned. "What?"

"The Purple Heart. Yeah. I've got one, plus like, four clusters. You get one anytime you're hurt in the line of duty. And when you're a SEAL, that's pretty common. All the guys I served with have one. They don't mean much to us."

"Clusters?"

Stone waved his hand. "You get an oak leaf cluster for each injury received after the initial award."

"So you've been injured in combat five times?" Her eyes were wide with awe.

Stone forced himself to sound nonchalant. *Don't play into it.* "That's just what got reported. You have to meet certain criteria, and it has to be a matter of official record. Not everything we do as SEALs is part of official, public military record."

"I don't understand."

"You know the difference between Navy SEALs and regular servicemen?"

"Special Forces, right? It means you're more trained."

He nodded. "Well, yeah. But it means, because we received special training, that we get sent on special missions. A lot of what I did, meaning, pretty much all of it, is classified. Meaning, I couldn't tell you specifics even if I wanted to. And when we're on those special missions, if one of us gets wounded, it's not likely to get reported in such a way as to meet the criteria for a Purple Heart. And we don't really want them, anyway. We don't do what we do for medals."

"Do you have any other medals?"

Stone shifted in his seat, slowing the car to drift around a wide turn. "Yeah."

"Really? Which one?"

Stone sighed, not wanting to talk about it, but knowing he couldn't just clam up now. "Silver Star."

"Is that the highest one?"

"No. The highest is the Medal of Honor. The Silver Star is the third highest."

"So what did you do to earn it?" Wren's eyes were getting wider with every exchange.

It made Stone uncomfortable, but it also had the egotistical part of him swelling up and wanting to keep impressing her.

"Look, we're getting into territory that I'm not comfortable with. I'm sorry. Do you know any other combat vets?" Wren shook her head. "Well, we don't really like talking about our experiences. Combat isn't something we like to relive. As to how I received the Silver Star…it's a classified mission. Meaning I can't tell you much about it. What I can tell you is it's the same mission that got me wounded and discharged. All that's really important is that I did what I had to do to save a few of my buddies. It was a tight spot, and I…had to get us out of it. It was my job, so I did it. I'd trade the medal a hundred times over to have my guys back. To have my career back."

"You lost friends on the mission?"

"Yeah. More than one. The whole thing went FUBAR."

"Foo-what?"

"Effed up beyond all recognition. It means it went really, really bad." Wren colored at the vulgar acronym, and Stone had to laugh.

"So have you ever—"

"I'd rather not talk about that," Stone interrupted. He hated that question.

Wren kept going. "I was going to ask if you've ever told anyone that story. I wouldn't ask…what you thought."

"Oh. Sorry. No, I never have." He'd brought them onto the U of V campus, and Wren pointed to a cluster of residence buildings. He parked in front of the one she indicated, and then left the car idling. "It's the kind of thing you'd rather forget."

"Would you ever consider telling anyone? Someone really special, maybe?"

"Someone special?"

"Yeah." She didn't quite look at him, toying with a rivet on the pocket of her jeans. "Someone you were with."

Stone let his head thump against the headrest. "Wren, I don't know if I'm—if I could be that guy for you."

She didn't respond right away. "Why not?"

"Why do you want to know what happened so bad?"

"It's not about that. I just…I'm curious. About you." She ducked her head. "I like you. I want to know what makes you…you."

"Well, like I said. I'm not sure I'm—"

"Isn't that my decision?"

"It's a two-way thing, I'm pretty sure."

"So do you like me?"

Stone laughed. "Should I check yes or no, too?"

Wren blushed, and then her expression tightened into anger. "I'm not a little girl, Stone. Excuse me for putting my feelings out there." She shoved open the door, slid out, and slammed it behind her.

Stone watched her walk away, feeling bad for having hurt her feelings, and mixed up about what he should have done differently. He wasn't right for her. Maybe it was for the best that she got mad and left. Maybe she'd shift her interest to someone more appropriate.

But, as he drove home, he couldn't help the disappointment from bubbling up. He did like her. He just didn't think that was a good thing for her.

He ended up back in the gym, lifting free weights until his arms trembled, and then running on the treadmill until his legs were jelly and his scarred thigh was throbbing with hot aching agony. And still, despite the physical exhaustion, Stone couldn't fall asleep for the longest time.

Dark eyes and bright smiles and thick black hair haunted his dreams when he did finally fall asleep. It was a damn sight better than the recurring nightmares he usually experienced, dreamed memories of the mission that went bad.

3

—Now—

SHE COULDN'T MOVE, COULDN'T SPEAK. She woke instantly, and this time the pain was what woke her. She was on her back, hog-tied. Voices spoke above her in rapid Filipino. *His* voice, and three others.

Her jaw hurt, and she realized she was gagged.

She couldn't see, and she realized she was blindfolded.

She was dizzy, disoriented, sludgy. The drug was in her system, muddling her brain.

The four voices were arguing, angry. She tried not to let them know she was awake. Whenever they knew she was awake, they shot her full of that awful drug, and they hit her. Sometimes they fed her, gave her water. Never enough, though. And sometimes, the food had things in it that wriggled as she chewed.

It was something in her belly, though, and that was better than nothing. She was so hungry. All the time. And so thirsty.

She hurt.

My name is Wren Morgan. She focused on that. Held on to it. It was all she had. All she knew.

A hand slapped her face, but she refused to give in to the pain, refused to give away the fact that she was awake.

The hand slapped her hard, again and again. "Up, American girl. Up." The gag was removed.

"Okay! Stop hitting me, please…I'm awake." Her jaw ached and her throat was raw, vocal chords scraping. Even her voice hurt.

"I tink you play games. You awake, play like you not. Stupid American. I know when you lie." *His* voice. Dark and evil and slithering like serpents in tall grass.

"I'm sorry. I'm sorry. Please. Let me go."

He just laughed. "Oh no. I tink no. You make me bery rich."

"My parents, they'll pay ransom. Please."

"I got petter idea." He slapped her again, but perfunctorily. "I sell you."

"Sell? Sell me? To…to who?"

"Dat we find out. Pretty American girl? You wort a *lot* of money."

She felt something cold against her breastbone. She fought to remember what it was, that cold metal thing between her breasts. Her cross. Her little silver cross. Her mom had given it to her as an adoption-day present four years ago, and it was her most prized possession.

A hand grabbed her chin, pushed her face from one side to another. Fingers pried her mouth open, dirty fingers tasting foul. She twisted her face away, and a closed-fist blow rocked her to one side. Her cheek throbbed, and she fought tears. Hands groped her, poked her arms, felt her biceps, rubbed a strand of her hair. Squeezed her breasts cruelly, pinching, lifting, weighing. She fought this violation as best she could, fought, fought. Until a fist bashed her into stillness, and the hands continued to grope and pinch. Her shirt was lifted, her bra jerked down to bare her skin. Her breasts were examined. That was what this was: an examination. A perusal of goods. When the examination ended, hinges squealed and the voices moved away, discussing her in low, quick Filipino. She was left alone, tied up, clothes rucked and her chest exposed. Her cheek throbbed, her skin ached. A tooth was loose in her mouth.

But they hadn't drugged her again.

And they hadn't raped her, yet.

Yet.

It was coming, and Wren Morgan knew it.

She refused to cry.

4

—Three weeks earlier—

STONE SAT AT THE LONG CONFERENCE TABLE, second from the end, next to Nick. He held his tongue, and his temper. So far. But he wouldn't be able to hold on to either much longer.

"…a great opportunity to do some real good," Nick was saying. "This is an area with a huge need. And I think this particular focus will go a long way to showing the people of Manila that we're serious about making a difference in their community."

Len, the executive pastor, nodded. He was a slim, fit, older man with silver hair, steel-gray eyes, and a closely-trimmed Van Dyke beard. "I agree. I think, though, due to the nature of our mission, we should keep it to high school seniors and the college ministry."

Nick nodded. "Absolutely."

Len shuffled through the papers in front of him—Nick's proposal. "Tell me more. I know I have it here on paper, but I want to hear it from you, Nick."

Nick nodded slowly, staring down at his notes before answering. "I've really thought about this, Len. I've spent the last week in prayer over it, and I really believe this is the best way to touch lives. I think we're all aware of how huge a problem sex trafficking is, especially in places like the Philippines and Thailand, as well as Russia. My plan is to go to Manila and set up a kind of safe house outside Manila itself. We'd identify problem areas in the city, where trafficking seems to be focused. Older members of the trip would be in charge of finding those at risk, the young girls and boys who have been sold into prostitution, and we'd bring them to the safe house. We would feed them, and help them understand that we can get them out. That they don't have to keep doing that. We'd help them turn their lives around. And this would be the first short foray into the area. My hope is to turn this into an ongoing effort, so there will eventually be a constant presence working against the evils of sex trafficking."

Stone couldn't keep silent any longer. "I'm sorry, but this is...it won't work. You're not going to accomplish anything like this. Worse, it's actively dangerous. You can't just...go in there and yank those kids away and think that's solving anything. You're just going to stir up trouble."

Len, who had never been Stone's biggest fan, narrowed his eyes. "What makes you say this?"

"I've worked in that area, sir. In my previous career. I agree that sex trafficking is a problem, and I agree that the issue needs to be addressed, but...a group of high school and college kids? Not smart. I'm sorry, Nick, I know you mean well, but this is a really, *really* bad idea. You need a team of trained specialists. Psychologist, security, social workers. People who know how to deal with the particular problems that will come up. The victims of sex trafficking...they're not just forced into prostitution, okay? They're drugged and brainwashed. They're made dependent on the drugs, and they're taught to fear their pimps. For good reason. You really don't know what you're trying to tackle. This isn't just isolated thugs. It's criminal organizations."

Len blew out a long breath. "I appreciate your concern, but I've known Nicholas for his entire life, and I believe that he knows what he's doing. He wouldn't set this up if he thought it would endanger the students."

Stone wanted to scream, but he knew it wouldn't do any good. "I'm not trying to undermine Nick.

He's my friend. I've known him since grade school, and I know he wants to help. He's got the best intentions in the world, and I *know* that." He glanced at Nick, who was shifting in his seat, clearly uncomfortable. "Just…please. Focus on other things. Build homes. That's a huge need in Manila. Bring food and fresh water, medical attention. Just bring the Gospel and friendship. They'll respond. I promise."

Len drummed his fingers. He turned to Nick. "What do you think, Nick?"

"I…I…" Nick looked stricken. He wouldn't meet Stone's eyes. "I think my idea is solid, sir. I know there are risks, but I've got a huge team of volunteers, and most of those who've expressed interest in the trip are adults. Sorry, Stone."

Stone leaned back in his chair. "I want my dissension recorded. This is a bad idea. Please reconsider. Please. I've got experience in this that ya'll don't understand. You really don't know what you're tangling with."

"It's been decided, son," Len said.

"You're coming, right?" Nick clapped his friend's shoulder. "You can be our security."

"I guess I am." Stone pinched the bridge of his nose and tried to ignore the roiling in his belly, the warning bells in his head.

The problem was, he'd been in the Navy for almost ten years. The first lesson he learned, on his first combat mission, was to always, *always* listen to the warnings in his gut.

Stone parked his Monte Carlo at the rear of the church parking lot, heaved his black duffel bag from the back seat, and locked his car. Once approval from Pastor Len had been granted, the trip had come together quickly. Stone had put in his opinions, and on most matters, Nick listened. Still, he'd voiced his disapproval and worry at every step of the way, but no one heeded him. They had the bone in their teeth, and they weren't letting go.

Stone had nearly gone postal when he saw Wren's name on the list of students. He'd gone so far as to corner her the day before, when the group was meeting for one final discussion of the itinerary.

"Don't go, Wren. *Please*," he'd said. "There are other ways to do good in this world."

Wren had stared back at him, seeming perplexed. "Stone…I'm going. I've paid—"

"I'll refund your money myself, right now. I'll write you a check, pull the cash from the ATM. Just…" he wiped his hand down his face and started over. "Wren, listen. I have a bad feeling about this. This trip isn't…I—none of you understand what you're getting yourselves into."

"And you do?" She had propped her fist on her hip, eyes narrowed.

"Yes!" He'd heard the word burst from him, vehement and too loud. "Yes, I do. There was a mission… look, I can't get into that, it's classified. Just please listen to me. Don't go. I'm begging you, *please*…stay home."

A myriad of emotions crossed Wren's expressive face. "Stone, I know you mean well. I do. But this is a once-in-a-lifetime opportunity to do some real good in the world, to change lives and save souls. I *have* to go. If there's risk involved, I'm willing to accept it. I trust that God will protect me."

Stone had wanted to scream. Instead, he'd groaned, spinning in place and pressing the heels of his palms into his eye sockets. "A once-in-a-lifetime opportunity to get yourself raped and killed, you mean."

"Aren't you exaggerating a little bit?" Wren had come up behind him and touched his arm.

"No. If anything, I'm understating how dangerous this trip is."

"I can't back out now, Stone. I *won't*."

Wren had walked away without a backward glance, leaving Stone to watch her go.

Now Stone found himself approaching the two church vans that would take the group to the airport, his heart heavy and his stomach turbulent. Most of the group was already in place, stacking their suitcases and duffel bags in a pile in front of the vans. They were chattering excitedly, a group of eighteen evenly divided by gender. Most were college students, with a handful of high school seniors tossed in. Wren was already bouncing on her toes, full of energy, spouting facts about Manila that she'd researched over the last few days.

This trip was a bad idea. Stone knew it. At least he would be there to make sure Wren stayed safe.

He packed the pile of luggage into the backs of the white Econoline vans while Nick did a head count against the roster. After the last few stragglers showed up, Nick drove one van, and Stone the other. Aside from the eighteen students, there was Nick, Amy, Jimmy, Stone, and three other non-staff adults, parents of the high school seniors on the trip.

All throughout the trip to the airport, boarding, and the flight, Stone's worry increased. It wasn't helped by the fact that he was returning to Manila.

As he dozed in his window seat and fell deeper into sleep, the dream-memory sunk its claws into him, and he was helpless to stop it.

Humidity was like a blanket, smothering him in sweat and heat. It would've been more bearable had he not been in full tactical gear. Par for the course though, and nothing he couldn't handle.

It was better than being cold, if you asked him.

They'd infiltrated from the sea, swimming from a blacked-out freighter to shore, more than a mile in full gear. The target was a cluster of shanties in the middle of a wilderness of makeshift dwellings. It was a damned effective disguise, putting their base of operations in the middle of the slumtown. They could operate in secrecy, right out in the open. No one would say anything, because they were all too busy scrabbling to stay alive.

The mission was to take down a ring of sex traffickers and drug smugglers. The ring was small in terms of numbers of members, but they moved huge amounts of product, both chemical and human. They were brutal, organized, and effective. Local authorities were terrified of them. No one would touch them.

Except Stone and his men. It was a mission unofficially sanctioned by the US government, the kind of mission that you had to volunteer for, and for which you wouldn't draw official pay.

Stone had seen the files. The photos of girls no more than seven or eight, beaten, forced into addiction to heroin, and sold into sexual slavery. Sixteen year old girls sold by their own families for paltry sums. Twenty-year olds kidnapped right off the street, found dead months later, raped and beaten into something unrecognizable as human. Most of the victims were Filipino, locals. Part of the massive South Pacific sex trade.

But—and this was the reason Stone and his men were silently sneaking through the midnight shadows—there were increasingly common cases of American tourists disappearing in the shantytowns. Some had been found dead—brutalized and viciously used, like the locals—but most had never turned up. There had been others, too, not just Americans. Canadians, Brits, Aussies, Germans. Young women from all over the world, traveling through Manila and vanishing without a trace. The clincher came when Lisa Johnson went missing—the nineteen year old daughter of Senator Alan Johnson, who just happened to be part of a spec-ops oversight committee. The senator gathered his enormous bundle of strings and pulled them all.

Find her, *came the orders.* Do whatever you have to do, but find Lisa and get her out at all costs.

Sources were pressed for information, a location was determined, and a plan came together. A two-fireteam unit swam ashore in the dead of a July night. Even then, Manila wasn't asleep. But, there were shadows enough for Stone and his men to slip unnoticed deeper and deeper into the shantytown slumbering beneath the shadowy bulk of Smokey Mountain, the smoldering, two-story high hill of trash that was Manila's sordid claim to fame.

Stone, running point, came to a stop outside a shanty identical to the millions of others. There was a slab of corrugated iron for the roof, broken hunks of plywood and stacks of crumbling bricks comprising the walls. It was so tiny he couldn't have stood upright in it, and probably could have touched all four walls standing in the center, but it was home to a family. Or the others were. This particular shanty was a little different. It had a door, for one thing. And if you looked carefully, you'd see evidence of more careful and skillful construction.

Stone pointed to the door, and then glanced at Benny, who consulted a handheld GPS unit and gave a thumbs up. Stone gestured at another team member, Blake, who examined the door and picked the lock open within seconds, shoving the door open with one hand. Stone rolled through the opening in a tactical crouch, HK MP5SD-N at the ready. His night vision goggles revealed a figure in the small room, and he had a matter of milliseconds to determine if the target was hostile or not.

The AK in his hands made the decision easy. He tugged the trigger twice, and the suppressed automatic submachine gun fired with a whispering click of a bolt. The tango dropped to the ground in a heap.

And then all hell broke loose.

AK fire racketed in the tiny space, shouts in Filipino. Shouts in English.

"Ambush!"

Benny was next to Stone, MP5 clicking, tangos dropping. The shanty was a front, leading to a maze of interconnected buildings. An AK-47 blasted, and Benny dropped, dead. Stone gave the order to retreat, but the street behind them was already bathed in the blood of his fireteam.

There was only Blake, Stone, and Nancy—Jimmy Naninsky—left. They were cut off from the street by the blaze of suppressing fire.

Blake had the door to the street open and was picking off muzzle-bursts with unerring and methodical accuracy. Nancy covered Stone, offering suppressing fire as Stone tried to come up with a plan that would get his remaining three men home alive. The second fireteam was in place still, covering the extraction zone a few miles north. But Benny, Dozens, and Zane were all down. Dozens and Zane hadn't had a chance, mown down from behind at the initial onslaught of the ambush.

Half his men.

Friends, men he'd served with for the last five years. Men with families.

Stone pushed those thoughts aside and focused on the problem at hand. He reached for a flashbang, pulled the pin, and tossed it through the entryway. It went off with a deafening bang and a disorienting flash of light, and shouts told Stone he'd bought them time. Nancy was already through and covering the door, so Stone loped in, dropped the first three tangos in view, bam-bam-bam. Blake came next, leap-frogging to the next doorway, kicking it in with a boot next to the handle.

It caved in, revealing half a dozen terrified girls, all naked and starvation-skinny, huddling on the floor. A tango had one in a hostage-hold, his arm around her throat and a gun to her head. Stone didn't hesitate: a single full metal jacket slug entered the tango's forehead and exited in a spray of gore. The girl slumped to the dirt floor, sobbing silently. Blake herded the girls through the open doorway and out into the street, rejoining Stone and Nancy as they leap-frogged through the maze of connected shanties. They found a few clusters of girls, and set them free. They burst through another closed door, surprising a young man in the act of raping a girl no more than fourteen. He had an automatic pistol in one hand, and as Nancy burst through the door, he lifted it and fired blindly. Nancy dropped him with two slugs through the skull, but took a round to the knee in return.

Stone felt something stinging his eyes, and wiped blood away with his gloved hand; a ricochet had grazed his forehead. He ignored the sting and shoved the dead man away from girl, cursing under his breath when he saw the ragged ricochet-hole piercing her throat.

Through another doorway, moving blindly, hoping to find an exit to the street. Another group of naked, *terrified girls. Then, in a cell in the floor, dug into the dirt and covered over with a thick piece of sheetrock, a group of Caucasian girls. Seven of them, blond and brown hair and blue eyes and green, naked, dirty, blood-crusted, beaten. As he lifted them from the cell, Stone heard a laugh and the thump of something heavy hitting the dirt. He rolled to one side and saw the grenade.*

He lunged to his feet, shoved Blake and Nancy through the doorway, shielding the rescued girls with his body as the grenade detonated. He felt the explosion first, a crumping pressure, then heard it, a sound so loud his hearing popped. And then he felt rockets of agony burst through him, fires burning in his leg. His thigh was exploding, giving way, but he couldn't fall. Wouldn't.

Stone clutched the doorway, his MP5 held in one hand, peering through the mask of blood across his face. He saw a short, squat form, and unleashed a hail of lead. The body twisted and fell, and Stone pushed through the pain, watched the girls scrambling to their feet, watched Nancy wind a belt around his knee.

He was dizzy and disoriented, and he knew he had to do something, but couldn't remember what. He felt something happening to him, glanced down to see Blake wrapping a bandage around his thigh. His leg was a ruin. It was bad. He knew it was bad. Nothing to be done now, though, except keep going.

One of the Caucasian girls was chattering in what sounded like German or a Slavic language, pointing at another door, and then to the floor. Blake, the only one uninjured, followed her and returned a few seconds later with another knot of naked, bloody, frightened girls. Few were older than eighteen. Among them, he saw the target, Lisa, a young blonde barely recognizable from the photo they'd been shown during the brief.

Around him, the maze of shanties burned. Voices yelled. Screamed. Stone shuffled behind the now-sizable group of girls, limping as he tried to avoid putting weight on his destroyed left thigh. A jagged shard of shrapnel was embedded in the muscle, shifting with every step, causing pain so fierce Stone could barely see through the blurry haze.

He couldn't stop, though. He heard voices behind them, caught enough of the Filipino to know those approaching weren't coming to help.

Run.

He pushed the girls ahead of him, pushed at Nancy and Blake. Run. There were too many.

They navigated the maze slowly, following the doorways, ducking through curtains of beads, and then they were out in the dim charcoal light of pre-dawn, three bloody men in tactical gear and at least a dozen naked teenaged girls.

A blast of AK-47 fire came from behind them, and Nancy twisted, stumbled. Stone caught him as Blake returned fire. The girls scattered, screaming. Stone staggered under Nancy's weight, his wounded leg unable to support himself, let alone someone else.

Get to the extraction point, *he told himself. Blake took Nancy's weight, shouting and gesturing at their frightened charges, pointing them north. Stone was wet, covered in blood.*

Nancy was gone.

He heard sounds behind them, let himself lean against a rickety shanty wall, aiming his submachine gun at waist height. The bolt clicked, sending a three-round burst whispering into the darkness, racketing off walls. Pained screams in Filipino told him he'd hit someone. Return fire shattered the silence, a blinding muzzle-burst giving Stone a target. He sent another three-round burst into the shadows above the muzzle-burst, and was rewarded by another scream.

He waited a beat, then shoved himself away from the wall, dragging his useless, agonizing leg behind him as fast as he could manage. Ahead of him, Blake carried Nancy's limp form over his shoulder, arms and legs dangling and flopping, dripping a trail of blood. The girls were huddled together, moving in shuffling knots, holding on to each other, mumbling in a plethora of languages.

Stone's leg was hot, tingling. A glance down revealed that it was seeping through the bandage. All he could do was limp onward and hope he didn't bleed out before they reached the extraction point.

His head was spinning and each step cost him pain, and he stumbled several times, but then black-clad figures were swarming around him, taking his rifle and catching his weight on strong shoulders.

"What the fuck happened, Stone?" Miguel, his voice a low rasp.

"They were...waiting for us."

"Where're the others?"

Stone let his head rest against Miguel, tried to breathe and tried to speak. "Back there. Gone. Never... never had a chance. Nancy? He's—?"

"Gone, man. Blake caught one too."

"Bad?"

"Pretty bad. You're worse, though. That leg looks fucked."

"Feels fucked." Stone couldn't stay upright any longer. Darkness washed over him. "Did we get them all out? Did we get the girls out? Lisa?"

"You got 'em, bro. Lisa is on the other chopper." Miguel's voice held that rough note of male tenderness as he lifted Stone onto the waiting chopper. "You got 'em all out. You shut 'em down."

Stone managed a downward glance as the helicopter banked away. Shanties burned. People streamed away in thin lines, running from the spreading flames.

Except one figure. Stone was too far away and moving too fast to make out his features, but one man remained behind, near the flames, staring up at the departing helicopters.

He heard Blake cough, then spit something up, something wet. He forced himself to meet Blake's eyes. "You're fine," he ordered. "Buyin' me a beer when we get back."

Blake grinned, red smeared on his chin. His breathing was labored. "You got it, L-T. A whole pitcher."

Stone nodded, then let himself succumb to the darkness once more. Someone sobbed quietly. It may have been him.

A hand shook him, and for a brief moment, Stone thought he was back on the chopper. He could almost hear the familiar *whump-whump-whump* of the rotors over his head, the crackle of a headset in his ear. The hand shook him again, and he jolted upright, clutching at the rifle that would have been angled downward across his torso.

Except it wasn't there, and he wasn't on a chopper. He was on a trans-Pacific airliner heading toward Manila.

And the hand belonged to Wren. "Bad dream?" Her voice was quiet. Her eyes conveyed her worry.

Stone blinked, and was relieved that he hadn't

woken up with wet eyes. That happened, sometimes, when the nightmares took him back. Especially when it came to the delivery of flags to wives and mothers and girlfriends, the 21-gun salutes. The first shovel of dirt and the snapped salutes. Nancy's wife, crying silently, stoically, as his casket was lowered into the dark hole. Blake's girlfriend sitting at his bedside for three months as he recuperated from the slug through the lung.

"Yeah," Stone mumbled, his voice gruffer than it needed to be. "Something like that."

"Talk about it?" Wren's hand drifted over to rest on top of his. Apparently she'd switched spots with Jimmy, who had been sitting next to Stone when the flight started.

Stone stared at her small, dark hand touching his lighter, bigger one. "Nothing to talk about. Just a bad dream."

"Dream, or memory?"

"Same thing, most of the time."

"But you won't talk about it?"

Stone felt a rush of irritation. "You're really pushing this, aren't you? No, I'm not talking about it. It's nothing you need to hear."

"Does it have anything to do with why you're so against this trip?"

Stone took several deep breaths. "Yeah, I guess it does. But we're here, and I've said my piece. Just…do me a favor, okay?"

"Anything." Her hand tightened around his.

"Never go anywhere alone while we're in Manila. Always go in a group, and don't ever wander away from where you're supposed to be. No exploring."

"Why?"

"Manila's a dangerous place. What we're going there to do? A bunch of white girls traipsing around the red-light district? It's like handing ya'll up on a silver platter."

"I'm not white."

Stone couldn't help the smirk. "No you're not, I guess. What are you, then?"

Wren shrugged, but he could tell she was trying hard to affect nonchalance. "I don't know. I was adopted. My adoptive parents think I'm Filipino, though. They're not sure, because my adoption was closed."

Stone examined her features, nodding. "I think they're right."

"That's why I needed to go on this trip. I want to know my heritage."

"Understandable."

Wren was silent for awhile, lost in thought. Eventually, she glanced at Stone. "What about you? What's your background?"

Stone shrugged. "All-American good ol' boy. Grew up in Virginia, near Arlington. My dad's an Admiral in the Navy. Spent most of my life on the base with the other Navy brats. Joined the Navy at seventeen."

"What about your mom?"

He stared out the window at the rippling field of ocean waves growing larger as the airliner made its descent. "She was a typical Navy wife. Not much to say. I'm not really close to my family."

"Brothers or sisters?"

Stone shook his head. "Nope. Just me. I've got an uncle, my dad's brother, but he's a colonel in the Marines, stationed in Okinawa for the last twenty years. I've seen him twice in my life. Once at Christmas when I was eleven, and once when my unit passed through Oki."

Wren shifted in her seat, clicked the buckle into place. "Why aren't you close to your parents?"

Stone chuckled. "You ask a hell of a lot of questions, you know that?"

She ducked her head, embarrassed. "I'm sorry, I'm just curious."

"It's fine, I guess." He hated talking about himself. "My dad was never around. He was always on base, being important. When he was home, he was an asshole. Sorry, a jerk. I shouldn't cuss, probably. My mom was always busy too, you know? Always off at fundraisers and brass-wives parties. I just…spent most of my childhood alone, fending for myself. I don't have any reason to like them. I don't hate my folks, I just…don't care about them."

Wren didn't seem to know what to do with this information. "That's…sad. I love my parents. They're my best friends. I can't imagine not…not caring whether I ever saw them or not."

Stone shrugged. "It is what it is. I had my unit. They're my family. I still talk to them a lot." *The ones that are left, at least.* His stomach lifted as the jet lowered to the tarmac, and Wren clutched his hand even tighter, her tan face paling. "First time landing?" Stone asked.

Wren nodded. "I've never been on a plane before. Taking off was kind of fun, but this is…scary. What if we crash?" She fished her cross from beneath her shirt, rubbing it between her thumb and index finger.

"We won't." There was a soft bump, and Stone squeezed her hand. "See? We're already down."

"You've probably flown a lot, huh?"

He laughed at that. "Babe, you have no idea. Big old airliners like this are nothing. Try sitting in the back seat of an F-22 making a night landing on a carrier during a thunderstorm. *That's* scary. Jumping out of a Hercules at 100,000 feet up is scary. That's what you call a HALO jump. High-altitude, low-opening. You've got to wear special gear, an oxygen mask and an altimeter and a whole bunch of other shi—stuff, along with your regular combat gear. You're up so high you're basically in space. You can see the whole earth beneath you, and it's so cold your spit would freeze the moment it left your mouth. You jump out, and you're free-falling for minutes. Not seconds, like a normal jump. Literally you're in the air, falling at hundreds of miles per hour, for *minutes*. Then the 'chute opens, and your whole body jerks. It hurts, because you've gone from rocketing earth-ward at two hundred miles per hour to a full-stop, in an instant. You have to time your chute just right, too. Too soon, and you'll basically free-fall, since the 'chute isn't big enough to let you drift. Too late, and you'll splat on the ground."

Wren's eyes were wide. "You did that? A HALO jump?"

"Dozens of times."

"Were you scared?"

"Every single time. The first time, I peed myself. No lie. I actually wet my pants. The guys ragged on me for months about that, but then, they all did, too, their first time." He grinned, remembering the way Benny had teased him, only to reveal later that he'd done the same thing.

"What do you do when you're afraid? How do you deal with it?"

Stone shrugged. "Well, for us, spec-ops guys, I mean, you're trained to deal with it. Basic training teaches you to keep going no matter what. BUD/S training takes it that much farther. We learn to let the fear have its way, but not stop us. Fear keeps you alert. It keeps you alive. If you're afraid, you're still fighting to stay alive. When you stop feeling fear, you've stopped caring whether you live or die. And that's when you make mistakes." They were taxiing across the tarmac, and Stone was rambling in order to keep the memories of Manila at bay. "You just do what you have to do."

"What's the most afraid you've ever been?"

Stone looked at her. "You really want to know what happened, don't you?"

Wren wouldn't meet his gaze. "Am I making you mad?"

"No, not mad. I just…I don't want you to…look, it's not a pleasant thing. You're a sweet, innocent girl. You don't really understand what you're asking about."

"We're back to that, are we?" Wren said, sounding irritated. "I'm not as innocent as you think. And I want to know because I want to know you. I want you to trust me. I want…I want you to think of me as more than just a 'sweet, innocent girl.'"

Stone groaned. "Wren, that's not a good idea. Not with me."

She stared at him, clearly angry again. The flight attendant announced the gate information, local time, the usual post-landing welcoming spiel. When the doors were opened, Wren lurched out of her seat, grabbed her carry-on from the overhead compartment and stormed off the plane, losing herself in the cluster of disembarking students. Stone let her go, hating the glimmer of tears he'd seen in her eyes.

Once off the plane and through baggage claim, he felt the wave of heat and humidity roll over him. The sun was high and hot, the sky the bluest blue. The smell came next, the familiar burn of Manila.

His stomach roiled, the churning of buried fear, the knowledge of approaching danger.

5

—Now—

SHE HAD TO FIGHT IT. It was coming, it was going to happen, and soon. She'd rather die than endure that. As *he* clomped down the creaking wooden steps, Wren realized with a bolt of horrified awareness, that she very literally would rather die than let him—or anyone else—rape her.

He knelt in front of her, a cruel smile on his lips. "I got prends come to see you. Pretty American girl, not look like no American girl. Dese prends, dey come see. Maybe, dey want try you. Yes? I make a good deal." He grabbed her upper lip and twisted it so hard she couldn't stop the yelp of pain and the start of tears. "You keep shut up, I don't let them try you before buy you. You like dat? No, I don't tink so. You keep shut your stupid mout, dey look, dey touch, but dey not gonna *fuck* you." He hissed the vile, vulgar word, spitting vitriol, making the 'f' sound almost a 'p', but not quite: *ppffuck*.

He smacked her none-too-gently, hard enough to make her ears ring and the cross around her neck swing free and dangle in the darkness. Then he left.

And that was when Wren understood, fully, that he wasn't just an opportunistic animal. He'd hit her, but he hadn't damaged her. He'd forced drugs on her, but he hadn't raped her, or let anyone else do so. He was saving her, keeping her intact. Keeping a product in prime condition so he could reap a maximum profit.

Wren was young and sheltered, and she knew she was naive in some ways, especially when it came to men, but she was far from stupid. She wasn't a virgin, but the few experiences she'd had only served to emphasize how awful things were going to get.

Unless a miracle happened. Unless someone saved her.

Someone like Stone.

Even tied up, in pain, drug-fogged and addled, terrified and alone, she shivered at the thought of Stone Pressfield. Huge, hard, mysterious, and difficult, Stone was…everything a girl could want. Six-foot-four, a body Adonis would be jealous of, close-cropped dark blond hair and deep brown, almost black eyes. But he was out of reach. He'd made it clear he wasn't interested. Not like that, at least. He'd made it clear she wasn't enough for him.

That didn't stop her, in the darkness of a dirty, bug-infested, smelly hole in the ground prison cell, from wishing for him, from hoping and praying that he would come for her.

As she fell into an exhausted, frightened doze, Wren let herself imagine Stone bursting through the trap door and rescuing her.

It was small comfort, but it was something.

6

—One week earlier—

IT WAS AS IF HE WAS DRAWN TO HER by some strange magnetic force. For the last two and a half weeks, Stone had run himself ragged, scouting locations before the missions team arrived, operating as security while they did their futile, dangerous work in the slums and the red light district, talking to prostitutes and paying them to spend time in the hostel, feeding them, offering them Bible tracts and prayer and smiles and promises of freedom from prostitution.

And all the while, Wren had stayed on the edges of his awareness. Crouching beside a frail nineteen year old Taiwanese girl who'd been a prostitute since the age of six, smiling as she mixed poorly accented Filipino phrases with too-loud English. Playing checkers with a ten year old girl who'd been sold by her own parents. Serving food and bottles of water, never shrinking away from bad smells or harsh, distrustful glares. Stone would stand a few feet away from Wren, watching for the pimps and dealers who signaled trouble, and he would find himself unable to keep his eyes off her. Her ink-black hair would fall across her eyes, and she would brush it away with her graceful fingers. Her tank-top would ride up, revealing a sliver of dark skin, and she would tug it down absently. Sweat would run down her forehead, and she would wipe it away carelessly. Stone couldn't *not* watch her. She was beautiful—and always, always kind. She never ran out of patience, and she was always the last one to stop working. The first one to volunteer.

How could he not be attracted to her? But it wouldn't—couldn't—go anywhere past that.

Not when he still had nightmares of bullet-riddled bodies, and memories of pulling the trigger that sent those bullets. He woke up sweating and terrified most nights, reliving and remembering. Wren didn't deserve that.

So, he kept to himself, watched the students, and watched the streets. Followed behind the group as they made their way to dinner, guarded the bathrooms while they took showers. Kept his hand near the cheap but functional 9mm pistol he'd gotten ahold of within hours of wheels-down.

He was starting to think his intuition had been wrong. The trip was days from completion and nothing bad had happened. Less than a week to go, and the students would be boarding a plane for the States. Which meant Wren would be safe. He prayed the next five days would go quickly. Yet, the feeling persisted. The troubled, gnawing sense of unease in his belly.

He refused to let anyone from the group leave the hostel without him, and without at least four other people. He slept with his pistol under his pillow, as lightly as if he was in the field with his unit again.

When he didn't dream of the raid in Manila, he dreamed of Wren, of the hopeful gleam in her eyes when she'd told him she wished he would see her as someone other than a sweet, innocent girl.

Friday. Less than forty-eight hours before their flight out of Manila. They'd spent the last twelve hours going out in groups of six, Stone as escort and tour-guide, seeing sights and having fun, unwinding before leaving for home. Now, he was at the head of the last bunch of students, leading them through the thronging crowds. They'd had *pho* for dinner, bought trinkets and t-shirts and postcards and souvenirs. Having been on his feet since eight that morning, Stone was exhausted. Holding up the level of vigilance he had over the last three weeks was like tensing his muscles, not just for hours on end, but for days and weeks without stop. The mind and body just weren't made for it. But he couldn't relax. Not yet.

He stopped at an intersection and did a head count: all six students were there, including Wren. The traffic light turned, and he led them across the street, watching the traffic on all sides, scanning the crowds.

A squeal of tires. Angry shouts in Filipino. Stone whirled in place, shoving back through the crowd to the edge of the sidewalk. Wren and three others hadn't made it across the street, and had been nearly run over by a taxi before scrambling back to the far sidewalk. Stone cursed under his breath. He met Wren's eyes, pointed at her and mouthed *stay there.* She nodded, and Stone turned back to the two students who'd made it with him.

He herded them up against the wall, next to the doorway of a liquor store. "Stay here," he ordered, his voice gruff, taking on the tone of command. "I mean it. Don't move, not for anything. Don't talk to anyone, don't answer questions, nothing. Just stand right the f—right here. Got it?" The two students, a high school senior named Brett and a college freshman named Leslie, nodded, eyes wide. They clutched hands, and Stone clapped Brett on the shoulder. "I'll be right back."

Stone brushed his hand against the butt of the pistol at the small of his back, hidden under his loose gray Navy T-shirt. Wren and the other students were still standing on the corner, waiting for the light to turn. It was a busy intersection, four lanes of crazy, honking, speeding traffic. The crowds were growing as evening neared, bringing with it relief from the heat and humidity. Stone bounced on his toes, keeping his eyes locked on the small knot of students, then burst into a run as the light turned and the waiting crowd on the other side surged into motion, carrying Wren and the other three with them. He caught Wren's arm in his right hand, wrapping his left arm around the other three, and hustled them across the street, not breathing until they were safe on the other side with Brett and Leslie.

"Next time, run across. Don't get separated again." He met each of their eyes, received serious nods in return.

They made it back to the hostel, and Stone rested his aching feet before rounding up the last group, mostly volunteer staff and older college students. As they ate tacos and shopped, his sense of unease heightened. Every step had him scanning the crowds, hunting for the source of his fear. But like every day for the past two weeks, he saw nothing unusual. No tails, no suspicious faces.

Nonetheless, his gut churned as he led the last group back to the hostel.

And that was when it came, the disaster he'd been waiting for, half a block from the hostel.

"Stone! Stone!" Emily, one of Wren's friends—a tall, slim girl with nut-brown hair. She was running toward him, panic scarring her face.

"Emily? Are you hurt?"

"No, no. I don't know what happened! We went to the corner store to get some water, all four of us together. It wasn't even a block, and we were all together the whole way, I promise! We even told John we were going. And then we turned around and she just wasn't there, and we can't find her!"

Stone felt his gut clench. "Take a breath, Em. Slow down. What happened? Who's not there?"

"Wren! We can't find her! She was with us, right there with us the whole time. And then she just wasn't. We went back to the store but they hadn't seen her since we left, and she's not here, and—What if something happened to her? Where would she go? We have to find her! Please!" Emily was sobbing now, trying not to and failing.

Stone swore under his breath. "Where are the others you were with?"

"There." She pointed to two guys, sophomores at UV with Emily and Wren.

The guys weren't crying, but they were clearly upset. "What happened?" Stone demanded.

Doug told a version of Emily's story. "We were like, a hundred feet from the hostel, and I turned around and realized Wren wasn't with us. She just… she just vanished, man! I don't know what happened. She didn't say anything, didn't make a noise, just… poof, gone."

"Show me where you realized she was gone." He pointed to other two. "You two, back to hostel. Tell John I said no one leaves. No one, for anything."

Doug brought Stone to a spot a few hundred feet from the hostel, a random location on the sidewalk, just like any other. No sign of Wren, no clues. He stood and tried to think. Wren wouldn't just run off without telling her friends. If she'd been hurt, she would have told them, made a noise. There wasn't any blood anywhere, no dropped articles. Just a hole-in-the-wall restaurant, an electronics shop, and the entrance to an alley, dark, wet, and smelly.

"Anything else you can think of? Anything?"

Doug shook his head, long blond surfer-style shaggy hair flopping. "No, man. Nothing."

Stone took a few steps into the alley. The concrete was wet and rucked and puddled, a dumpster on one wall, bags of trash and an abandoned men's shoe, a broken wooden crate. A rusted, red-metal doorway led into the electronics shop on the left side, and on the right, a blank stone wall. At the end, another street, cars passing intermittently. Power lines overhead.

He turned in place, desperate for any clues, anything.

There. A cigarette butt on the ground. Crushed underfoot, but the white end of the cigarette was still white, recent. Not mud-stained or faded.

"Did a vehicle come out of this alley?"

Doug started to shake his head, then stopped. "Actually, yeah. A van or a truck or something. I don't know. I was looking for Wren, but I do remember seeing some kind of vehicle pull out of here. I only noticed it because I was facing the alley, wondering if she'd gone back for something."

Stone guided Doug back to the hostel, then found Pastor Nick and John, a parent volunteer and one of the deacons of the church. "Wren is missing."

Nick paled. "What? What do you mean she's missing?"

Stone didn't try to mask the anger in his voice. "She and three other students went to the corner store to buy water, and Wren vanished on the way back." He looked at John. "They said they asked you first, and you let them go, *against* the policy we've gone by for the last three weeks."

John nodded numbly. "They told me they were just going to the corner. It's not even half a block. I thought it would be fine."

Nick wiped his face with both hands. "What's the next step then?"

"Contact the US embassy, file a missing persons report. I'll look for her while you do that. John, you stay here with the students. Gather everyone and stay together. No one goes anywhere. Not ten steps out of your sight." He stabbed John in the shoulder with a finger. "I mean that, deadly serious. Not one person takes one fucking step out of your sight. Not for water, not to pee, not for anything."

John nodded, his eyes wide with fear. "Yeah, yeah, I got it."

"Nick, go to the embassy. Give them Wren's information, show them her picture."

"Don't you have contacts in the embassy?" Nick asked.

"I'll follow up with them later if I need to, but for now I need to look for Wren. Every second counts."

"What do you think happened?" Nick kept his voice down, but his worry was palpable.

"I don't know. Maybe she just got turned around or something." He met Nick's eyes, and knew he had to give his friend the truth. "I'm worried she got snatched, though."

"Snatched by who?"

"The bad guys." Stone couldn't make himself say it. He pulled his pistol from his waistband, ejected the clip and checked the loads, more for something to do than anything else. It was a familiar action, one that helped him feel more like a Navy SEAL than a helpless church worship leader. "Get the kids home. Get them to the airport tomorrow, and get them home. I'll find Wren."

He shoved the pistol back in his waistband and left the hostel, mind whirling with possibilities, contacts, potential locations, people he could shake down for information.

He returned to the alley where his gut told him Wren had been abducted. There weren't any extra clues, just that one cigarette butt. Some oil on the ground, dripped from an old engine. Stone felt the rage of helplessness bite at him. Where to begin? He was a warrior, not an investigator. Others sniffed out the information. He acted on it.

His gaze flicked across the street, landed on an abandoned, shuttered shopfront, graffiti-tagged and piled up with trash. There, almost completely hidden in the piles of trash in one corner, was an old man. He was nothing but a dirty, straggly beard and small, beady eyes lost amidst the newspapers and food wrappers and Coke bottles and plastic bags.

Stone felt a fleeting glimmer of hope as he jogged through traffic and crouched in front of the derelict.

"You see something happen there?" Stone asked in rough but passable Filipino.

"See nothing." The old man spoke Filipino as roughly as Stone. He probably spoke some obscure dialect. He claimed ignorance, but grime-crusted fingers made themselves visible through the trash.

"You sure?" He dug a wad of Philippine Pesos from his jeans pocket, stuffed a few bills into the outstretched fingers.

"A truck. Some men. They take a girl, American, look Filipino."

Stone bit back a curse. He shoved a few more bills into the now-empty hand. *"Who take her? You know?"*

The old man shook his head, beard waggling. True terror flashed in his eyes. *"Not say. Not say. You look Smokey Mountain. Maybe find her there."*

Stone peeled yet more pesos from the wad and shoved them at the old man, who only shook his head and refused to take them, burrowing down into the trash. A stump protruded from the garbage, where a foot had once been. *"Who was it? Who are they?"*

"Not say! They know."

That in itself told Stone several things. First, if an old homeless cripple was afraid of talking about them, then he knew who they were. And if he was afraid of talking about them, they were organized, and brutal. He remembered the briefings before his team had landed in Manila, rumors of informants disappearing. Snitches turning up dead. Sources of information drying up cold, frozen by terror.

Stone also remembered debriefing interviews with the girls he and his team had rescued at such great cost. They spoke of quick and silent abductions. Needles in the arm, brutal beatings and forced addictions, being sold to the highest bidder into sexual slavery.

Something told Stone that his team's strike had only set back the trafficking ring, hadn't killed the beast entirely. Organizations like that were hydras, seven heads emerging for every one you cut off.

And now they were back, and they had Wren.

He left the old man cowering in his den of garbage, flagged a passing taxi and named an intersection far across the city. He set out on foot, navigating narrow streets and busy intersections. In the distance, a mountain of trash loomed, a two-story monument of waste covering several acres, wreathed in smoke and fumes. The closer he got, the more looks his presence received. He was a lone white man in a place most residents of Manila avoided. To one side were the tenement apartments the government had built several years ago, which now housed thousands of people who used to live on the trash mountain itself.

The shantytown spreading from the base of the mountain was a world of its own, a maze of tin and rot and desperation, tumbledown heaps of refuse serving as homes for starving millions. It was into this place, this fever-dream nightmare of abject poverty that Stone ventured.

Vacant eyes watched him, apathetic, resigned. Faces peered from glassless windows, watching him shuffle warily from one shadow to another. He wasn't safe here. He knew that.

Ropes were strung from pole to window, strung with shirts and pants and bras. Stacks of cinder blocks formed walls, and often, roofs were the floors of the residence above. The shanties were stacked two and three high in places, patchwork squares of rickety homes. Most were barely six or eight feet wide, and perhaps the same high. Flaps in the wood fronts could be let down to function as windows. Stone hadn't ever been inside the stacked shanties, and had no idea how the residents got from the street level to the top. Perhaps there were ladders somewhere within. Belongings were hung from the windows, clothes, pots and pans, buckets, water coolers. Bicycles were lined up along the streets, often the only means of transportation for entire families. Where the shanties were only one story high, the roofs served as storage, sidewalk, and homes for those with nowhere else to go.

Where the shantytown followed the river, homes often sat mere feet above the water, which was stagnant and green and thick and slurried with trash.

Stone tried to ignore the eyes on him, ignore the warning prickle of hairs on his neck. He was following old memories, lost in the maze now, swallowed by Manila. He ignored the futility of wandering in this place, ignored the fear. He could disappear here and never be found. He had no idea what he was looking for, where he was going, what he was doing.

Nonetheless, he picked his way through the shanties, eyes raking and roving, watching and assessing.

Sheer blind, dumb luck brought him his first break. A middle-aged Filipino man, dressed a little too nicely, hands a little too clean, hair a little too neatly cut and combed, stepping gingerly through the dirt, avoiding bits of trash. Stone's instincts screamed, and he listened. The man didn't see him pressed against a wooden wall, hidden in shadows cast by the trembling bulk of the jury-rigged buildings above him. Stone followed at a distance, noting his surroundings and the route through the maze back to a main road. The man waited at a curbside bus stop with half a dozen others. After a few minutes, a bus rumbled to a stop, belching diesel fumes. Stone burst into a run, falling into line several places behind his quarry, digging out change. On the bus, he slumped against a railing, peering out the window at the passing cityscape, hoping his prey wouldn't notice him. The man rode for nearly a dozen stops, de-boarding in the middle of the metropolitan city center. Stone followed, keeping as many people between himself and his target as he could without losing visual. As he made his way through the city on foot, the Filipino man fished an older model flip-style cell phone from his hip pocket, hit a speed dial number, spoke briefly, and hung up, the entire conversation lasting less than ten seconds.

And then, between one breath and another, the man vanished. Stone stopped in the middle of the sidewalk, scanning the crowds, the street-side carts and vendors of tourist trinkets, the alleys and door-ways. All to no avail. He cursed under his breath, moving into the lee of a doorway, and scanned the crowd again, hunting for some clue to where his target had gone—a closing doorway, a knot of people disrupted, as if pushed aside by someone in a hurry.

Something cold and hard pressed into Stone's ribs, and fetid breath huffed in his face. "What you want, huh?" The voice was pitched low, thickly accented but fluent.

Stone shifted slightly, and saw the man he'd been following standing beside him, a pistol pressed against Stone's side, hidden from view by their bodies. "I'm looking for a girl."

The man chuckled. "I know lots of girls. Maybe you new here, yeah? Pollow me not smart. Pind girls some odder way."

Stone clenched his fist and forced himself to play a role. "I'm looking for a certain kind of girl."

"Keep talking."

"I think you can find the right girl for me. Young. American. I'll pay good money."

Silence strung out a little too long, and Stone braced for the shot that would kill him, but it never came. "Show me money. American dollars."

Stone held his hand out to show it was empty, then rooted in his hip pocket for his emergency stash of US dollars. "There's a thousand here. I can get more."

The man laughed again. "You need more. Much more. Dat kind of girl, she not cheap, huh? Maybe you a cop? Work por goberment? Yeah. You smell bad. You smell like po-liss-man."

"Fuck that. I just wanna get off. You know? Stick my dick in someone warm. She ain't even gotta be willing, know what I'm saying?" Stone grated the words out. "But I like American girls, and I heard you got 'em around here."

"Sometin' wrong with Pilippines girl? Not so sexy por you, huh?"

Stone shrugged, affecting nonchalance. "Nah, they're fine. You just get homesick, you know?"

The pistol barrel was still touching his ribs, but wasn't pressed quite so hard. And then it was gone and the man was gesturing for Stone to follow him. "Dis way. Dis way. I got girls. You got dollars, I got girls."

Stone tamped down his disgust and followed as the man led him down a block and into an apartment building, up and up and up around endless stairs. Through a doorway marked with a tilted brass number and into a low, dank, dark apartment. Threadbare blankets hung over the windows, sunlight streaming in through cracks along the edges. A drooping couch faced away from the doorway, and a coffee table stood just beyond, covered in empty beer bottles, full ashtrays, empty baggies that had once held drugs. Three girls were draped on the couch, slumped sideways against each other, one resting on the armrest, another drooling onto the first girl's shoulder, and the third across both their laps. All three were mostly naked, clad in nothing but panties. They were skinny, ribs showing, arms and legs like sticks, hair lank and greasy and unwashed. They didn't look up as the door opened, but when they saw Stone's escort, they righted themselves quickly, blinking, eyes going wide and fearful. They cringed as the man rounded the couch.

Stone made himself stay still and not react. The man latched his fist around one girl's wrist, yanking her upright. She stumbled, bleary-eyed, clearly strung out into dazed incoherency. She stood awkwardly, weight on one leg, the other bent slightly and turned inward, arms hanging at her sides. Her eyes were green, bright moss-green, her hair black. Her filthy, scarred, needle-tracked skin had once been porcelain.

She had once been beautiful.

Now, as the man shoved her toward Stone, she blinked once, slowly, realizing this was a cue. She glanced up at Stone, forced an empty smile onto her slack, dry lips, and shoved her panties down around her thighs, stepped out of them. She pushed herself against him, fumbling for his belt.

The pimp, or whatever he was, stood with his back to the window, watching, a leering grin on his face.

"What, are you gonna just gonna fuckin' stand there and watch?" Stone growled.

"Ha, no. You want, I charge extra for dat. Tree hundred dollar, you do what you want with all dese girls. Couch, fine. Room ova dere, fine." He pointed at a slightly ajar door at the end of a short, narrow hallway. There was one other door, leading to a bathroom, and a tiny galley kitchen.

"What about you?" Stone asked.

"Smoke, out da door. Not far." He stepped between Stone and the girl, who was waiting apathetically, eyes crossing as she fought to stay conscious. He pinched her nipple hard enough that she whined and stumbled away, but didn't try to stop him. "Only rule, no cutting, no burning, no makin' dem bleed. Yeah?"

Stone nodded, and made himself look at the girls as if he wanted them. Inside, his gut was churning, clenching, revolting. This girl couldn't be more than twenty, but she looked old and used, uncaring and empty, as if this was a scene she'd experienced too many times to count. There was no hope in her eyes, no life.

The pimp held out his hand, and Stone fished the American money from his pocket, peeled three bills away, and shoved the rest back into his pants. When the pimp took the money and smoothed a bill out, holding it up to the light, Stone struck. He lashed out with his hand, jabbing the "Y" between his thumb and index finger against the man's throat.

The pimp gasped, surprised, choking, dropping the money and clutching his throat. Stone lunged, driving his knee upward into the pimp's groin. The girl stumbled backward, fell against the couch and sat down hard. Stone knocked the pimp to the floor and, kneeling astride him, pulled his pistol and pressed the barrel against the man's exposed throat, knee in his sternum.

"I'm looking for a girl," Stone growled.

"I—got you girl," he gasped. "Tree girls. No charge, do what you want. No charge."

Stone slammed the butt of the pistol against the Filipino man's forehead, gashing it open and loosing rivulets of blood. "No, see, I'm looking for a particular girl. New. American. Not on the market yet. I think you took her. I want her back."

"No new girls. I don't—please, I don't know!" He writhed, trying to get at his own gun.

Stone put the barrel between his eyes and pulled the hammer back. "Liar."

"Okay, okay! I know! I don't take her. I gonna buy her, but I don't take. I know where she is. Please, I show you."

"Tell me."

"Ha, you neber pind it alone. You kill me, you neber pind your girlpriend."

Stone gritted his teeth, knowing the pimp was right. There were no addresses, no streets, no way to navigate unless you'd been there already. He reached under the Filipino man and extracted the pistol, tucked it into his own waistband. He hauled the man to his feet, keeping the 9mm trained on him. How was he going to manage this? If he took his eyes off the pimp for even a split second, he'd be gone, but he couldn't very well navigate Manila with a handgun out in broad daylight. There wasn't any good solution to the problem, but the longer he stood here trying to think through it, the worse off Wren would be. Stone gathered the dropped bills, shoved them back into his pocket, and gestured with the barrel of his pistol.

"Go," he grunted. "Show me. And don't think I won't shoot you if you try to run."

"You pind da girl, den what? Dey won' let you go wit' her."

"Let me worry about that. Just take me to her."

"Okay, dead man."

Stone followed him out of the apartment, down the stairs and onto the street, back onto the bus, returning the way they'd come. Stone kept close to his guide, his pistol tucked into the front of his jeans, wedged uncomfortably and not entirely safely, but within easy reach.

As the built-up, modern downtown faded into tumbledown shanties and the wasteland of poverty, Stone felt his gnawing unease ratchet into outright fear. His guide was constantly turning his head around to grin at him, shaking his head and laughing at if at some private joke.

The joke, Stone knew, was on him. He was walking alone into the lion's den, basically unarmed. A couple of 9mm pistols weren't going to do much good against a criminal organization that had all of Manila quaking.

Off the bus and into the maze of sheds and crates and garbage and stench and human suffering, left and right and left and right until Stone was thoroughly lost. People hung their heads out of windows and watched, stared, listless and uninterested, as Stone and the other man passed through, squeezing between buildings, avoiding packs of snarling dogs fighting over scraps, burning heaps of trash, open doorways echoing with the sounds of sex, acrid clouds of drug fumes. Shouting voices, arguments, fights. The sound of a hand smacking flesh and a small voice crying. Rot, the miasma of death and sickness. Puddles of muddy water underfoot, raw sewage. Clothes hanging from wires overhead like multi-colored flags all in a row.

And then, the faces began to vanish. Windows were closed. No one watched. The scent of fear was palpable. Even his guide had slowed and was scanning the rooftops, the narrow alleys, the street behind them.

Eventually, he stopped. "No closer. They see me, you, *bam-bam*. We bot' dead." He pointed down the street, little more than a narrow gap slicing between stacks of shanties. "See da red door? In dere."

Stone eyed the door in question, a small crimson slab of wood, the paint peeling and marked with Filipino graffiti. Or, rather, what was supposed to be graffiti, but was more likely an identifying marker of some kind.

"How many are in there?" Stone asked.

The man shrugged. "Girls? Or men wit guns?"

"Both."

"Many, and many. Maybe…tirty girls. Men? More dan dat, men. Maybe? I only know Cervantes, but I see odders, many many."

"Who's Cervantes?"

Another shrug. "Cervantes is…Cervantes. Bad, bad. I scare ob him. Ebry-one scare ob him." A pause, and then: "You really gonna go in dere? One girl, she not wort' it, I tink."

"This one is."

"You crazy. Crazy, and dead." He spat in the dirt. "I go now, or you kill me."

"What are you gonna do if I let you go?" Stone asked, turning to watch the man to see if he would lie.

"Run. Go home fast. Get big drunk."

Stone saw truth in his eyes, and waved his hand. The pimp scurried off into the late evening gloom, not looking back. Guilt washed over Stone. He hadn't done anything to help the girls in the apartment. Maybe he could go back. But first, he'd be lucky to do anything to help the one girl he came to rescue.

He pushed all thoughts from his mind and turned his attention to examining the doorway and the windows around it. He saw no sign of anyone watching, but that didn't mean anything. He leaned against the wall, mud sucking at his boot, sweat dotting his forehead, unease rumbling in his gut.

It was now or never. Stone blinked a bead of sweat out of his eye and moved toward the red door, reminding himself to breathe.

You crazy, the man had said. *Crazy, and dead.* Stone was worried he was right. The red door swung open slowly, resisting motion, scraping against the dirt. Stone entered with his pistol drawn, sliding through the doorway in a tactical crouch.

Here we go, he thought.

And then hell broke loose.

7

—Now—

WREN WOKE TO THE SENSE of being watched. She hurt all over. Stifling a groan, she opened her eyes, starting as *his* eyes bored into her from a foot away.

"Time to go, little bird," he rasped in his accented voice.

Does he know my name? Wren wondered? Or maybe it was just a coincidence. She didn't think she'd been asked her name. Would it matter if she told them? Was anyone looking for her?

She forced herself to stay still when he reached into his pants pocket and pulled out a slim, long rectangle of silver, then flicked his wrist. Metal flashed and spun, the knife in his hands glinting and gleaming in the dim light shed from above. The blade wavered, serpentine, looking razor-sharp. He leaned against her, sniffing the skin of her neck as he slid the blade between her hands, tied at her back. Pain lanced through her palm as the edge sliced her skin, and then the bindings gave way and her hands were free. She brought her arms around front and shook them to erase the numbness. Blood sprayed from her cut palm, dotting her captor's face.

He reared back, wiping at his face and cursing in Filipino. "Hey, watch it, bitch," he said in English. He slapped her with his empty hand, knocking her sideways. "I don't want your blood on me."

Wren couldn't sob, couldn't breathe. Pain was a vise clamped around her ribs and lungs as her cracked rib protested the way she'd slammed into the ground. Her palm stung as dirt caked on the open cut, but that was a distant twinge in comparison to the agony of her ribs.

She felt her feet being freed, and then an iron-hard hand latched around her arm, just beneath her armpit, and yanked her to her feet. Her arm socket joined the chorus of aches, but she ignored it, focusing on remaining upright and drawing air into her lungs. Tears leaked down her cheeks, but she kept silent. She forced one foot in front of the other, up the stairs and into relative brightness. She squinted. It was still dark, she realized, but after the total darkness of the pit she'd been in, any light was blinding. He mounted the stairs behind her, pushing her into a corner and lowering the trapdoor, laying a thick square of cast-off carpeting to hide it.

Around her, the walls were bare, the roof low, not even two feet over her head. There was no window, nothing except a tiny card table in one corner with two folding chairs, an electric camp lantern shedding blue-white light. Each chair held a man, both short but muscular Filipinos, one with a nasty scar pulling his left eye down. They both had guns across their laps, black machine guns with tan wood stocks, the kind she saw terrorists on the news holding, and army men from third-world countries. The one with the scarred face had a cigarette pinched in the corner of his mouth, the smoke curling around his nose and narrowed eyes. They both watched her in silence, until the scarred one spoke in Filipino, gesturing at Wren with the barrel of his gun. It sounded like a question, judging by the tone of his voice.

Her captor responded with a single syllable, a harsh negation. He pushed Wren by the center of her back, sending her stumbling toward a doorway. Each step made her ribs scream and stole her breath, but she forced herself to walk anyway, gasping and trying not to cry, trying to keep her wits about her. She was still dizzy and foggy from whatever drug he'd given her, and she felt a hot, needy ache in her belly, deep down. A kind of craving, a desperation. For what, she didn't know. For something. She needed it, her body needed it.

She moved through another room, this one empty but for a stained blue and white mattress on the ground, and then another one identical to the last, except a Chinese girl (or was she Japanese? Wren didn't know) lay on the mattress, naked butexcept for dirty white underwear. Her ribs showed, expanding as she drew a deep breath and depressed the plunger of a needle stuck into her forearm. A blissful expression swept over her features as Wren watched, and then the needle went slack, tumbling to the mattress beside her. A man Wren hadn't noticed scooped up the syringe and vanished, nodding at Wren's captor.

Through another room, this one larger, wider, with a higher ceiling. Couches lined three walls, an ancient TV flickering on the fourth wall. Except for the TV, she hadn't seen any other sign of electricity. A clear plastic liter bottle hung down from a hole in the ceiling, fastened in place, filled with water. Sunlight refracted through the water in the bottle, shedding light into the room.

Wren had assumed it was nighttime, since every room she'd been in was dark or dimly light, but now she realized it was daytime, there were simply no windows to let it natural light.

In the center of the room was a long, low table littered with bottles of alcohol, ashtrays, needles, packets of various kinds of drugs, bongs, pipes, pistols, boxes of condoms, clips for guns. Men sat on the couches, watching a soccer game on the TV. When Wren entered, a dozen pairs of eyes focused on her. All of them went narrow and hooded with lust. Against all reason, she shrank against her captor, who only laughed and pushed her away from him.

"You aren't for dem," he said. "Dey can't afford you."

One of the men said something, and her captor responded with the same short barking negative. The man who'd spoken adjusted his crotch, and then leaned over the arm of the couch and shouted something through a doorless entryway. He was short, heavyset with beady eyes and skin greasy with sweat, a scar twisting his mouth into a permanent snarl. At his shout, a girl entered the room, a small, petite Asian girl no more than eighteen, with long, tangled hair and bloodshot eyes. She stood by the arm of the couch, head down, waiting. She was clad in a dress, a barely-there thing that left her chest mostly bare and didn't quite hit mid-thigh. The man spoke again, tugging at the zipper of his jeans. The girl responded immediately, sinking to her knees.

Wren couldn't look away, although she wanted to. Beside her, the man she'd come to think of as her captor spoke quietly into a cell phone. She didn't dare move, or speak, so she was left watching the unfolding events on the other side of the room. None of the other men so much as glanced away from the soccer game, although one of them reached for a pipe and flicked a lighter, sucking at the pipe and holding the smoke in his lungs for a long time before blowing it out with a hacking cough.

Wren's heart lurched as the Asian girl undid the man's pants and lowered her mouth to his member, bobbing her head and making a faint slurping noise. The man let his head thump back against the couch and fisted his hand in her hair. After a few moments, he began shoving her head down with increasing force, and every time he did, the girl gagged audibly. Wren's heart lurched, and her stomach twisted. But she couldn't look away. She closed her eyes, but she could hear the girl gagging, the man shoving her head down, and that was almost worse. She opened her eyes again to see him lift his hips once, gagging the girl, who made an audible gulping noise, twice, and then he released her. She fell back onto her bottom, wiping at her mouth. The man grinned at her, and then, as she struggled to her feet, he slapped her. It was a desultory blow, not meant to really hurt her, and she stumbled, sagging against the doorframe.

Beside her, Wren's captor uttered a short command without moving the phone from his ear. The other man grumbled, digging in his pocket and tossing a wadded peso bill at the girl. She scooped it up hastily, and then hesitated again, as if awaiting a command. The man who summoned her waved his hand in dismissal, and the girl scurried away. Before she vanished, the girl met Wren's eyes.

The brief glimmer of sympathy Wren saw in those otherwise dead brown eyes frightened her more than anything else.

Her captor ended the call, stuffing his phone in the back pocket of his shorts. She'd never noticed his attire, before, or really much about him, but she did now. He was young-looking. No more than thirty, and he wore baggy khaki cargo shorts and a skinny black tank-top clinging to his wiry, muscular frame. He had a round face, rotten teeth, cruel, intelligent eyes, a small crescent-shaped scar beneath his right eye. And the green flip-flops. She knew those. She saw those every time he visited her.

He reached behind himself, withdrawing a black pistol, ejected the clip, checked it, and then returned it to the small of his back. He said something in Filipino, and one of the men grabbed a clip from the table and tossed it. Her captor caught it easily and shoved it into one of his pockets.

He glanced at Wren and seemed to see her thoughts. "Good show, huh? Miguel, he's crazy for blow job. No regular sex, only dat. All da time, blow job, blow job. I don't get it." He pinched Wren's cheek, shaking her face. "Maybe I let him teach you how to give a good one, huh? You gonna have to learn, yeah?"

Wren could only shake her head, couldn't get the word *no* out. She backed away, but had nowhere to go. He grabbed her wrist, tugged her away from the wall. "Don't like dat idea?" He grinned, evil, amused. "You had it easy. Good time to learn sometin' new." He shoved Wren toward Miguel, whose lips curled into a gleeful smile as he reached for her.

She stumbled, and scrambled away, tripping backward into the TV, blocking the view of the soccer game. Angry shouts erupted, and Wren moved away from the TV, watching Miguel, who'd stood up, and her nameless captor, who just watched, scratching a chicken-pox scar on his cheek.

Miguel dug his hand into his pants, adjusting himself, and then grinned again. "You come." He twitched two fingers at Wren, an imperious gesture. "You come now."

Wren shook her head, sliding along one wall, into the corner farthest from Miguel. She was cornered now, as Miguel stalked toward her, slipping a long folding knife from his pocket and opening it. Terror flooded Wren's veins as he stopped a foot away from her, running his tongue over his bottom lip. He held the tip of the knife in her general direction, reaching down to his pants with his other hand. He opened the button, the zipper, and then pulled his privates out and held his member in his fist. Wren whimpered, shrinking away, closing her eyes, covering her mouth. Laughter filled the room, amused male guffaws. A fist grabbed her hair, and something sharp and cold pricked her cheek.

A command in Filipino. Then, in English. "Suck," the last syllable emphasized with a click.

Wren shook her head, the movement cutting her cheek open on the knife point. Eyes clenched tight, she let the sharp pain sear her, expecting death. Still she waited, refusing. She felt the knife dig in, sharper, and then her captor spoke, emphasizing his order with the distinctive sliding-click of a pistol being racked. The knife point withdrew, the hand left her hair, and Wren opened her eyes. The man was gone, sitting back in his place on the couch, touching himself almost idly, despite the room full of other men. He called out, and a girl appeared, a different one, and she seemed to know what was expected of her, because she knelt between his knees immediately.

Her captor grabbed her and pushed her through the doorway beside Miguel. Wren focused on breathing, ignoring the wrenching agony of her rib, wiping the trickle of blood from her face. The room she found herself in was filled with girls, all of them her age or younger. Most were horrifyingly young, twelve to sixteen. Most were naked, some in underwear, others in short sort-of-dresses. They were crowded into bunk beds stacked three high against all four walls, a small gap left for the doorways in opposite corners of the room. Some were on the beds, others sat on the floor or beside other girls. One was reading a book. All looked skinny to the point of starvation, and all of them had tell-tale scars on their arms.

His cell phone rang, then, and he stopped Wren, answering his phone with a harsh syllable. He listened, spoke briefly, and then hung up. He grinned at Wren. "Good ting I didn't let Miguel hurt you, huh? He woulda kill you, you know. He don't like 'no'. Dat was my buyer. He comin' right now. He don't like his girls wit' marks on dem."

"Buyer? You're...you're selling me?" Wren couldn't stop the question.

"Yeah, yeah." He scratched his cheek with his thumb. "Lotsa money. Lots and lots."

"What...who are you selling me to? What are they going to make me—make me do?"

He just laughed. "What you tink? Lotsa men pay good money to fuck pretty American girl. Dat's you. Pretty American girl. Best part is, you don't even look American. He can charge more extra."

"No...no. Please. Don't."

He leaned close and his breath stank as he spoke. "You tink I'm nice? Tink I like you? Tink again. I won't kill you. I lose money, dat way. Know what I do? I'll fuck you just to teach you a lesson. Right here, in dis room, on dis floor. So you best shut up.

Huh? Shut up and you won't see me again. Keep talking, and I'll fuck you hard. Teach you a lesson you never gonna forget."

Wren shrank back, sucking in a terrified breath that had her wincing in pain. "Please, I'm sorry. No. Don't....I'm sorry."

"Better. Now shut up." He shoved Wren through another doorway, and this one led to a room with a small round table and four chairs, an old refrigerator that didn't seem to be plugged in to anything, and a big red cooler with a white top, the same kind she used to help her parents pack full of Coke and salami and Gatorade and cheese and bread for a day on the lake. He shoved her toward the table and she sat down, pressing her palm to her screaming ribs, focusing on each breath in, each breath out, refusing to consider her fate, what was coming, what would happen.

She breathed, and she prayed.

He pulled on a length of metal bar fastened vertically to one of the walls, and it slid aside, the entire wall serving as a door. He only opened it a few inches, peering out into the street beyond. Wren peered hard at that gap, the sliver of freedom. What if she made a break for it? Knocked him aside and ran? He would kill her. But wouldn't she rather be dead than forced into prostitution? Wren thought she probably would rather be dead. She tensed her legs, gathering them beneath her, focusing on the few inches of space between the door and the wall, planning her motions. If she tried to knee him in the groin, it might buy her some time.

She lifted up out of her seat, sucking in a deep, preparatory breath...

But something inside stopped her. It wasn't an audible voice, not really. But she heard it within herself, nonetheless: *WAIT. WAIT.*

She settled back down, confused. Now was her chance. It might be the only one she'd get. And she'd missed it. He shut the door, pulled his phone from his pocket and checked the screen, cursing in Filipino.

"Where da fuck he is?"

Wren shifted in her seat, glancing at the refrigerator and cooler, wishing she had something to drink, or eat. She couldn't remember the last time they'd fed her, or given her water. She was so hungry it was painful, so thirsty her mouth felt withered and drawn.

She had nothing to lose, she realized. "Could... could I have something to drink? Please?"

He glanced at her, amused. "You got balls, huh? Sure, look in dere, see what you see."

Wren struggled to her feet and pulled open the fridge. It wasn't plugged in, but there were bottles of booze, beer, and something else, some local brand of soda. It was better than nothing. She grabbed one and opened it, sipped from it, tasted citrus, something like Sprite. He was watching as if interested in the way she drank, so she grabbed one of the bottles of beer and extended it to him. He lifted an eyebrow, but took it, twisted the top off, and drank.

A few minutes passed in silence, Wren sipping her soda and feeling stronger with each swallow of liquid.

And then she heard gunfire, loud bursts from somewhere behind them. Her captor swore in Filipino, grabbed Wren's arm and dragged her from the kitchen and out into the street. She was running, trotting behind him, dragged by his iron-hard fist around her bicep. The soda can slipped from her fingers and splashed onto the dirt road. An engine roared, and then a van swung around the corner, skidded to a stop in front of them. More gunfire blasted from the maze of shanties, and Wren knew in her heart that it was Stone, coming for her. The sliding door was wrenched open from within, and her captor shoved her into the van and leaped in after her.

She grabbed the chain of her cross and yanked it so the clasp broke. As she was being thrown into the van, Wren tossed the cross into the dirt, hoping and praying that Stone would find it and recognize it, and know she'd been there.

8

—Now—

STONE'S INSTINCTS AND TRAINING kicked in automatically. It wasn't reaction that had him lunging to one side. He wasn't even through the door yet, his eyes hadn't adjusted and he couldn't see a damn thing. It was a voice whispering in his brain, compelling him to move. Gunfire hacked, muzzle-burst flashing, blinding, illuminating. Stone squeezed the trigger of his pistol, felt it jerk in his hands, the double bounce of the recoil in his fist as familiar as his own heartbeat.

BANGBANG.

A body dropped, and Stone kept moving, wishing he had a flashlight. He stooped and scooped up the AK-47, slung it by the strap over his back.

The gunfire had awakened the beast, he knew. Voices shouted, male and angry, female screams. He noted the closest doorway, but also saw that another wall had a doorway cut into the wood. This wasn't one building, he realized, but a maze of connected shacks. He followed the female voices, the screams, and the shouts trying to corral them.

He caught words in Filipino: *"tahimik!" Shut up!*

Another doorway, an empty room, right turn, through another doorway, a stained mattress. He heard footsteps, ducked backward into a corner, crouching, pistol held in a Weaver stance. Two men stomped through the doorway, assault rifles held at hip-level, sweeping the room haphazardly. They didn't check the corners, though. A pair of slugs each, and two bodies dropped. Stone waited for others, crouched, legs tensed, pistol ready.

Another figure entered, and this one clearly had some kind of military training. He swept the corners first, unfazed by the sight of two dead bodies spreading pools of blood. He didn't see Stone fast enough. A squeeze of the trigger, and Stone watched a small round hole begin to weep ruby in the darkness.

Three bodies. Stone moved on, shutting away the images in the dark mental place where he pushed all such images. He kept moving, passing through room after room. Most were empty of people, although he did pass through one room full of frightened girls in varying states of nudity, packed into a tiny barracks, bunk beds stacked three high. They shrank away from him when he entered. None of them spoke.

He fixed his gaze on one girl, Filipino by the looks of her. "New girl?" He asked it in English. None of them responded, or seemed to understand him. He tried in his limited Filipino: *"Bagong babae?"*

She pointed, and then shrank against the wall.

Stone indicated the other door, opposite the one she'd pointed to. *"Tumakas,"* he said. *Run away.*

None of them moved. Stone wanted to yell at them, beg them to save themselves. He did none of these things, though. He couldn't help them more than he already was. Shouts were echoing through the rooms: they'd found the bodies he'd left behind. He didn't have much time.

He moved through the doorway, sweeping the room as he went, checking corners, seeing nothing. Another room, empty. And then a room that wasn't empty. A man stood with his back to a corner, a long knife in his hand. He had a scar on his cheek, pulling his mouth down. The knife was held to the throat of a prostitute, her eyes wide and terrified, a trickle of blood snaking down her throat where the blade creased her skin.

"Drop gun." His voice was a low hiss.

Stone considered his chances. It was a small room, barely six feet across. If he dropped his gun, it was over. Wren would be killed or disappear. He lifted his pistol slightly, and the girl's eyes widened, shaking her head, sending fresh rivets of blood down her throat.

He held his breath as he centered the bead on the scarred thug's face, squeezed the trigger. His pistol jerked, barked. Blood and brains painted the wall, and the man sagged, the knife going limp. The girl whimpered, then shoved the arm away, stumbling forward with her hand clapped to her throat, blood leaking between her fingers. Stone cursed, then caught the girl as she fell. He settled her on her back on the floor, then reached out and ripped a chunk free from the dead man's shirt, pressed it to her throat, moving her hand to hold it down. The skin had been sliced deeply, but he didn't think her windpipe had been severed. She stared at him, trying to swallow, tears sliding down her cheeks, chest heaving as she struggled for breath against the pain.

Stone was wrenched by guilt. He wasn't sure she would live, but he couldn't afford the time to stay with her until he was sure. He rose to his feet, and the girl reached for him with her free hand, making a whimpering noise. Guilt ate at him as he forced himself to turn away, thinking of Wren. Behind him, he heard feet scrabble at dirt, and he twisted to see the girl stumbling through the opposite doorway, toward the barracks room. If she could walk, she would likely be okay, he told himself.

Through another series of empty rooms. Footsteps echoed behind him, and then more shouts. He glanced over his shoulder and saw shadows and forms passing through doorways, following him, just a few rooms behind. He entered a small kitchen of sorts, an unplugged refrigerator, a small table, a big red cooler with a white top. A door was open, leading to the street.

Goddammit! Stone whirled in place and slammed his fist into the wall, splitting his knuckles. His blow splintered the plywood of the wall, leaving a faint red smear.

A can of soda sat on its side in the middle of the street, glugging clear liquid into the dirt. He kicked the can viciously, sending it flying. He spun in place, seeing tire tracks in the ground, but with no way to know if the tracks meant Wren had even been here or not.

He was about to jog away, following the tracks northward, when his gaze caught a glimmer of sunlight on silver. He knelt, brushing dirt away to reveal a thin chain. He lifted it up, and his heart wrenched at the sight of the slim silver cross. It was Wren's cross. She'd been here.

Gunfire blasted behind him, kicking dirt up around him, and Stone spun in place and lurched to one side, lifting his rifle and firing. His rounds caught the gunman in the chest, knocked him back several paces, red blossoming from the holes in his chest. He kept his muzzle pointed at the fallen thug as he approached and knelt beside him.

Stone grabbed a fistful of shirt. "Where'd he take her?"

"Never know…you never gonna know." Blood bubbled from grinning lips.

"Tell me!" Stone shouted, fury pulsing through him. "Where is she?" The thug just laughed, coughing bloody froth. Stone drew his pistol and jammed the tip against the dying man's crotch. "You're already dying, you sick fuck, but I can make it a hell of lot more painful for you. I'll ask one more time. Where…the *fuck…is* she?"

This got a reaction. "Don't, please! I tell, okay, I tell you. Nice Hotel. Mandaluyong. He sell new girl dere. Different room all da time, same hotel." He coughed again, spewing pink froth from his mouth, eyes blinking, body shaking and shivering.

Stone nodded once and stood up, striding away, following the tire tracks through the maze of shanties until they disappeared onto the main road leading east over the river. He boarded a bus heading east, and then transferred to another line heading south toward Mandaluyong City. As the bus trundled the long journey south and eastward from the

Tondo district toward Mandaluyong, Stone considered his options and tried to formulate a plan.

The problem was, he discovered, there wasn't much to plan for. He had the name of a hotel and nothing else. How would he find Wren?

Nearly half an hour later, he was standing outside the Nice Hotel. Train tracks ran behind the building, ending in the Shaw Boulevard MRT station, a huge white building connected to the even more mammoth Pavilion Mall. This was, Stone realized, a brilliant place to have a human-trafficking auction. It was close to several forms of transportation, the mall provided crowd cover as well as any number of hiding places, and the Nice Hotel, while not as seedy as some of the other no-tell motels a bit west of Mandaluyong, still offered a suite for six hours at an affordable rate—PHP675 for six hours, Stone discovered after inquiring at the front desk.

He booked a suite, simply for the chance to nose around, if nothing else. He found his room, and then wandered the corridors, listening and watching. This turned up nothing, so he made his way down to the lobby and loitered, watching people come and go, hoping for a glimmer of a clue, someone out of place, someone he recognized.

After forty-five minutes of fruitless waiting, his attention was drawn to two well-dressed younger men entering together. There wasn't anything overtly suspicious about them, but for some reason, Stone's gut was telling him to follow them. Maybe it was the constant roving of their eyes, the way they assessed the room upon entering. Their gazes settled on Stone, who busied himself with a brochure for the nearby mall.

His heart rate ratcheted up to a blitzing hammer when the two men approached him, eyes hard.

"Why you watch us, American?" one of them asked, his hand lingering near what was the butt of his gun, no doubt.

Stone shrugged, barely glancing up from his brochure. "I wasn't watching you."

"You lie."

Stone turned his gaze to the speaker, a young man with slicked back black hair and small gold hoops through his ears. Stone decided to gamble with the truth. "I heard there was...I heard I could find some friends here. Know what I mean?"

"Maybe I know. Maybe I don't." The young man glanced at his friend, and the two seemed to have a silent conversation. "Some kind of prends, dey be esspensib. You know? Cost money. Maybe you show me dollars."

Stone glanced around, then dug his stash of US dollars from his pocket. "Seen enough?"

With a nod, the young man set off toward the elevators, gesturing for Stone to follow him with a flick of two fingers. Stone rode the elevator with the two other men in awkward silence. His heart was hammering and his palms were sweating. Something was off. His senses were jangling. He tensed, preparing.

When the elevator stopped on the fifth floor, the one who'd spoken gestured for Stone to precede him into the hallway. As he did so, Stone snuck a sideways glance, just in time to see a flash of metal. Stone's instincts kept him alive. His body arced away from the blade, spine bowing outward and his hands curling around the extended wrist. With a twist of his arm and a pivot on the ball of his foot, he wrenched his opponent's knife arm to bend against the joint, then slammed the butt of his palm against the elbow, breaking it with a loud *crunch*. The knife fell to the carpet, and Stone dropped his shoulder, jerking the man toward him so his momentum carried him up and over Stone's head. With a soft grunt, Stone lifted the man clear off the ground, keeping the momentum going so the knife-wielding thug flew a foot or two and then crashed into the floor. Before the first opponent had hit the carpet, Stone was scooping up the knife and lunging into the elevator. The entire process had taken less than ten seconds, so the second man wasn't ready for Stone's lunge. Stone held the knife so the blade was horizontal and jabbed upward with all the force he possessed. The blade bounced off a rib, sending the man backward but not seriously injuring him. Stone lashed out with his other hand, slamming his fist into his opponent's diaphragm. This bought Stone enough time to lever the knife upward again, this time passing cleanly between ribs to puncture a lung.

Stone let him drop and turned back to the first man, dragging him into the stairwell and kneeling on his throat. "Which room?" The thug struggled for breath, writhing and gasping. He shook his head, and Stone dug the tip of the knife against the man's throat. "I won't ask again. Talk." He eased his weight off enough to allow speech.

"Six...nineteen."

"How many are in there?"

"Don't...don't know. Tree men? Only da one girl."

"Will they hurt her in the room?" He dug the knife-tip in farther, drawing blood.

"I don't know!" Fear brought his words in a rush, nearly incomprehensible. "Depends on da buyer. Cervantes won't touch, he hab his own girl. Don't use da ones he sell. Buyer? Maybe do what he want. Not here, I tink. He take her somewhere else."

Stone rose off his prisoner, intending to tie him up. As soon as his weight was off completely, however, the thug rolled away and drew a pistol. Before he could squeeze off a shot, Stone was on top of him, knife scraping between ribs and slicing through muscle. He watched as the man gasped for breath, but his punctured lung wouldn't allow it.

Stone turned, forcing the weight of guilt away. He buried it, swallowed it. He didn't have time for guilt, didn't have the luxury of it. Wren needed him. He would spill as much blood as it took to save her from the fate awaiting her.

He dragged the dead man on the elevator into the stairwell with his friend and then wound his way through the corridor until he came to room six-nineteen. He heard voices on the other side of the door, male voices. The slap of fist on flesh and a soft female whimper of pain.

Rage blew through him, setting him on fire. He couldn't just kick the door down and barge in with guns blazing. That would get Wren killed for sure. He had to be smarter about it.

Stone hefted the bloody knife, testing its weight, considering.

9

Wren sat on the edge of the bed, fighting to stay calm. Three men filled the room with her, one of them her captor—she'd learned from other men that his name was Cervantes; the other two men she'd never seen before. Both were older than her captor, maybe middle-aged. One wore a business suit, the other a pair of wrinkled chinos and a red-and-blue-striped polo shirt. They eyed Wren with obvious lust as they discussed terms. She couldn't understand their words, but they held up fingers and argued, clearly bickering over price. That thought made her shiver with horror. They were discussing the price of her body, how much she was worth.

She steeled herself for the worst. Part of her wanted to charge at them, knowing they'd kill her.

That part of her welcomed death over rape. Not just rape, but a lifetime of sexual slavery. But then, just before her body left the bed, her instinct for survival kicked in. If she stayed alive, maybe she could escape eventually. Maybe someone would rescue her.

As she battled with herself, she began to feel a gnawing, prickling need deep inside. Hunger for something. Need. Not for food, but for...the drug. The needle. She hated it, but her body was beginning to crave it.

The arguments grew worse, loud and angry, verging on violent.

Wren spotted a glass ashtray on the bedside table, and when the men weren't looking, reached out and grabbed it, stuffed it between her thighs to hide it. The glass was cold on her skin.

One of the men let out a disgusted groan and turned away, clearly incensed, waving his hand in dismissal. He spat out something in Filipino, then stomped toward the door and jerked it open. He stopped, though, surprised by something on the other side. The bark of a pistol echoed, and red spray burst from the back of his head. He staggered, fell, blood gushing across the carpet in a flood.

Cervantes' face contorted in shock, and then twisted into fury. He reached behind his back and pulled out a gun, darting to the side of the room closest to the window. The second buyer dropped to a crouch in the corner as the deafening explosions of gunfire filled the room, bullets digging into the floor where Cervantes had been. Cervantes fired his own pistol, and then cast a glance toward Wren. She was frozen, the crash of guns terrifying her into momentary paralysis.

A shape filled the doorway, a huge figure in khaki shorts and a gray Navy T-shirt, a pistol clutched in his hands.

Stone.

Relief flooded through Wren, but it was short lived. Cervantes leapt over the bed and wrapped his arm around Wren's throat.

He jerked her off the bed, while Stone kicked aside the dying man in the doorway. He glanced at the second buyer, cracking off a single shot before returning his stare to Wren. She heard the slump of a body hitting the floor, and her gaze was drawn to the red painting the wall, trailing messily down to the carpeting.

She felt dizzy, whether from fear or from how tightly the arm was clenched around her throat, she wasn't sure. She fought for breath and for calmness. She had the ashtray clutched in one fist, and Cervantes hadn't seen it yet. Stone was watching her—watching them—tensed, crouched, one finger on the trigger, the other palm cupping the butt of the pistol. He looked perfectly at ease with the fact that he'd just killed two men.

Wren felt something cold against her temple.

"We goin' now. You move, she die." Cervantes' voice was low and calm.

"Let her go, Cervantes. Let her go now, and you won't die." Stone's eyes were hard, brown shards exuding mercilessness. "If you make me chase you, I'll make sure you die slowly. If you hurt her, I'll make sure you stay alive long enough to regret every single breath you've ever taken. If you hurt her, you'll beg me to let you die."

Cervantes laughed. "Big words, American. You sure you want her back?" He licked the skin of her neck slowly, then laughed again, an low, nasty sound. "You know how many times I fuck her? She beg me to stop, and then—and then she beg me to fuck her again. Jus' like she beg me for da drugs. She not your innocent little girl no more. She *mine*. She a *whore* now."

Stone's face shifted, and even Wren was afraid of the rage and the promise of death she saw in his expression. She wanted to tell him it was lies, but she couldn't. She couldn't speak. She could barely breathe. And…she realized, in some kind of nebulous way, that maybe Stone should believe it. Maybe if he believed it, he'd make Cervantes pay.

She felt a shiver of something awful wriggle in her gut. It was something terribly like glee. The thought of Cervantes bleeding for what he'd done to her…it made a part of her happy to consider. And that scared her witless. What was happening to her? She shouldn't wish pain on anyone, not even her worst enemy. She should pray for Cervantes. Turn the other cheek. Trust God to have a plan, even in the midst of this terror.

But…she just couldn't. Not any of that.

She wanted Cervantes to *hurt*. She wanted him to hurt like she hurt. She wanted him to feel the kind of fear she felt.

She wanted him to pay for the need she felt in her veins, the horrible, itching, crawling, hot and then cold *need* she felt in her skin and in her blood and in her belly.

Need for the needle to pierce her vein and send the evil chemicals into her.

Need for the needle. Perhaps that was where the term came from. The word *need* was buried inside *needle*, after all.

"You gonna let us go, American. Count to thirty, *slow*. I see you, I hear you, she dead." He nodded at the bathroom door. "Go in dere. Sit, wait, count, or I kill her."

She watched in despair as Stone reluctantly moved into the bathroom and sat down. Wren felt herself dragged through the doorway, her heels scrabbling on the threadbare carpeting. She smelled Stone, faint cologne, sweat, and blood. She managed to meet his eyes briefly, saw the hate there, saw the anger and the sadness and the determination. She tried to comfort him with a single glance. She tried to pour all of her heart into that fleeting meeting of eyes.

And then she was out of sight of Stone, and she missed him so much, needed him. She knew he wouldn't stop until he had her safe. All she had to do was stay alive.

But Cervantes wasn't taking any chances. He dragged her down the stairwell, her feet slipping on the concrete, missing a stair or two at a time, off-balance and gasping for breath. The gun barrel wasn't pressed against her anymore, but she still had no chance to break free. Not yet, she knew. Not yet.

Then they were out on the street and his arm was gone from her throat, but the gun was pressed against her back, his arm now draped casually over her chest, cradling her almost tenderly, like a man with his girlfriend out for a stroll on a hot afternoon. Into the mall, into the wild and bustling crowds, the ceiling high, high overhead, bright lights and sunshine streaming, voices chattering in Filipino and a smattering of other languages, even English...*found a purse...only a hundred pesos...Daddy please...*

A purse. A girl begging her father for money to buy a purse. She had been that girl before. Now she just wanted to be free, to survive this hell.

Wren sucked air into her lungs, trotted to keep up with Cervantes as he wended through the crowd, angling across the cavernous space as if he knew exactly where he was going. She scanned the signs, looking for one in English that would give her some kind of clue. Then she saw a sign pointing the way toward a train station, and realized what his plan was.

If she got on a train with Cervantes, she'd never be free. Stone would never be able to find her again. She wasn't even sure how he had in the first place, but if Cervantes got them onto a train, she was as good as dead. Or worse.

It wasn't time to fight, yet. She had to wait until he was distracted.

They left the mall and entered the train station.

This was her chance; the crowds in the station—which the signs announced to be the Shaw Boulevard MRT station—were thick and chaotic, jostling elbow to elbow. She waited, waited, let Cervantes push her through the crowd. She felt her pulse pounding, readying her for action. She tried to breathe slowly and evenly, tried to take in everything. A door, there. A bathroom? No, no way out except the way in. A security guard? Perhaps. Her best bet was to simply get away and try to lose herself in the chaos.

They approached the ticketing counter. Cervantes kept the pistol between their bodies, shielding it from view while digging in his pocket for money. Once he had the tickets he wanted, his arm went back around her and guided her down to the platform level. The bustle of people was worse here, barely room to breathe or move without bumping into half a dozen people. An elderly man in front of them moved with glacial slowness, and Wren could feel Cervantes growing impatient, trying to push around him. But the thickness of the crowd wouldn't allow it.

And then the moment came. A woman stumbled, her three-inch heel catching on the floor and careening her into Cervantes. He cursed angrily, shoving the woman away. In that moment, a split second, the barrel of the pistol wasn't pressed into her flesh. Wren whirled, holding the thick glass ashtray in her fist with the edge leading. She bashed Cervantes in the skull, near the temple, and felt bone crunch, give. He stumbled, blood immediately masking his face.

People screamed, pointed. Wren ignored it all.

She struck again, aiming for the same place. Cervantes fell to his knees, his gun slipping from his fingers. She kicked it away and ran, pushing through the crowd. She was in full panic, now, adrenaline bursting through her, putting speed into her movement, strength in her tired, pain-ridden body. She elbowed people away, pushed and kicked and shoved, striving for as much distance as possible.

She found the escalator, made her way back up to L3, where the bridge to the Pavilion Mall was.

She thanked God that she'd been paying attention, so she knew exactly where to go. Run. Run. Run. She heard shouts behind her, heard Cervantes' voice, and she poured on speed, zigzagging through the crowds at a breakneck pace, crashing into people, knocking them aside and earning curses and shouts, not heeding them but only running faster. She saw the entrance to the bridge to the Pavilion Mall, choked with people. Her eyes scanned the crowd, seeking one face, one blond head standing over the rest. She didn't see him, and felt despair. Surely he'd followed them?

Shouts of pursuit echoed behind her, and she knew she had to get out of this complex, away from the mall and Shaw. Running full sprint now, Wren found a stairway leading down, toward the street level, and she tore down it, slipping and tripping, slamming into walls. She exited, and felt the humid wall of heat blast her like a fist as she stumbled out into the open.

Hide, she had to hide. People would see her running and talk.

There: a Starbucks across the street, full of locals and tourists alike. She crossed the street at a fast walk, trying to slow down and not attract attention. She realized she looked just like everyone else, here, except few had the bruises on her face and the dried blood on her nose. Her clothes were ripped and filthy, showing too much skin in places. The shirt had been a blue V-neck, scooped low, but it had been torn at some point and now revealed the dirty white lace of her bra and the tan expanse of flesh it contained. People stared and pointed, and she knew all Cervantes had to do was question a few people in order to follow her trail.

She hurried through the congested traffic, causing a taxi to brake hard and nearly hit her. She entered the Starbucks, the familiar sight and sound and smell of the coffee shop comforting her. She was so thirsty, so hungry, so tired. She wanted to sink into a deep red suede chair and sip a latte, nibble on a blueberry muffin. Read back issues of *The New York Times*. Pretend to do the crossword.

She couldn't do any of that, though. She pushed toward the back of the crowded store, past the clang of the espresso machine wands and the hiss of the steamer, ignoring the chatter and the music, jostling a display of travel mugs and pound-bags of exotic coffee beans. Cool air washed over her skin, drying the sweat and making her shiver. The ladies bathroom door swung open and a woman stepped out, blond hair and blue eyes, wearing an open white button-down shirt over a pink tank top and cut off jean shorts.

The woman cast a critical glance at Wren, and then her expression changed to concern. "You all right?" she asked, her accent faintly German.

Wren wanted to beg for help, plead, weep. "I just...I ripped my shirt."

"Looks like more than that, sweetheart. You need a doctor."

"I'm...I'm fine." She resisted a glance over her shoulder for Cervantes, not wanting to look as desperate and terrified as she really was. "Can I borrow your button-down?"

The woman immediately shed the shirt and handed it to her. "Sure, honey. Here. Do you need anything else? Are you sure I can't bring you to a doctor?" She leaned in close. "You don't have to stay with him, honey. Don't let him keep hurting you. Okay?" The woman turned away, and as she passed, she pressed a tightly folded wad of bills into Wren's palm.

Wren slipped into the bathroom and locked it, then sat, trembling, on the toilet. She buried her face in her hands and let herself shake, but refused to cry. If she started crying, she'd never stop. After a moment, she forced herself to her feet and peeled the dirty, ripped T-shirt off her body, groaning in pain as her injured ribs protested. In the mirror, she saw the bruises on her torso and her face. No wonder the woman had assumed Wren was in an abusive relationship.

If only the truth were that easy. She wet a length of paper towel and scrubbed the worst of the dirt and dried blood from her face and around her nose. There wasn't much she could do for her knotted and snarled hair, but she ripped a piece of her old shirt and used it to tie it back so it didn't look as bad. Then she put on the new shirt and buttoned it, feeling more human.

She dug the money the woman had given her from the pocket of her shorts and counted out $20USD. Enough for a bottle of water and something to eat, at least. Assuming Cervantes wasn't just beyond the door waiting for her.

Wren hesitated with her fingers on the door handle. Her heart was pounding so loud she could no longer hear the café's music. What if he was out there, waiting? She couldn't, wouldn't let him take her again. She'd fight to the death, if she had to.

Where was Stone? Had he followed her? Had he stopped to deal with Cervantes? Was he even alive?

She knew in her gut that Cervantes wasn't dead, wasn't going to stop. He'd find her.

Wren pushed through the door, tensed for the worst.

10

STONE SLID BETWEEN PEOPLE, scanning faces. Shaw was insanely busy, people streaming in all directions. Ahead, he saw a commotion, a cluster of onlookers crowded in a circle around someone. Stone used his height to peer over their heads, caught a glimpse of Cervantes climbing to his feet, his face a mask of blood.

"She went that way," someone said in Filipino, pointing toward the escalators. *"She looked like she'd been through some shit."*

Cervantes had ripped off his shirt and had it pressed to his temple. He was sagging against a pillar, clearly in pain, dizzy and disoriented. Stone wished he could finish the job, but Wren was his first priority. He'd have to deal with Cervantes, but he couldn't do anything at the moment. Stone pushed through the crowd toward the escalators. Where would Wren have gone?

Out of the mall. Out, away. Somewhere familiar, probably. Stone headed toward the mall's entrance, scanning, searching. Outside, he paused, watching the crowds and cars move in an endless stream.

There: a Starbucks. Probably the most familiar place of all for a lost and afraid American girl. The first place Cervantes would check, too, most likely. Stone ran across the street, dodging traffic and nearly getting hit a few times before reaching the sidewalk, leaving stopped cars and shouted curses in his wake. He jerked the door open and sucked in a breath of the familiar coffee shop air. He didn't see her in the dining room, didn't see her in line or waiting for a drink. Maybe she wasn't here.

Then the bathroom door opened, and there she was. She'd cleaned up a bit, found a new shirt. Good girl.

She still looked battered and in pain and terrified, but she was scanning the shop with wary, alert eyes. Stone's gut twisted at the sight of her. Bruises darkened her face, and she looked sweaty, even though it was cool—almost cold—inside Starbucks. He saw her reach a hand to her forearm and scratch absently, then notice what she was doing and stop, shaking her hand as if flinging away the need to scratch.

He slipped through the crowd, willing Wren to glance his way, to see him. He dared not call out, knowing she'd bolt, and that would make a scene. He needed to get her away from this area without drawing any more attention than necessary. He closed to within three feet before she spotted him.

Her entire being lit up, as if merely seeing him was salvation. She flew through the air and slammed into his chest, her arms wrapping around his neck. His arms clutched her waist and he buried his face in her hair.

A moment passed, and then another, and then he felt her body jerk and shudder, a sob ripping from her. "Stone...oh God, Stone. Don't—please don't let him—"

"I've got you, Wren. You're safe, baby. I promise." Baby? Stone thought. *Where did that come from?* "I won't let him hurt you again."

Wren sobbed again, and then drew a deep breath and seemed to physically force herself to stop crying. "Did you...did you see him? In the mall? I hit him with an ashtray, but I'm not sure how good I got him."

Stone chuckled. "You got him good."

She lifted her chin to look up at him. Her eyes were wet, brown and wide and afraid and relieved.

"Is it horrible that I'm glad I hurt him? He's...he's evil, Stone. You don't even know..."

"That's a perfectly normal emotional response," he said. "And I do have a pretty good idea what he's like." Stone refused to think about that mission. He was positive it was Cervantes he'd seen, there at the last, watching them fly away.

He pulled Wren out of the Starbucks, his gaze roving the street for any sign of Cervantes, mind racing. *Cross the street, just move, keep moving.* Find a cab, put distance between them and Cervantes. He walked quickly, almost carrying Wren with one arm. A jeepney hauled past them, then braked at a stop. Stone tugged Wren into a jog and pushed her onto the flamboyantly colored vehicle, which was crowded well past any logical capacity. He held her against his front, shielding her from the view of anyone on the street.

She was panting, pressing one hand to her side, sheened with sweat.

"Are you hurt?"

She nodded. "Ribs. He...he kicked me. A few times. Not broken, I'm pretty sure, but it hurts."

"Did he...hurt you in any other way?" He hated asking, but he had to know, if only so he'd be aware of her psychological mindset.

Wren shook her head. "No. He was...saving me. For whoever bought me." She scratched her left forearm again, then stopped with a curse under her breath. "They...forced drugs on me. Not sure what. With a needle."

"Probably heroin. How are you feeling? Symptom-wise, I mean."

"I don't...I don't know. Achy. Nauseous. I think I have a fever. It's...it's awful. Sometimes it feels like bugs are crawling on me. Under my skin. A million...a million bugs with sharp little feet crawling inside me...I want to scratch, and I want them out, I want...oh God, I hate it. But it's the drugs. I know it's the drugs, and I can't...I *won't* let it take control. I can't be addicted. I didn't want this." She had her head leaned against Stone's chest, and she was whispering quietly, fiercely. "Make it *stop*, Stone. Please."

"That's the heroin, babe. The fever can do that too. It's gonna be okay, Wren. I promise. I'll get you through it. I won't let anything happen."

"But...I *need* it. You don't understand. I don't *want* the drugs, but I...my body—my body *needs* it."

Stone held her with one arm, gripping the railing with the other as the jeepney wound through the Ortigas Complex, jerked to a stop, disgorged passengers and absorbed others. He was listening to her, but part of him was on high-alert, watching for Cervantes or someone who might work for him. The problem was that Cervantes would have a massive network of informants, paid and otherwise.

They rode the jeepney for several stops, and then Stone pulled Wren off and boarded another one, letting it take them farther away. The second jeepney took them northward, and then they transferred yet again, this time back onto Ortigas Avenue, heading northwest. Wren clung to him, sweating and mumbling, shivering, scratching.

He had to get her off the street so he could help her through the worst of the withdrawal. He wanted to go back to the hostel, but he wasn't sure exactly where that was, for one thing, and for another, the group had already left, making the hostel no better a place to go than anywhere else.

Another transfer, this time to a regular bus line heading north. Wren couldn't even walk. He had to lift her bodily up on to the bus. As they swayed with the motion of the bus, he pulled his cell phone from his pocket, intending to find someone to help them. He swore when he discovered that the battery had died.

Stone couldn't remember how long he'd been awake at that point, how long he'd been scouring the city, how long it had been since he'd raided the brothel. He'd been exhausted when she had gone missing; he was dead on his feet now.

He wasn't sure when he'd eaten last, or had anything to drink.

He wasn't sure where they were going. He didn't know what to do, how to get Wren out of Manila without risking another shootout with Cervantes and his army of goons.

He may have dozed off. Wren was a heavy weight against him. The bus had emptied significantly, and he no longer had even the slightest clue where they were. His best guess was somewhere between San Juan and Northern Calocoon City. His dim understanding of Manila's geography told him a northerly route from Mandaluyong would take them into Quezon City. It was far from where they'd been, and that was good enough for that particular moment.

The bus juddered to a stop, belching diesel, and Stone dragged Wren off, held her in the shelter of a building. The late evening sun was hot, and they were both about to pass out.

Gnawing instinct had Stone turning his head around just in time to see a black sedan with tinted windows soar past them. It slowed abruptly, squealing brakes and skidding. Stone buried his face in Wren's shoulder, and she murmured, mumbled.

"Wren, baby. Gotta wake up. We gotta move. We got trouble."

"Cold…so cold. Tired." She sagged against Stone, shaking her head and trembling violently.

He shook her. "Wren!" he hissed into her ear. "He's back. He's after us. It's Cervantes. If you want to stay alive, I need you to pull it together."

"He's back?" She turned her face up to peer at him through slitted eyelids.

"Yes. I think he saw us. Get ready to run."

"I'm not sure I can."

He lifted his head enough to meet her gaze. "You have to. If you want to get out of this, you have to."

He watched her visibly focus, struggle, strengthen. She straightened, blinking hard and setting her jaw. "I'm ready," she said. Her body betrayed her bravado, shaking with feverish violence.

"That's my girl." Stone twisted slightly. "Do you see a car behind us? A black one with tinted windows?"

Wren nodded. "Yes. There's a guy staring at us." She lifted up on her toes to peer past Stone's shoulder. "Oh…shit. He's—he's getting out."

A shout rang out from behind them. *"Ayun, ayun sila!" It's them!*

Stone whipped around, drawing his pistol and firing in one motion. The man who'd exited the car and shouted and stumbled backward, blood flowering from his chest. The car's doors opened and several men swarmed out, one of them Cervantes, who had been driving.

Stone pulled Wren along, shoving her ahead of him onto a side street that was more of an alley than a street, narrow and clogged with trash. He twisted around as he ran, adrenaline burning through him. A face appeared, and Stone cracked off a wild shot, missing, and then another, and a third. He wasn't sure if he hit with the second two shots, but the pursuit slowed, and he stumbled around a corner, hauling Wren by the bicep. He turned aimlessly, left and then right, lungs aching and fear dogging his steps. Wren was flagging quickly.

The street ended in a T-intersection, and to Stone's horror, Cervantes was waiting for them. He had a big, blocky, chrome pistol in his fist, and he raised it, squeezed the trigger. Stone shoved Wren to the side. She crashed into a wall and stumbled backward, then ducked when Cervantes' pistol cracked, hiding behind an overflowing dumpster.

Stone felt something slam into him, not exactly pain at first, more of a tremendous sense of impact, pressure, like a wrecking ball bashing into his side. He dropped the pistol, felt his toe send it skidding away. He stumbled, tripped, cursing, and jerked the other pistol from his waistband and sent round after round at Cervantes. He saw red at Cervantes' shoulder and on his arm, so he knew he'd hit him at least once, maybe twice.

Stone was hit too, though. Bad. His entire side was in agony, on fire. He couldn't breathe for the pain, but he had to move. He pressed his hand to his side, felt it come away wet and sticky and warm with blood. No time for anything but as much pressure as he could manage with one hand. Cervantes was gone, but he heard tires squealing behind them, shouts, sirens.

Wren was beside him, saying something. He shook his head, pushed her none too gently by the shoulder blades. "Just go. Run."

"But Stone, you're—"

"Just fucking run!" He pushed her again, and she stumbled into a run, left out of the alley.

He clenched his teeth and followed, twisting as he ran to watch for pursuit. Steps pounded, shouts echoed, and then three men burst from the alley, pistols in hand. They caught sight of Stone and Wren, and shots rang out, bullets buzzed angrily past their heads. Sirens howled not far away, southward somewhere and approaching. Stone leveled a few shots at their pursuers, thought he winged one, then tugged Wren down another alley and into an open doorway, hiding in the farthest, darkest corner.

An old man with white hair and a long white beard sat in a tattered wicker rocking chair, smoking something acrid and heavy from a pipe. He didn't speak, but his eyes pierced. He rocked twice, paused, inhaled, rocked twice, exhaled, rocked twice, inhaled. Stone lifted a finger to his lips, and the old man's head bobbed. He sucked at his pipe until his cheeks went hollow, and he held the smoke in his lungs for a long moment, then spewed it out in a slow, thin stream, then rocked twice more.

Footsteps thumped past, voices chattered breathlessly. Stone held his breath, felt Wren beside him doing the same. The voices stopped just beyond their hiding place, sounding angry. Stone was in too much pain to bother translating.

Smoke billowed from the old man's pipe, wreathing Wren and Stone and the small room in thick, acrid clouds. He tried not to breathe it in, but to do so was inevitable. He felt himself floating slightly, dizzy from the contact high. Long moments passed, and finally he dared to peek out of the doorway. He saw nothing, no one. He had one spare clip in the cargo pocket of his shorts, and he switched it for the mostly emptied one. He took a deep breath and led Wren out of the tiny, smoke-hazed room, away from the silent old man, out into the wild, sprawling slums of Manila.

11

WREN'S HEART POUNDED. She followed close behind Stone as he wended a dizzy path through a strange world of leaning shacks and muddy roads and stench and noise. She couldn't help staring around her in horror and pity.

"What is this place?" she asked, trying gamely to ignore the stiffness in her muscles, the soreness all over, the ache and the hunger and the gnawing fear and the residual terror at what had almost happened to her.

Stone didn't slow down or turn around. "This is Manila. The real Manila. One of the most densely populated and poorest cities on Earth." He stopped at an intersection of sorts, the wider road they were on sliced by a narrow track between shanties. He turned down this narrower track. "Most families live on something like $6 per day. Around here, more like $2 per day."

"How is that possible? How can someone live on $2 per day?"

"That's a family living on that, not a single person. It's about 250 Philippines Pesos per day for a family of three or four, sometimes more." He tossed this over his shoulder, his head always moving, eyes scanning.

Tripping over a cluster of empty brown glass bottles, Wren clutched at Stone's shoulder for balance. His skin was feverishly hot under her hand, and he was shivering, although he gave no indication of pain and showed no signs of slowing down.

"Are you okay?" Wren asked, then realized how stupid a question that was. He'd been shot; of course he wasn't okay. She'd watched it happen, kept seeing the way he'd jerked, stumbled backward, blood blossoming scarlet at his back. "We have to get you to a doctor, Stone."

Another turn, this time onto a road so skinny they had to nearly turn sideways to fit. Stone rolled his shoulders, pressing a palm to his side. "I'm fine."

Wren huffed. "You've been shot."

"And?"

"And you need medical attention."

"I need to clean it out, and I need bandages. And a shirt." He wiped sweat from his forehead while suppressing a shiver. "I'm not going to a hospital. Number one, they'll find us in a hospital. Two, we can't afford the time, or the money. Three, I'm just not going to a doctor, especially not one around here." He stopped and looked around, scanning the rooftops, glancing behind them. "Cervantes isn't going to give up. He's going to come after us again, and he's going to bring friends. Lots of friends with lots of guns."

"But how can he get away with that? We're American citizens."

Stone snorted. "This is his turf, babe. We disappear, they'll look, they won't find us, and they'll have a memorial service. We'll just be two more tourists who vanished into the slums."

"How did he find us so fast?"

Stone shrugged. "He's a crime boss. A sex slaver and probably a drug dealer, maybe even small arms dealer. He's got a huge network of informants, meaning he's got people all over Manila who do nothing but watch and report back to him."

Not knowing what to say to that, she just kept walking, trying desperately to ignore the feverish shaking and trembling need inside her, the crawling of her skin and the heavy ache in her soul.

Wren glanced above her head and saw clothes hanging on a line. She gestured. "Can't you just... borrow a shirt?"

Stone smirked at her. "You mean steal one? From someone who probably can't afford another one?"

Wren blushed. "I just meant—I mean—"

Stone laughed, then winced. "Relax. I know what you meant. I want to get out of this area first, and then I'll send you into a store to buy one for me." He leaned against a shanty, sheened with sweat and taking deep, slow breaths.

"Do you know the way out?"

Stone shrugged. "Out? There is no out. There's only somewhere else."

"So no."

"Not really." He coughed, and Wren watched the way his body shivered violently. She watched as he visibly forced himself upright.

"How'd you find me?" she asked, trying to distract him.

"I had a...guide."

Wren wasn't sure she wanted to know what that meant. There were a lot of things simmering in the back of her head that she couldn't afford to think about at that moment.

Stone set off at a stiff lope, forcing her to trot to keep up with him. Suddenly her foot slid in a puddle of mud, and she pitched forward. Her face smashed against Stone's back, and he twisted in place, catching her as she fell. His arms circled around her back, his hands pressing against her spine and shoulder blades. He took a step backward and leaned back against the building, sheltering her in his arms.

She smelled sweat, felt flesh under her cheek, hot and hard and slick. She heard his breathing and the faint thump of his heart, and for the briefest moment, the nightmare of the last few days slipped into the recesses of her mind. She shifted her feet, regaining her balance, but she didn't push away from Stone, and he didn't let go.

Wren felt herself drifting in his embrace, tilting and spinning and floating, breathing in his scent.

She'd wanted this for so long, it seemed. She'd spent an hour every Wednesday night for months sitting across from him, barely able to focus on his words, his instructions. She been hypnotized by the way the muscles in his forearms had shifted under his tanned, weathered skin. She hadn't been able to take her eyes off his biceps stretching the sleeves of his T-shirt, or off his fingers flexing on the guitar strings, nimble and sure. She watched his every movement, trying not to stare. Trying not to feel like a little girl with a hopeless crush.

She'd lain in her bed in her dorm room, wondering what it would feel like to have his arms around her, his hands on her. She wasn't a virgin—she'd had a couple boyfriends in college, but none of them had inspired the kind of feelings in her that Stone did. Jon, her last boyfriend, had been nice enough, attractive in a Virginia country good ole boy sort of way. He was a guy, definitely all-male, well-built, and attentive as a lover, given to wearing camo hats and ripped blue jeans and dirty Timberland boots and Browning T-shirts. He rode dirt bikes and went mudding and fished every Sunday morning, rain or shine. Wren had had a good time with him, but it hadn't meant anything. They'd been friends, more than anything. Friends who slept together, but friends. She hadn't felt the kind of...*need* that she felt for Stone.

She remembered the first time she'd seen him. He'd arrived at LifeBridge just as Nick was getting ready to start his message, had stood in the back with his arms crossed over his chest. He was a huge, dominating presence, even from a distance. She'd been sitting at the far edge of the semi-circular arrangement of padded church chairs, so she'd seen him slip in, and she'd been immediately struck by him. He was six foot four and muscled in the lean, lupine sort of way. He wasn't classically beautiful, not in the Hollywood way. Taken individually, his facial features were too hard and rough to be classified as "hot" or "handsome". His nose had been broken more than once, it looked like, and his eyes were deep-set, permanently narrowed and squinting, his jaw square and so hard it looked like you could break rocks on it. He had a white scar on his right cheekbone, a crescent-shaped ridge of puckered flesh. When you put all those features together, you had a person who was masculine in the extreme, the very picture of raw manhood. His beauty was in his brutal power and lethal grace.

"Okay, babe?" Stone's deep, gravelly voice brought Wren back to the present. The sun was setting, shedding orange light on the city.

She nodded against his chest. "I just slipped."

"Uh huh." Something in Stone's voice told Wren he knew she wasn't okay. "We should keep moving."

"Where are we going?"

He sighed. "I'm not sure. A hostel or motel, somewhere cheap that won't ask any questions. You need food and rest."

"What about you?"

Stone's hands were rubbing circles on her back, soothing, comforting. "I'm fine. This isn't the first time I've been shot."

Wren wasn't sure what to say. "Thank you for—"

Stone didn't let her finish. "Not now. Don't think about it. Don't say it." He looked down at her, and Wren tilted her head to meet his brown eyes. "I won't let anything happen to you. I don't care what I have to do. I'll get you home, I promise."

Her hands had found their way to his shoulders, curled under his armpits to clutch him tightly. "Stone…" She wanted to try to express what was in her head, in her heart, tried to let it out through her eyes.

He wouldn't let her finish. "I know, okay? But not now. We're not safe yet." He shivered, squeezing his eyes shut and shifting his torso. He pushed forward and twisted Wren in place, gently nudging her into a walk. "Come on. Let's try and find our way out of here."

Wren felt eyes on her as they wound their way through disorienting maze of ramshackle huts and crudely assembled shelters. She glanced around as frequently as Stone did, the back of her neck tingling. She never saw anyone other than the occasional local peeking through windows, children watching from doorways, or huddled under awnings and overhangs.

A thin, mangy, matted dog trotted past, tongue lolling. It watched them, one bent and drooping ear twitching, the other upright.

The sounds of traffic coming from ahead of them had Stone increasing his pace, but their progress was constantly frustrated by the fact that the shantytown roads didn't follow any kind of plan, and they constantly had to backtrack and find another way when their path gave out at a dead end.

And then Stone made a turn, cursed, and came to a stop, the pistol in his right fist rising. From behind him, Wren couldn't see anything around his broad back, but the way his body tensed told her all she needed to know.

She risked a peek around him, and saw that the way ahead was blocked by three men with short, compact machine guns. Cervantes wasn't one of them, thank God.

"Be ready," Stone breathed, not taking his eyes off the men in front of them.

Wren nodded, not sure what to be ready for, but she tried to mentally prepare herself to move. She glanced around, saw a narrow opening just ahead on their right. She would break for that opening. Her hand trembled, and she realized she was panting, almost hyperventilating. She slowed her breathing and focused on Stone's back. She wasn't ready for gunfire, for blood and death. She wasn't ready. There were too many men, and she wasn't going to be any help.

The moment drew out until Wren's nerves were shredded.

It happened between one breath and the next. She saw, almost in slow motion, Stone's back flex, his arm lift, hands coming up to cup the pistol, his body twisting slightly. The pistol jerked in his hands, popping with a deafening blast, once, twice, three times. As soon as the first *BANG!* reached her ears, Wren jerked into a run, lunging for the opening, feet slipping in the mud. She slammed into the side of the building, pain wracking through her as something sharp scraped her arm through her shirt, her bruised or cracked rib screaming until she couldn't breathe, couldn't see, but she kept moving, twisting away from the building, through the opening, slipping again, feet shooting out from beneath her, sending her into the mud. The slimy wetness splashed, coating her, smelling awful and dripping in her hair, down her skin, coating her khaki shorts and white shirt.

It wasn't entirely mud, she realized.

Wren choked back the vomit and struggled to her feet. Gunfire barked just feet away, chains of single rounds from Stone, chainsaw chatter ripping from the machine guns. Several rounds thunked and cracked into the side of the building, spitting shards of wood and splinters of concrete, dinging off metal, ricocheting into the alley. Something hot and angry buzzed past her ear, causing her to lurch forward, slip, and stagger toward the opening.

Silence reigned, then, deafening and thick. Where was Stone? Was he dead?

She peered around the corner, crouching low, ignoring the howl of pain and the stench now coating her. Two bodies lay in the street, bleeding red into the mud. Something bright flashed from a window, accompanied by a deafening racket. The mud at her feet exploded, the building by her face exploded, and something stung her eyes, flecked her cheek.

"Get back!" Stone's voice shouted from several feet away. "Get the fuck back, Wren! Stay down, goddammit!"

She threw herself backward as the fire flashed again, and the buzzing, snapping, whizzing of bees past her face had her tumbling to her backside into the muddy sewage. Stone's gun banged twice, and she heard a grunt and a harsh fading curse in Filipino. Silent moments passed, and then she heard Stone's angry voice, Filipino denials, and then...

BANGBANG.

Stone appeared in the mouth of the alley, a fresh red crease along his stomach weeping crimson. Blood was spattered on his chest and face, tiny red dots. It wasn't his blood, she realized. He was breathing hard, each breath making his muscles swell and his chest expand. His eyes were hot and dangerous, but they softened as he approached her. He reached out with a slightly shaky hand and plucked slivers and shards from her hair, and then wiped a palm over her cheeks, one side and then the other. She hissed when his hand ran over something sharp embedded in her skin.

"Shit, sorry." He bent closer to her face, eyes narrowed, and pulled a splinter from her skin, tossing it aside. His eyes met hers. "That was stupid, Wren. Next time, stay out of the way."

"I just…I'm—I'm sorry," she mumbled. "I just needed to know if you were—"

"If I'm worried about you staying out of the way, I'm not focused on *them*, and that's what'll get us killed." His eyes flashed. "If shit gets hairy, get out of the way and stay out of the way until I get you. All right?"

Wren nodded. "I get it. I'm sorry I distracted you."

Stone's gaze raked over her. "Fell into the mud, did you?" His tone was jocular, although the tight wrinkles at the corner of his eyes betrayed the fact that he was in pain.

Wren tried to bury her nausea, but couldn't entirely. "It's not just mud."

Stone's eyes widened. "Oh…oh, shit." He seemed to be suppressing laughter.

"Yeah. Exactly." She glared up at him. "I'm glad you think it's so funny."

"Sorry, it's not funny." His expression sobered up, but then he leaned close and took a whiff. "We gotta get you cleaned up. You stink, babe."

Wren wanted to come up with a witty reply, but everything hurt. She sagged, feeling herself stumble, and then she was caught in strong arms. She was so tired. She was trying to be strong, but…she just couldn't anymore. She felt something hot curling in her throat, something wet sliding down her face. "I'm sorry, Stone. I'm just so tired. And it hurts. It hurts."

"What hurts?" His voice was tender.

She tried to breathe through the need to cry, refusing to let it out. "Everything."

Stone cursed and pressed his fingertips to her side, prodding gently until his touch, gentle as it was, found her hurt rib. She couldn't mute her agonized whimper. "Shit. How the hell are you upright?"

She liked the raw admiration in his tone. "Didn't have a choice, did I?" She was so close to crying, to just breaking down.

But there were dead men in the alley, and someone would find them soon. She levered herself out of Stone's warm embrace, breathed deeply and wiped her hands on a clean part of her shirt, then brushed away the tears that had escaped. Shallow breaths, careful movements. Adrenaline was wearing off, she realized, and reality was setting in.

"Let's go," she said, trying to sound stronger than she was.

Stone watched her, as if assessing. She took shallow breaths and tried not to move. Stone shook his head. "Try to take deep breaths regularly. I know it hurts, but it's important, since it'll prevent infection, hopefully." He took her shoulders and gingerly helped her twist at the waist. "Does it hurt more when you move like this?"

Wren couldn't get words out, could only gasp and nod. "Yes," she said, when she could breathe again.

"That's a good thing, actually. It means it's just muscle and tissue damage, maybe some bruising to the bone. I don't think it's broken." He peered around the corner, and then moved out into the open. As they neared the bodies of the men he'd killed, Stone gathered her close to his side. "Don't look."

Wren didn't want to. She buried her face against his arm, letting him guide her past the bodies. She smelled blood, and something else, something indefinable. It was, she realized, the smell of death.

She opened her eyes as they turned a corner and heard the sounds of traffic. They'd left the shantytown, which hopefully meant access to food, water, and somewhere to rest.

She wasn't sure how much longer she could go on.

12

Stone held Wren tight against his uninjured side, trying not to let her get jostled. They were on a bus heading north; he was thinking of Quezon City, a lively area of Manila where two Americans wouldn't be quite so out of place. He wasn't heading south toward downtown commercial Manila, though. That's where they'd be expected to go. They were both a mess, and drawing stares. Stone was clearly gunshot. Wren was covered in mud and shit, barely conscious, and obviously in pain. He'd stuffed the pistol into his waistband, but the butt was still visible.

Inconspicuous they were not.

They rode the bus for around twenty minutes, and then, simply to throw off any possible pursuit, switched lines. As they transferred, Stone grabbed a guide to the Manila bus lines, consulting the map as he held onto a vertical bar. Four stops later, they were heading toward Quezon City, part of the massive, sprawling Metro Manila area. It had been the capital of the Philippines for a few decades, and was still the wealthiest part of the country. Which meant access to better food and hopefully some kind of medicine.

After far too long on the rumbling, rattling bus, Stone half-carried Wren off the vehicle and onto Visayas Avenue where it dead-ended into Tandang Sora Avenue. Here, their rough and ragged appearance drew even more stares from the scurrying crowds. Cars rushed by, honking, squealing brakes, buses rumbled, voices chattered. Stone tried to push away the burning shriek of pain in his side, and the stares.

He pointed. "There, a Savemore." He directed them toward it, then found a small gap between buildings and slumped into it, wedging himself in place. "Go in, buy us some supplies. Bottles of water, as many as you can carry. Some tampons. A shirt for me. Bandages and medical tape. Antiseptic spray, if they have it." He handed Wren a wad of pesos.

Wren took it, and hesitated. "Tampons? Why? I'm not—I mean—"

Stone grunted as he shifted to a more comfortable position. "Not for you. Me. Small ones, light ones. Best thing for through-and-through wounds. We'll need food too. A backpack to carry everything."

"I'm going in by myself?" she asked.

Stone nodded. "You're less...conspicuous than I am. Don't talk to anyone. Keep your eyes peeled, watch around you, behind you. You feel anything weird, like a bad feeling, or if you see anyone suspicious, get out of there ASAP. Don't stop, don't come back for me, just run."

"But what if—" Wren's eyes were wide, her voice tremulous.

Stone cut her off. "You can only deal with the here and now, babe. This is all there is. What ifs won't keep you alive." He took her hand in his and tried to send courage through his gaze. "You'll be fine. You're just getting some supplies. Don't worry about me. Don't even think about me. Get in, get out."

Wren nodded, straightening the folded, wadded, colorful pesos. "You won't...you won't leave without me?" She wouldn't look at him, staring at the ground between her feet.

Stone shifted upright, gathered her against his chest. She felt small and warm against him, fit perfectly underneath his chin. "No, Wren. I'll never leave you. I'll be right here. Promise."

She took a deep breath and stepped away, folded the pesos in half and straightened her body, wincing as the movement stretched her injured ribs. "Okay. I'll be right back."

"Remember, water, a shirt, tampons, food."

"Got it."

"And Wren?" Stone didn't let her hand go just yet. "I need you to hustle, okay? On the double, babe."

She nodded, swallowed hard, and backed away, entering the market. Stone moved deeper into the space between buildings. It was a gap, really, not even properly an alley, so narrow he had stay sideways to fit. Now that Wren was out of sight, he let himself slump, let himself hiss and groan as he pressed a hand to the wound. It hurt so bad, so bad. He was worried about infection, but he doubted he'd find any antibiotics. He'd just have to keep it clean and hope. And pray.

He was struggling to stay upright, beyond exhausted. Then he felt the tingling at the back of his neck, the tightening of his gut. Warning signs. Apprehension.

He slid a pistol from his waistband and shifted farther back, deeper into the gap, ignoring the heat and the pain. He felt his senses sharpen, his focus tuning in. He heard a heavy footfall, voices. The sounds stopped near his hiding place, and then he heard two voices conversing.

"Nakita sila nung matandang babae na bumaba malapit dito." The old woman saw them get off the bus near here.

"Hanapin sila. Ibalik nyo yung babae kay Cervantes. Patayin yung lalaki." Find them. Cervantes wants the girl. Kill the man.

Stone's Filipino was sketchy at best, but he caught enough to know they were talking about him and Wren. He tightened his grip on the pistol and held his breath. He heard them move forward, saw them pass by him, one and then a second. He waited a few more seconds, then moved to the street, peering out from his hiding place. They were readily identifiable, two powerfully built men with submachine guns out in plain sight, interrogating people on the street. They cornered a man sitting in the lee of a building, old and wrinkled and tired, hunched over a bottle. The old man pointed with an unsteady hand, seemed to be speaking at length, gesturing. When the two thugs had the information they wanted, they turned away. The old derelict lifted a hand in supplication. Even from a few hundred feet away, he could see the cruelty in the way the two thugs stopped, turned around, tossed a peso to the dirt in front of the old man, and then kicked him when he reached for it. He hunched into a ball as kicks rained down, the thugs laughing as they brutalized him.

Stone's fury burned hot as he watched the two men stroll away, laughing and shoving each other. They were heading directly toward the market. Wrenching himself into action, Stone followed.

Ahead, he could see the entrance to the Savemore, where Wren had gone for supplies. The two men wove through the crowds, scanning, shoving people aside, casually ignoring the glances and curses. Stone had to stop them before they spotted Wren. But he had to do it without attracting attention.

A vendor stood at a cart, chopping vegetables with a large knife. Stone dug another wad of pesos from his pocket, pointed at the knife and held out the money. The vendor looked baffled, but shrugged and handed over the knife. Stone shoved his pistol back into his waistband and returned his attention to the market. The thugs were inside the pharmacy. Stone broke into a run, pressing his palm to his side and stifling the groans of pain. He headed through the door, down an aisle, behind one of the men. They'd split up, providing him with an excellent opportunity to take them out one at a time.

The first thug was alone in the aisle near the corner, surrounded by deodorant and shampoo and soap and toothbrushes. Stone gathered his nerves, tightened his grip on the knife, and lunged. The thug heard or sensed something at the last second, whirling, and the blade missed his throat—Stone's original target. The tip glanced off his cheekbone, and Stone sent his fist into the thug's face, buying a split-second. With a quick slash, he dragged the blade across the man's exposed throat, unleashing a sluice of blood. It was messy, but effective. Stone danced away from the hot spray, moving past the falling body, around the corner before it hit the tile. He had to search three more aisles before he found the second thug, who had taken a bottle of soda, opened it and was chugging it, earning the irate scolding of an apron-clad worker. As he approached from behind, Stone heard the thug laughing, telling the terrified but determined young man to get lost. When the thug hefted his gun, the worker scurried away. Guzzling the soda, the thug didn't hear Stone come up behind him, nor did he notice the blade as it flashed upward, under his diaphragm and into his lung, collapsing it. Stone lurched toward the exit once more. Shouts and screams erupted as the bodies were discovered, and Stone used the sudden chaos as an excuse to slip away, hopefully unnoticed. As he stumbled back toward his previous hiding place, he saw Wren spinning in circles. She had a child's pink *Hello Kitty* backpack on her back, and a terrified expression on her face.

Stone whistled, and she whirled around, relief flooding her features as she saw him approaching. Horror replaced relief when she saw the knife in his fist, the blood coating his hand and forearm. He cleaned the knife on his shirt, and then slid it between his belt and shorts.

"You—you weren't here," Wren said. "Where—what happened?"

"We had company." He turned Wren around and unzipped the backpack, scooped up the shirt and one of four liter-bottles of water.

The shirt was several sizes too big, but it would cover him. He uncapped the water and took several gulps, then dumped it over his crimson-coated forearm, scrubbing away the worst of the blood.

Wren took the bottle when he handed it to her. She drank, closing her eyes in obvious bliss. Recapping it, she eyed him. "So we had company? And you...you killed them?"

"Couldn't let them find us, or get word back to Cervantes."

"Are you...did they hurt you?"

Stone shook his head. "No, babe. They never even saw me." He stuffed the nearly empty water bottle back into the backpack, rummaged again and pulled two energy bars out, unwrapping one and handing the other to Wren. "Good job, Wren. You got some good stuff. Eat this. We gotta hole up, get off the street."

He led her back to the intersection, where he stopped and scanned, spotting a hotel across the road. He pointed, and Wren nodded, understanding. It turned out to be a fancy place, nicer than Stone would have chosen as a hideaway. He didn't have enough Philippines Pesos, so he had to pay for a room with some of his American dollars. The clerk behind the counter eyed them carefully, suspicion filling his features as he took in their ragged appearances.

Stone peeled a hundred dollar bill and slid it across the counter to the clean, groomed, neat-looking Filipino man. "My girlfriend and I had a bit too much fun, know what I mean?" He let the number on the bill show, but didn't give it to the clerk yet. "We lost our luggage, but we're too exhausted to go buy new stuff."

The clerk reached for the money. "I will get new, no problems, no problems."

Stone jerked it back. "See, the other issue is, we're kind of eloping. So we need it to be kept quiet."

The clerk narrowed his eyes. "Eloping? What dis?"

Stone leaned close, whispering conspiratorially, dragging Wren against his side. "Getting married, but her parents don't know. It's a secret."

Smiling wide, the clerk nodded. "Ah, yes, yes. Run away, get married."

Stone let him take the money. "So, if any of her brothers comes looking, you haven't seen us, huh?"

"You need doctor, yeah?" The clerk's eyes focused on Stone's blood-soaked shirt.

"No. I just...fell. I'm fine."

"Sure, okay, man." The clerk clearly knew exactly how Stone had gotten hurt, but he said nothing.

"I'm feeling kinda sick, you know?" Stone said. "So, if you happened to know where to get some antibiotics, there'd be another one of those in it for you." He tapped the $100 bill with his forefinger, which was crusted with blood he hadn't managed to clean off.

"I might. Not cheap, but I get it." He glanced at Wren, his expression openly curious, if not lustful.

She blushed under his scrutiny and giggled, pressing closer to Stone and nuzzling his neck. Stone had to force himself to stay calm, to play the part. It was difficult, though, with Wren's mouth against his throat, her shy laugh in his ear, her arms around his neck. It was a game, an act, though it felt like anything but.

It was purely to convince the clerk, then, that he pressed a kiss to her cheek, and then her lips. It wasn't that he wanted to kiss her, obviously. He just had to play the part. That's all. Yet he couldn't catch his breath as he tasted her mouth, felt her warmth, her tongue touching his upper lip. She was responding, giving in, playing the part back.

Only, the kiss went on longer than it needed to, and when they broke apart, Wren's flushed face and widened eyes didn't look faked. Nor did her surprise, or her raw desire.

"I tink you need room for dat, huh?" The clerk handed them the envelope with two key-cards, the room number written in marker across the front. "Number two-two-tree."

Stone took the envelope with the keycard and tugged Wren to elevator. She clung to him, but now it wasn't merely for support. There was another element to way she held on to him. It was closer, somehow. More intimate. Her palms were flat on his chest and her eyes were locked on his face. Her full breasts were pressed against him, showing him tantalizing glimpses of her tan skin.

The elevator opened, and a young Caucasian couple stumbled out, laughing uproariously, holding on to each other, reeking of alcohol. The man had dreadlocks held back by a white bandana, and he wore khaki capri pants, flip flops, and a tie-dyed Grateful Dead shirt. The girl was dressed similarly.

"Dude, you're like, bleeding, man," the dreadlocked drunk said. "You okay, dude?"

Stone growled. "Dude, I'm, like, fine. Mind your own, like, fucking business."

The guy held up his hands. "Sure thing man. Whatever. I was just thinking, I've got some vikes in my room. Thought you might want one, you know?"

"Vicodin?"

He nodded. "Yeah, man. They ain't, like, legal or whatever, but they're the real deal."

Stone fished out a $50. "I could use one."

The couple lurched back onto the elevator, and Stone and Wren followed them to their fourth-floor room, which stank of pot and cigarettes. Empty bottles of vodka were scattered everywhere, and Stone saw an ashtray full of joint roaches. Dreadlocks picked up a small cellophane packet with four large white pills stamped with the word "Vicodin".

"Here, man. The fifty should cover it." He took the bill and handed Stone the baggie. "Anybody asks, you didn't get that shit from me."

"And you never saw us," Stone said.

"Saw who?" Dreadlocks answered.

Stone just nodded, prodding Wren out of the room and toward the elevator. As the door left, he heard the girl ask her boyfriend, "Are you sure he wasn't a cop? He kind of looked like a cop. And that looked like a gunshot wound."

"I don't know, man. He might've been. But he didn't arrest us, did he?" A thoughtful pause. "Besides, we're in the fucking Philippines, aren't we? I don't think an American cop can arrest us here. Juris-duty, or something."

"You mean *jurisdiction*, you moron."

Stone shook his head and led Wren back to the elevator. A thought struck him, and he dug into his pants pocket, withdrawing Wren's cross. He dangled it in front of her by the chain. "I thought you might want this back."

Wren took it in a trembling palm. "Oh, my god, Stone. Thank you." She pressed the cross to her lips. "This was an adoption gift from my parents."

Stone hugged her briefly as the elevator doors whooshed open. As soon as they found their room, Wren dropped the backpack onto the floor and fell onto the bed, then winced.

"God, a real bed. Thank you, Jesus." She pressed a hand to her ribs, taking a deep breath and shifting her torso.

Stone watched her sprawl, watched her breathing slow and become even, and then she was asleep. He watched her for a few minutes more, and then snatched the backpack up and moved into the bathroom. He lowered himself onto the closed toilet seat and then, holding his breath, peeled his shirt away from the wound, expelling his pent-up breath in an explosive hiss as the clotted, drying blood snatched at his skin and at the open wound.

Before he did anything else, Stone needed to be clean. He turned the shower on, washed down one of the Vicodin while he waited for the water to get hot, and then stripped out of his shorts and stepped in. The water scoured his skin and the torn flesh, but the heat felt good, relaxing his exhausted muscles. He stood under the spray for a moment, and then washed up and got out, wrapping a towel around his waist.

Taking a seat on the toilet, he grabbed the closest towel and pressed beneath the wound. He took an unopened bottle of water, and, using the tip of the knife, worked a small hole into the bottom of the bottle. The spray from the shower had set the wound bleeding again, so Stone held the towel beneath the entrance wound, and then, tilting his body back as far as he could, squeezed the bottle so water squirted in a thin, high-pressure stream into the bullet hole. His breath expelled in a gasping moan, but he gritted his teeth and squirted more water in, catching the excess as it sluiced away, pink with blood. He soaked through one towel, tossed it into the tub, and grabbed another, pouring water into the wound until the bottle was gone. Then he fished the small bottle of antiseptic spray from the backpack, opened it, and sprayed the entrance hole.

The next part was trickier. He had to do the same to the exit hole, which he couldn't really reach on his own. He debated trying, but knew it would ineffective. Pressing the towel to the opening, he shook Wren awake.

She moaned, murmured, and then finally cracked her eyes open.

"Sorry, babe, but I need your help."

Wren sat up and blinked, shivered. Her forehead was dotted with sweat, and she scratched at her skin, then caught herself and stopped. "Help with what?"

Stone crossed the room to resume his seat on the toilet, this time facing the tub to give her access to the exit hole. "Squirt some water into the hole for me."

Wren knelt behind him in the small bathroom, taking the red-soaked towel from him. She handed him one of the unopened bottles of water, and he poked a hole into it, then handed the bottle back to her.

"Will it hurt?" she asked.

"I've got a bullet hole in my side," Stone said. "Everything about it hurts. I'll be fine."

Wren cupped the towel against his back and poured the water onto the hole. Stone suppressed the hiss of pain, grinding his teeth until they hurt.

After she'd used the entire bottle, he nodded. "Good," he said. "Now spray the antiseptic on it. A lot, from an inch or two away." She sprayed it liberally, and he couldn't stop a groan from escaping. "Good. Okay, now open the tampon for me."

She did so, and Stone slid it into the hole, grimacing and growling as the cotton scraped the raw edges of open flesh. The string hung down his side, and he ripped a piece of the medical tape and fastened the string to his skin so he could pull the tampon free later. Wren had bought a roll of gauze, so he wrapped that tightly around his body, covering the wound and applying a bit of pressure. He taped the ends to his skin and then sank back against the cold porcelain, trying to even out his ragged breathing.

It would have to do for now. He was lightheaded and weak, which meant he'd lost a lot of blood.

"What now?" Wren asked.

"Now we hope I don't pick up an infection. If that clerk can find some antibiotics, I'd be happier, but if not, we'll just have to pray."

Stone uncapped the bottle he'd already opened and drank from it. He finished the liter and then forced himself to his feet. He was dizzy, exhausted, hungry, and tense. He checked the latch on the door, then slid the chain into place, and propped a chair under the handle. Finally, he couldn't stay upright any longer.

"One of us should really keep watch, but I don't think either of us is capable. I'm dead on my feet." He sank gingerly onto the bed. "You should take a shower before you fall back asleep."

Wren nodded and went into the bathroom, closing the door behind her. After a moment, the shower turned on and Stone was left to picture her naked and wet beneath the water. Twenty minutes later, she emerged from the bathroom wrapped in a towel. She rounded the bed and lay down on the edge, stiff and seeming unsure. Stone wrestled with himself briefly, and then gave in.

"Get over here, babe."

"What?" Wren's eyes were wide.

Stone extended his arm and crooked his finger at her. "Come over here. Closer, so I can hold you." Wren wriggled over until her head was on his chest. He curled his arm around her, holding her waist and trying not to let his hand wander lower. "Better?"

Wren nodded, and within moments was asleep. Stone wasn't far behind, despite the fact that they were both wearing nothing but towels.

An unknowable time later, Stone woke up with Wren curled against his uninjured side. She was tensed, even pressed against him. He knew by her breathing that she was awake.

"Stone?" She rolled away slightly, clutching the towel in place. She searched his eyes. "In the lobby… was that just…I mean—did you—?"

"I don't know, Wren. Honestly I don't. I don't know what it means."

"Did you…feel anything?" Her voice was small and hesitant.

"Of course I did," he said. "How could I kiss you and not feel anything?"

She shrugged, and the towel slipped slightly, drawing Stone's attention to her cleavage. He forced his gaze to her eyes when she spoke. "I don't know. It's so hard to tell with you. You don't ever seem to show emotions. You don't show pain, or fear, or happiness, or anything. You're just this wall of...stone."

Stone laughed. "How do you think I got the nickname 'Stone' in the first place?"

Wren's face scrunched. "Nickname? Stone's not your real name?"

He shook his head. "Nope. I got it after my first combat mission."

"Why?"

"Well, like you said, I don't really...show much. I never have. And then during combat I was just stone-cold calm the whole time, and my L-T made some kind of casual remark, like, 'you're made of stone or something, Pressfield,' and the nickname Stone just stuck."

"So they gave the nickname to you for being unemotional?"

Stone wobbled his head side to side in a 'not really but sort of' gesture. "It's a little more complicated than that."

"What do you mean?"

Stone sighed. "It's another one of those things I don't like to talk about."

"I watched you kill men today, Stone. I think I can handle some old story."

"It's not just because I'm stone-cold emotionally; it's because I seemed like a stone-cold killer. That first combat mission, it went off the rails. Went bad. Old intel, the bad guys had more backup than we'd anticipated. One of them got the drop on L-T, and I was out of ammo. Rookie mistake, you know? Shooting too much, waiting till empty to reload. Supposed to reload when you've got a few rounds left, and you never just throw the clip away like in the movies. You save it. Reuse it. Anyway, a tango got the drop on L-T, and I was out of ammo. For some stupid reason, I went for my KA-BAR instead of my sidearm—"

"Kay-bar? What's that?"

"Combat knife. I should have shot the fucker, but I stabbed him instead. Of course, unless you know exactly what you're doing and where to stab and all that, you never get a guy on the first try with a knife. It's surprisingly hard to kill a man with a knife. That's why you always hear about someone being stabbed like twenty or thirty times. The human body can withstand a shitload of damage as long as it doesn't stop the heart immediately, or the brain. So I got the guy, but he had a gun and I had my knife, and L-T was down, wounded, so I just laid into him again. Not thinking, just doing." Stone flexed his hand, remembering the feel of the knife in his hand and the warmth of blood on his hands for the first time.

"Shooting someone from far away, that's one thing. Even from thirty feet away with a pistol. It still takes it out of you, hits you hard the first few times you do it. But to kill someone up close and personal like that? With your hands? You watch the light go out of his eyes. You watch him turn into a dead husk right in front of you. Watch him bleed out, knowing you did that to him. And because I don't show much emotion, and never have, it seemed to everyone else that I just did it easy as you please, no guilt, no remorse."

"Did you? Feel that stuff?" Wren asked, sounding shaken.

"Shit yeah. Of course. I wanted to puke afterward. I couldn't sleep for weeks, seeing his face every time I closed my eyes. That mission, those first kills? I'll never forget them. Not for as long as I live. I don't really remember most of the others, but you never forget the first man you kill."

Wren didn't answer for a long time. When she did, it was in a tiny whisper. "Have you killed a lot of people?"

Stone just nodded. "Too many."

"And today. You killed people today. For me."

He pulled her against him. "Yeah. And there will probably be more before we're safe."

"I'm sorry, I didn't plan on talking about this."

"It's inevitable. You've seen some awful shit. Experienced hell." He touched her cheek with the knuckle of his forefinger. "At least you're with me, now. Safe. And you weren't raped."

"I saw it, though. I saw...girls. A lot of them. Being...used. And that was almost me. If you hadn't—"

"But I did. I've got you."

Wren burrowed against him, relaxing into him, slipping a hand across his chest and holding him. "Thank you, Stone. Thank you, so much."

Stone felt his heart constrict and expand. She sounded so vulnerable. Felt so right, in his arms like this. "Of course, babe."

"What's your real name?"

Stone sighed. "I was born George Alexander Pressfield the third. My grandfather was the captain of an aircraft carrier in World War II, and my father commanded a PT boat during Vietnam. My great-grandfather was in the Navy, too. So that makes me a fourth-generation Navy brat."

"George? Really?" Wren sounded amused.

He pulled back and glared down at her. "Is that funny to you? Is it funny that I'm George the third?"

She nodded, laughing now. "Yes! It is funny, actually. George. Little Georgie."

Stone growled. "That's why I go by Stone. I was never so glad for a nickname in all my life."

"Maybe I'll call you George from now on," Wren suggested.

"You better not."

"Sensitive much?"

"I hate that name. I've always hated that name. Even in elementary school, I would introduce myself as Alex. I actually went by Alex until I got the nickname Stone." He laughed. "I refused to answer to anyone unless they called me Alex. I got detention almost every day for the first half of third grade because my teacher refused to call me anything but George. Eventually we compromised on 'Mr. Pressfield.'"

Wren shifted against him, and now the humor was gone from her eyes. In its place something else, something hot and desperate and alluring. "So you won't answer if I call you Georgie? Even if we're alone?"

Stone shook his head. "Nope."

She moved even closer, and now she was pressed against him, almost lying on top of him. Her legs were warm against his. "I like Georgie. It's cute."

"I'm a Navy SEAL. I don't do cute."

"Am I cute?"

Stone sighed. "Wren, are you sure this is—"

"You kissed me in the lobby," Wren cut in. "You can't pretend it didn't mean something to you. It did for me. And I saw your eyes. I'm learning to read you, you know."

"Wren—"

"You said you don't do cute. Well, what about me?"

"You're not cute," Stone growled. "You're beautiful. So much more than beautiful. You're strong. You're tough. You're sweet. And you're sexy."

Wren's face split into a smile, but it quickly faded into seriousness. "Will you kiss me again? Please?"

Stone closed his eyes briefly. "I'm not sure this is the best time or place."

"I'm not asking for anything else. Just a kiss."

"There's no such thing as 'just a kiss.'"

"Sure there is."

"Not with me, there's not." He had to look away from her, away from her desire-hot eyes. "You've been through hell. We're both hurt and filthy. And now all of a sudden we're gonna kiss?"

"This isn't sudden, Stone. I've wanted you to kiss me...for so long. For like—since the first time I met you. Every time we played guitar, I would have to make myself focus on the music instead of kissing you."

Stone exhaled noisily. "But you've seen what I do. What I am. And you're so sweet, so kind. So innocent."

She pushed away from him angrily. "I'm *not* innocent. I'm not a virgin. And with everything I've been through over the last few days, I'm even less innocent. I know what I want. I want you. I've always wanted you. And you know it, too. We talked about this before we left for Manila."

Stone scrubbed his face. "Dammit. I don't even know…I don't know what to say."

"Tell me how you feel. Tell me what you're thinking. Do you feel the same way? Do you really just see me as just a friend? Or just a student? If so, I'll drop this. But I don't think you do. I think there's more." Her hand, till now resting on his chest, slid upward, touched his jaw.

Stone swallowed hard. "Yeah, there's more."

"So what do you want to do about that?"

Her hand on his jaw was soft and delicate and warm. It made it hard for him to think. "I'm not sure it's right to do anything about it. I—I'm not…I'm not good. For…you."

Wren didn't answer right away. She just stared at him, into him. "I think your problem is you don't think you're good, full stop."

"I'm not."

"What if I don't agree, and don't care if you are or aren't?"

"You should."

She groaned in frustration, rolling away from him. "God, you're so stubborn."

"Wren, it's not a matter of desire. That's exactly the problem. I *do* desire. I just—I'm not sure it's okay to let it happen."

"Shouldn't I have some say in that?" She wasn't turning back to him.

"Maybe. But…right now?"

"All I wanted was another kiss. Just…to see how it felt again. To…distract myself."

"Distract yourself from what?"

She finally rolled back to face him, and her eyes were wet. "All this. Everything. Being here, in Manila. I…can't let myself cry about it, or I won't stop. And… the withdrawal is driving me crazy. I hurt. I'm tired. I'm scared. And I can't even begin to think about the things I've seen. Those girls getting raped. Almost being sold for sex myself. Men being killed in front of me. You getting shot. I just…I want to pretend, even for thirty *fucking* seconds, that it's just you and me in a hotel room, alone. Nothing else to deal with. Is that so wrong?" She wiped her eyes with both hands. "I just…I want to feel something else."

Stone let go, then. He couldn't help but draw her to him, wrap her in his arms. This time, she turned her face up, eyes closed, and he let it happen. He let his lips touch hers, gently, gently. Hesitantly.

He'd wanted it too, after all. Ever since the first time he'd walked in to his high school buddy Nick's church and saw her for the first time. Now here she was, basically begging him, and making a pretty damn good case for why it was okay to do this. To kiss her like this.

It was magical. The macho guy in Stone hated how girly that sounded in his head. But it was the truth. All the girls he'd kissed, on base and off, on deployment and on leave, none of them compared to the way this kiss felt.

Her lips touched his, and at first they merely touched. Soft, wet, and warm. And then her mouth moved, and she was kissing him, moving her lips against his, seeking, searching, opening, and he wanted more. He let his tongue slip out and she tasted it with her own. Her palm touched his face, lay flat against his cheek and she was writhing against him, lost in the kiss.

He was lost, too. He couldn't have stopped the kiss if he'd wanted to, and he didn't want to. He wanted to let it go on forever, just kiss her like this. It was just a kiss, but it was more. It was him giving in, letting the things he'd felt for so long, wanted for long, rise to the surface.

Stone's hand curled around her back, pulled her tighter against him, and then slipped back down to the small of her spine, rested and hesitated there, and then she pulled his lower lip into her mouth and sucked on it, and Stone's hand moved down a few more inches to cup her backside over the towel.

Wren moaned into his mouth, let his lip go and kissed the corner of his mouth. Her hand clutched the column of his neck, and she kissed him, deeper than ever, with complete abandon. Stone felt the male need in him take over, and he moved his hand beneath the towel, touching bare skin, holding the supple globe of her ass in his hand and kissing her, trying to hang on to the last vestige of control. Gunshot or not, he couldn't keep kissing her like this for much longer, or it would go where he couldn't hold back.

He was already nearing that place. He moved his grip to the other side of her ass, marveling at how firm yet soft she was. She kissed him voraciously, as if she couldn't get enough of him. It was primal, the way she kissed him, at odds with the sweet and innocent persona she gave off the rest of the time.

Stone's other hand brushed her hair out of her face and held the back of her head, and now he opened himself up even more to the kiss, to the feelings she engendered in him.

Finally, Wren broke away, and she was panting. "Stone..."

"Yeah?"

"I know we're both tired and hurt, but…stop holding back. Stop holding out on me."

"If I don't…this will—"

"You think I don't understand exactly where it will go?" She supported her weight on one elbow, then hissed at the pull on her ribs, and moved to lay on him once more, but angled so she could meet his eyes. "What if that's where I want it to go?" She still had the towel clamped closed around her chest, but she let go when she moved to lay against him, and Stone felt the fabric loosen.

If she moved away from him, the towel would fall open.

Stone knew his body had responded to the heat in her kiss, and she had her leg draped across his hips, so he knew she could feel the evidence of it. "Wren…" He wasn't sure what he was going to say, or what *to* say. His reasoning, his logic, his resistance was riddled and tattered and fading.

"Stone." She took his hand in hers and threaded their fingers together. "Stop trying to protect me from you."

"I'm just trying—"

"I know. But…I'm a grown woman, okay? Sure, I'm young, but I'm adult, and I can choose for myself what I want. And *this* is what I want. Whatever we have, whatever we can have, wherever it goes. I want that. All of it. All of you. Whatever you'll give me."

"But what if—"

"And don't say it's just because you saved me, or because we're going through this whole running from killers thing. It started before this, and will continue after it."

"You're assuming there is an after."

Wren squeezed his hand. "Yes. I am assuming there's an after. If I hadn't assumed there would be an 'after,' I wouldn't have had the courage to get away from Cervantes in the first place. Not like positive thinking will solve every problem there is, but it goes a long way towards it." She touched her lips to his chin, and then placed another kiss on his jaw line. "Stop trying to distract me."

"I though distracting you was the whole point?"

Wren frowned. "You know what I mean."

Stone laughed, but couldn't hold the humor for long; her kisses were drifting from his jaw to the shell of his ear, her breath tickling, her hands skating oh-so gently across his bare chest. Warm hands, warm mouth, soft body, soft skin.

He knew he should resist. It probably was at least partially the after-effects of adrenaline and danger driving them both to this. But, then again, he'd wanted her, desired her before any of this had ever happened. Their relationship had definitely been pushed beyond the student-staff model. It was something else, now. They'd witnessed death together. Stone had killed for her. That brought two people closer than anything else ever could, or would.

She was kissing the corner of his mouth and caressing his chest, his shoulders, letting her fingers explore his stomach—careful to avoid his wounded left side—and her touch was a drug all its own, pushing away the pain and the exhaustion, filling him with the burning energy of desire.

He still had his hand on her ass, and he explored the taut muscles, then found her bare thigh. She breathed a moan as his touch slipped up the back of her leg, from the crease of her knee to just beneath her ass. He hesitated there, but Wren's body writhed under his hand, silently begging him for more. His fingers pressed into the firm flesh, driving them both wild with need. She attacked his mouth with her own, devouring him, pleading with him.

Stone brushed a lock of black hair away from Wren's mouth, grazed her cheek with his knuckles, and then bent down to capture her mouth with his. He held nothing back, this time. His hands found their way to her shoulders and back, just above the towel, his touch loosening the wrapped fabric. She shivered at his touch, clutched his shoulders with fierce fingers.

And then she pulled away again, but this time, her gaze remained locked on his as she released her hold on the damp cotton of the towel. With a deep breath, Wren pulled the tucked-in end of the towel free. The fabric sagged, then fell away from her body to pile on the floor around her feet.

And just like that she was naked in front of him.

Stone felt his chest constrict at the sight of her. She was all tan skin and dark hair and endless curves, her brown eyes half-seductive and half fearful. She stood still, one leg bent at the knee, black hair cascading over one shoulder. He let himself really look at her, finally. Full breasts, high and heavy, bell-curve hips and strong legs, hands at her sides and lips pressed together. She was nervous, but refusing to cover herself, he realized. She was waiting for his reaction, for his approval.

Wren was barely able to contain the trembling. She was hot, and then cold, and then hot. Her skin itched, crawling with invisible bugs. Her knees knocked, threatened to buckle. Part of it was the withdrawal, part of it was sheer nerves. She'd wanted this with Stone for so long, and now it was happening.

She could barely focus on him. She was on fire. She was ice. She felt every moment as if she was on the verge of throwing up, nausea boiling in her stomach like magma beneath the Earth's crust.

She needed the heroin. It was the oddest sensation, needing something she didn't want, had never wanted. But yet she *needed*, somewhere in her bones, the heady, forgetting rush of euphoria. It was all she could think about. For as much as she wanted Stone's mouth on hers, for as much as she'd dreamed of Stone taking her in his arms and making love to her, all she wanted was to crawl into bed and hide from the sick need in her gut.

But Stone was waiting. She'd started this, approached him, forced him to face his desire for her. She couldn't let the drug control her. She *wouldn't* let it stop her from taking what might be her only chance to be with him.

She shivered as the cold hotel room air hit her bared skin. She felt her nipples pucker and go erect, both from the cold and from Stone's gaze, hot and molten brown and rife with lust. She fought the inclination to cross her arms over herself, and instead let Stone stare at her. He wanted her. She saw it in his eyes, saw in the way his fingers clawed into his biceps until his short-clipped fingernails left crescents imprinted in his sun-darkened skin.

Keep going, she told herself. She fought down the withdrawal-induced nausea and tried to focus on the memory of his kiss, his hands on her butt, his fingers caressing her skin. Chills overtook her, and she couldn't quite stop the chatter of her teeth.

"Are you sure you're okay?" Stone asked, his voice suspicious.

"Yeah," she said. "I'm just…excited. And a little nervous. It's been awhile."

"It's been awhile for me too," Stone said. "Look, we don't have to rush this. We'll go home and take this at our own pace. It doesn't have to be now."

Wren closed the gap between them so the rigid tips of her breasts just barely brushed his hard, hot chest. "I want to. I want it to be now. Besides, you're the one who said we may not make it out of this alive. Now may be all we have."

His hands circled her arms, slid up and down twice, and then moved to her shoulder blades, down her back and to her waist. "I know what I said. But I don't want you think I'm saying we won't make it. We will. I promise you we will."

Wren lifted up on her toes, clutched the back of Stone's neck, and kissed him. In a book, the kiss would erase all of her aches and doubts and fears and sickness. In a book, she would be able to forget it all and lose herself in the taste of his mouth. He really *did* taste wonderful. But this was reality, and she couldn't simply forget the blazing heat of chemical addiction. It was alive within her, boiling her blood in her veins, sending armies of crawling *things* itching under her skin.

She kissed him anyway, until she had to stop for breath.

His hands scoured her skin, scraped and stuttered over her hips, cupped her ass and squeezed it, tickled her thighs. His lips moved from her mouth to her neck, to the hollow of her throat and the delicate curve where neck became shoulder. Then, to her breastbone, and she shivered, hot all over and shaking, knees quaking. She couldn't breathe, and now his lips were touching the upward slope of her breasts and the nausea stomping in her belly was nearly forgotten in the sweet ache of arousal.

She felt his mouth close over her right nipple, and the tug of his lips was matched by a tug between her thighs. She held on to him, focused every ounce of her attention on feeling him, only him. One of his hands slid over her skin just above her aching core, and the other remained behind to cup the weight of her buttock. She wanted to gasp his name breathlessly, but she couldn't summon even that. She could only hold on to his neck and shoulders and give over to tactile sensation.

His fingers delved between her thighs, grazing the crease of her pussy with his long middle finger. She let her thighs move apart, clinging to his neck, pressing her lips to the warmth of his throat, kissing and nibbling and then giving way to gasps as his fingers slid inside her and began to explore.

He seemed to know exactly where to touch her, how to stroke her. Within seconds, she was unable to stand up on her own at all, and Stone was lowering her to the bed and kneeling over her, never slowing the slow sweep of his fingers, or the suckling of his lips on her nipple.

Wren bit her lip and tried to ignore the roiling of her stomach, tried gamely to focus on the raw fury of her building orgasm.

She moaned, scratching at his shoulders as he moved his mouth to her other breast. He shifted position, and she felt the hard bulge of arousal against her thigh. She lifted her hips into his touch, moving with his rhythm, seeking release from the ache. His fingers inside her accelerated and his teeth grazed the sensitive, erect nub of her nipple. She couldn't move or think or feel anything but the blasting pulse of heat low in her belly and the tugging in her breasts as he released her hand to gently twist and flick her nipple.

And then, just as the heat and pressure became too much to bear, Stone's fingers slid upward inside her and his thumb rolled over her throbbing clitoris and Wren came apart, crying out and clawing his back with her fingernails, pressing her lips to his throat and whimpering as the orgasm blasted through her.

She clung to Stone, shaking and quaking, heat raging in her veins, every ounce of strength within her leached away, now.

Wren felt herself going under, slipping beneath the surface of consciousness. She fought it, forcing her eyes open, rolling in place to face Stone, who was on his side now. His eyes were hooded, heavy-lidded, burning. Wren extended her hand, fighting the weight of her own limb, to touch his chest, tracing the outline of his pectoral muscle, the tan, hard flesh hot beneath her fingertips. His gaze raked over her, soaking up her body, then returned to meet her eyes.

"You're so beautiful, especially when you come for me like that." Stone's voice was pitched low, barely a murmur, rumbling like distant thunder.

"Stone." She carved a path down his chest, following the grooves of his cut abdominal muscles. "That was…incredible."

"It was a start."

"You finished me off, Stone. I can barely function." Wren struggled with her drowsing eyelids, forcing them open. "But you…I'm not done with you."

She touched the tightly rolled and tucked cotton of his towel, which he'd somehow managed to keep around his waist the entire time. The front of the white cotton was tented by his straining erection.

He tensed as she hooked her index finger under the towel at his waist, loosening it. "It doesn't have to be equal, Wren. I'll be fine."

She shook her head floppily. "It's not about equality. I want…this. You. More."

His lips quirked in an amused smile. "You're falling asleep as you talk, babe."

"Then I should save my energy, shouldn't I?" She smiled at him, but it was a soft, faint curve of her lips.

She tugged at the towel gently until the ends came apart and he was bare to the air and to her gaze. Wren couldn't stop a surprised gasp at the size of him, but quickly recovered, closing her fingers around his silky hardness. He gasped, then, as she slid her fist down his length.

Wren marveled as she touched him. Stone had always seemed larger than life to her, massively muscled yet as lithe and graceful in every movement as a lion, rugged and rough-hewn. And now, naked, she could barely fathom the raw power of the man. There was no spare fat on him, no imperfections in his muscular build.

She slid her hand around his cock, exploring him, and each stroke of his taut skin took an absurdly long time to complete. He was watching her with hungry eyes, still, letting her touch without moving, without trying to get more from her.

Sliding closer to him, she tucked her head against his chest and took her time stroking him. She used her fingertips to trace his length, then her fist to squeeze his thickness, now setting a rhythm of achingly slow strokes, thumbing his tip at the apex of the stroke and twisting her hand when she reached his base. He pressed his lips against her hair and kissed, tightened his grip on her shoulders, but otherwise remained completely still. The only sign of arousal was his increasingly ragged breathing. Then, as she began to increase the pace of her hand on him, he bucked his hips, meeting her hand.

A groan escaped him, and then another. "Wren, I'm not going to last much longer."

"Good," she murmured. "Let go."

"All over you?"

She only quickened her pace, until he was gasping and writhing. Wren watched him, gauging. She watched the tip of him leak as he pushed into her fist. Wren was aroused again, turned on just watching him grow frantic, savoring the growl that escaped him when she slowed down, and then let go of him.

Summoning all of her energy, forcing away everything but the need for this, for him, she slid her leg over his hips, clinging to his neck as she positioned him at her entrance.

"Wait, we don't have a—"

"It's fine. I'm on Depo."

"But—" He tried to slow her down, but she wasn't about to let that happen.

"I promise," Wren said, sinking him deep inside her. She groaned low in her throat as he filled her, stretched her. "Oh my god, Stone."

"Shit, Wren." Stone clutched her hips and held her still as he buried himself to the hilt. "How can anything feel so perfect?"

"That's what I was thinking." She pressed her feverish forehead to his chest and arched her back, whimpering as he slid out and buried himself once again. He was still holding her hips so she couldn't move, and she was growing frustrated, impatient. "Let me go. Let me move."

Stone chuckled. "I don't think so, babe. Just lay on me, let me do all the work."

Wren pressed her mouth to his pectoral and gasped as he set a slow pace. "Fine, but I need more. Faster."

Stone didn't answer verbally, only drove into her harder, faster, holding on to the crease of her hips and pulling her against him as he thrust. Wren couldn't figure out how he was still lasting, since he'd been on the edge when she let go of him, but he was still going, still driving her to madness. She was filled, burgeoning with need, gasping against him, moving unconsciously now, unable to stop the fluttering of her hips as she swelled closer and closer to a second climax.

Only her hips moved, the rest of her was boneless on top of him, and now her muscles tensed, coiled, and then she felt something break inside her, burst open and detonate. She stifled a scream against his skin, and then he was there with her, moaning and pulling her down on him, driving into her relentlessly, and she felt herself filled by him as he released, coming inside her with a primal growl in her ear.

They moved together for long minutes more, milking their united climaxes, slick and sated and exhausted.

When they were both about to pass out, Stone shifted Wren so she was cradled in his embrace. "God, Wren. You're fucking amazing."

"Mmmm. So are you." She could barely form words.

Even through her exhaustion, however, she felt the ache, the chemical need, the drowning desperation. She'd managed to push it away long enough to be with Stone, but now it was coming back with a vengeance. She shivered, cold now, and violently nauseous, but too exhausted to move.

Stone's arms clutched her tighter as she shook, and then he reached down to pull the blanket over them. "You're sick, babe."

"It's worse, all of a sudden." She swallowed hard against the rising of her gorge. "It was bad, before, but now...oh God, I don't want this. I hate this. Make it stop, Stone."

Stone groaned. "I knew I shouldn't have let us—"

"No." Wren forced herself to move, to meet his gaze. "No. I wanted that. I *needed* that."

"But now you're even sicker. You needed that energy to fight the withdrawal."

"I needed you emotionally, even more." She wished she could express what making love to him had meant to her, but she was too tired to think anymore, too burned out and too sick to speak anymore. "Just...hold me."

"That I can do."

"Don't let him get me again." It was her last thought.

She heard him curse. "Never. Never."

Blackness swarmed through her, sucked her under, and this time she welcomed it.

13

Stone held Wren in his arms, beyond exhausted but unable to fall asleep. She shook intermittently, her skin feverish. She moaned now and then, rolled away and then back, restless. Her fingers dug into her skin as she tried to scratch away things that weren't there.

He'd known she was starting to feel withdrawal from the heroin Cervantes had forced on her, but he didn't realize how bad it was until she'd collapsed in his arms after they'd made love. She was absolutely limp, yet unable to stop shaking, whimpering from the ache in her bones.

Part of him felt guilty, like he'd taken advantage of her somehow, but he knew that wasn't the case. She'd wanted him, beyond the need for safety as her rescuer. She wanted him, as a man. And having wanted her back for so long, he couldn't resist, and couldn't keep inventing reasons to try.

And it had been better than he'd ever imagined. Even with both of them being hurt, tense with the knowledge that they weren't out of danger, it had been the most intense and amazing experience of his life. And it had been making love, he realized. It was more than sex. He wasn't ready to admit how deep his feelings ran for her, but what they'd shared had been far more than mere sex, and certainly more than anything so meaningless as fucking. It had been…necessary, somehow. They couldn't have not gone there with each other.

Stone watched Wren as she tossed and turned and moaned, crying out in pain as her body tried to flush the poison from her system. She was soaked in sweat, wracked with constant tremors. And even then, she was beautiful.

He wanted to stay awake, guard her, protect her. But he also knew he couldn't do that properly if he didn't get some sleep. Calling on years of practice, he forced himself to shut down, to push away all thoughts of worry and love—was it love?—and sleep.

Stone woke to the sound of Wren screaming. She was tangled in the sheets, spine arched to breaking, head shaking, *"nonononono!"* shrieking from her lips. He reached for her, and she pulled away, kicked out, rolling off the bed and scrambling into the farthest corner against the wall and the nightstand. She clutched her left forearm in her fist, knees drawn up. Her breathing was ragged, drawn out whimpers and moans escaping with each breath.

Stone slid slowly off the bed, heedless of being naked. He crouched down near the foot of the bed, a few feet from her. "It's okay. You're safe." He extended his hand, palm up. "Wren, babe. It's me. It's Stone. You're with me, in a hotel. You're not there anymore. Look at me, baby."

Wren shook her head, trying to shrink farther back into the corner. "It's not real. You're not real."

Stone inched closer, until he was able to touch her foot. "Feel that? That's my hand on your foot. I'm real. You're safe."

Wren stopped breathing, blinking furiously, as if debating the veracity of her own senses. Then she glanced at her arms, her breathing going panicked again, her palms scrubbing at her skin, nails gouging her forearms. "Get them off. They're biting me. They're crawling on me, Stone! They're all over me. Get them off…please!"

"Look at me, Wren. Look at my eyes, okay?" He touched her knee with his palm. "It's me, it's just me. They're not real, Wren. I know it feels like it. It may even look real. But I promise you, there aren't any bugs. It's the drugs, the fever."

"No…You promise me you're real? I'm not dreaming again?" She uncurled slightly, and Stone took her arms in his hands. "I dreamed of us. Together. But now I'm back there, in the dark. He'll come and put the needle in me again, make me forget."

Stone slid his palms up and down her arms. "Feel that? That's real. That's me, touching your arms. And that dream of us, together? That was real. We did that. It wasn't a dream. You're not there."

She looked confused. "I was so hot. Now I'm cold. My skin hurts. I itch." She looked down at her arms and whimpered. "They're back. They're eating me. Crawling on me. Get them off!" She batted at invisible insects on her arms, hitting and scratching until Stone caught her hands in his.

"Listen to me, Wren. It's not real. I'm real. I'm here." He pulled her toward him, stood up and scooped her into his arms, sank onto the bed with her curled against him. "Feel that? Feel me? I'm right here. You're here. You're safe. No bugs, no drugs. Just me and you."

She touched his chest with her fingers, eyes shut tight, shivering and shaking. "You…you feel real. I'm so scared. I don't want to go back there. Back into the dark. It was so dark, Stone. No light, not at all.

I couldn't see my own hand in front of me. I could hear things, voices, footsteps, birds. But I couldn't see anything. And I was so confused. Like I was floating. Dreaming, lost in a cloud. Then I'd come down from the cloud and remember, and I'd try to hold on to the remembering, because even up in the clouds, I knew something was wrong, it was too dark and I was alone. All alone. And I was scared. Of *him*. He's *evil*, Stone. The square door in the ceiling opens, and I see his—his green flip-flops. That's all I'd see, until he was right in front of me, and he'd look at me. His eyes are dark, and they might almost look normal, like he looks almost normal. But then he looks into my eyes and I just know…he's evil. *Evil.* He wants me to be afraid, but I can't let him see. He wants me…he wants something from me. I don't know what. I always thought he was going to rape me. But he didn't. He hurt me. He'd hit me. Kick me. He brought men down to look at me. Like I was…a painting, or a sculpture. Something to be bought."

She shook her head, opened her eyes and stared up at Stone, her gaze pleading with him to never let go, to not let her slide back down into that nightmare. And he wouldn't. He'd never let go.

He rubbed her back with one hand and brushed the dark locks of hair from her eyes with the other. He felt the guilt like an acidic ball in his gut. "I knew something bad would happen. I knew it. I didn't stop it, and I'm so sorry, Wren."

She shifted, put her palm to his cheek. "No. Please no, Stone. It wasn't your fault. You told everyone, whether they wanted to listen or not, that we shouldn't do this, that it was a bad idea." She seemed to draw strength, spine stiffening and tears drying, though her body was still wracked by tremors and slick with fever sweat. "It wasn't your fault. You begged me not to go. You told me not to go anywhere without you."

Stone rubbed circles on her back, held her against his chest. "Enough. Enough blame. It happened, and you're out. I won't let anything else happen to you. I'll get you home."

"What about—what about the other girls? The ones who…who didn't have you to rescue them?"

Stone sighed. "I wish I could give you an answer you'd like. But…I can't. It's just not possible. There are too many, and only one of me. And even with a team of guys, a team of trained SEALs, I couldn't rescue them all. It's a trade that has gone on for…forever, I think. For as long as there's been prostitution, there's been a woman forced into it somehow. And this is just one corner of the world, one particular group of sex slavers." He closed his eyes and breathed in the reality of Wren in his arms. "You know that story you always wanted to hear? You guessed it had something to do with Manila. What this stupid trip was all about. You were right. It was my last mission. A bunch of American girls had gone missing, including a senator's daughter. She was backpacking around Europe and Asia with her girlfriends, except she never made it out of Manila. Well this senator had some sources, and they said his daughter had been kidnapped by sex traffickers. Nasty fuckers. Kidnap the girls, drug them, sell them, run a train of johns on them until the girls were just…gone. Drug them again, use them until they were useless, and then leave them dead. Kill them, dump them in the river. It was happening to girls from all over the world. Russians, Germans, Italians, Chinese, Japanese, local Filipinas, Americans. It wouldn't have involved us at all, my group of SEALs, I mean, until this senator decided to pull some strings. It was all to get his daughter back, of course, but it was wrapped up in a pretty little humanitarian package. Send a message, and all that."

Stone took a deep breath. "So we went in, my fireteam and Foxtrot. My guys were point, the ones who went in. Foxtrot was backup, extraction zone coverage. On the surface, the traders, whatever you want to call 'em, seem like just another group of thugs and smugglers, drug dealers, whatever. But they're organized. Smart. Someone in charge is smart, rather. Individually, they really are just drug dealers and common criminals, but they're run by someone sharp. We knew that going in. They had a network of informants, people on the street, people watching and reporting. Paid, or frightened into keeping an eye on anything that happened. Our intel even put out some false trails, misleading info. We went in dark. Swam from way out. You know those SEAL commercials, where the guys are coming out of the surf in full gear? That was us. We found the right place without trouble, which in Manila at night was quite a feat in itself, especially in somewhere like the Tondo district, just mile after mile of interconnected shanties with no direction or addresses or real streets or anything. We went in, and…they were ready for us. Six SEALs can do a shitload of damage, okay? We're the best of the best. But when we're up against twenty or thirty guys who are waiting for us with AKs and Uzis?"

He paused, rubbed his face with his palm and pushed on. Wren was silent and still, except for the shivers of the fever. "They were waiting for us. Dozens and Zane were covering our ingress point. Watching the door, I mean. Dozens got it first. I never saw it happen. Just heard the AKs open up, and then he was gone, Dozens, and then Zane. Gone, in less than thirty seconds. A blink of an eye, guys I'd known for five fucking years, just dead. I'd just gotten shitty with Dozens a couple days before.

We'd gone to the bar together, put down like, four pitchers between us.

"Well, the only way for us to go was in. The ambush was behind us, so we went in. Room by room, by the book. We saw…some awful shit. Girls too drugged and apathetic to respond even to automatic arms fire. Rescued, but too fried to care. Some we rescued. We found the senator's daughter, Lisa, and a few others. A bunch more. A dozen white girls, too many local girls to count. We got our target out. But we lost Dozens, Zane, Benny, Nancy. Blake almost didn't make it. I almost didn't make it. Took shrapnel to the knee, ended my career. Shredded my knee bad enough that I couldn't keep up, even after I healed. But we got the girls out, and we took out their operation.

"Shitty thing is, even though we killed—god, fucking dozens of guys, it wasn't enough. They came back. Started over, hired more, moved their ops to somewhere else. Cervantes, man. He's the one." Stone realized he was gripping Wren's arm too hard and forced himself to relax his hand. "All that, for one girl. Four of the best SEALs in the entire Navy, dead. They knew going in, every mission, it might be the last one. We all knew it. Wasn't the first time we'd lost guys. But…it was different. We all had sisters, girlfriends, wives, moms, friends, and when you see the pictures of the girls with ribs showing, beaten bloody, track marks on their arms, sold like fucking meat and killed, floating face down in the river… you'll do whatever you have to. It wasn't about Lisa Johnson. Not entirely. And then this stupid church and their goddamned idiotic mission trip. Save the prostitutes for Jesus. How goddamn stupid can you be? I tried to tell them. Build houses for Jesus. Feed the hungry, bring medicine, penicillin, water. Fuck, bring empty water bottles so they can have light. They fill these empty bottles with water and a little bleach, cut a hole in the ceiling and hang the bottle into the room, the sun shines through and it's free light. Fucking genius, really. But no, those holy-ass elders wanted to do something bigger. Nick meant well, but he's never left Virginia, he had no idea what he was planning, what he was getting you kids into. And it happened. And now I've got more blood on my hands. I've got Cervantes and his entire fucking operation on my ass, and all I've got is one pistol and my bare hands. This is the guy who managed to ambush US Navy SEALs, and I've got no back up. No extraction zone. No chopper waiting for me."

Wren curled her hand around the back of his neck, pressed her forehead to his. "But you're not alone. Just like I'm not alone. We're in this together. I know I'm not a Navy SEAL, but…I'm here with you."

Stone dragged in a shuddering breath and blew it out. "Babe, you're as tough as any SEAL I've ever known. I don't know many trained, battle-hardened soldiers who could have endured what you have." He kissed her temple, softly, slowly. "And you're sexy as hell, to boot."

"Not like this, I'm not. I'm a mess."

"Shower again?"

Wren nodded, then he saw her forehead wrinkle in a frown. "I'm not sure I can, though. It hurts. My side hurts. I'm...weak. Hot, and then cold. Achy."

Stone brushed her hair away from her eyes. "Together, then. I'll help you."

Wren grinned, a smile equal parts shy and eager. "You'll help me?" A lift of her eyebrow turned it into an innuendo.

Stone narrowed his eyes. "Help you get clean. How can you think that way at a time like this?"

"How can I not? I'm naked, you're naked. I may feel like shit, but I'm not dead."

Stone scooted toward the edge of the bed, holding on to Wren, helping her into the bathroom. He reached in to the shower stall and turned on the water, adjusting the temperature until it was hot. He nearly yelped when he felt Wren's hand skate across his ass, a soft touch. He glanced down at her, and she managed to keep an innocent expression on her face even as she palmed his left ass cheek, and then his right. He felt himself responding, hardening.

He tried to think about anything other than her hand on his skin, but it was impossible. Especially when she pushed to her feet and stood so she was pressed against him from behind, her breasts on his back, her hand on his ass, now sliding around his hip and brushing his stomach. He stepped into the shower, grabbing her wandering hand and pulling her in after him. The water was almost too hot, but perfectly so, sluicing over her hair and down her chest, between her breasts, over her thighs. She was upright on her own, despite her words. But then he felt her shake, felt her knees give. He turned with her and set her on the seat in the corner of the shower, adjusted the shower head so the water soaked her.

Standing in front of her, he opened the shampoo, dumped some on her scalp. Wren closed her eyes and held on to his waist as he massaged the shampoo into her hair, working it down to the tips. When she was lathered, he helped her stand up and rinsed her hair until it was clean once more. Then the conditioner, gobs of it smeared into her thick black hair, working it in from scalp to tips and back again. Then he massaged her scalp with his fingertips, reveling in the blissful expression on her face, the way she sighed in pleasure. Leaving the conditioner to set, he scrubbed a washcloth with soap until it lathered, and then held Wren against his chest, her front to his, forcing his thoughts away from where he'd like to touch her and the sounds he wanted her to make, focusing on scrubbing her dark skin with the soapy white cloth. Her washed her all over, shoulders, arms, back, crouching to scrub her thighs and calves and feet, the water beating on his head like hot rain. Then he turned her to lean back against him and washed her breastbone, between her breasts. As gently as he could, he ran the washcloth over the soft, heavy globes of her full breasts, reverently, tenderly.

When he moved the washcloth away, Wren took it from him, dropped it to the floor of the shower and took his hands in hers, moved them back to her breasts.

"Touch me, Stone." She moved one of his hands down her belly, between her thighs. "Touch me here."

All this time, Stone had nearly forgotten his own injury. He was reminded when he shifted in place, letting her weight sag against him as he obliged her request, indulging in his own desires. Pain screamed through him, but he ignored it, shifted her weight away just enough to ease the ache. His hands roamed her body, sliding over her soap-slick skin, feeling her nipples harden under his palms as he grazed her boobs with his hands, cupping their weight. Between her thighs, to the heat there, his fingers finding her softness ready for his touch. She moaned when he slid two fingers inside her. She wrapped one arm up over her head to cup his neck, and he bent his head to kiss her shoulder as he found her most sensitive places, found the ways she loved to be touched and brought her to climax, let her fall away from the edge and back up again.

He sat down and moved gingerly to his knees, tugged her bottom forward and nudged her knees aside.

"Stone? What…what are you doing?"

"This." He kissed the down-soft skin of her inner thigh, then again closer to her core. She sucked in a breath and held it as he licked at her opening, and he held his own breath as his side protested. The ache was nothing to the pleasure of hearing her moan as his tongue flicked against her slick wetness. He licked again, and Wren pressed toward him, seeking more. He gave her more, found her clit and sucked it into his mouth, suckled it until she couldn't hold back the moans. She leaned back against the wall, moaning, lifting her hips, pressing her opening to his mouth. He slid his hand beneath her ass and lifted her, lapped her sweetness, set her down and slid a finger inside her, curling to find the perfect spot, high inside, making her groan low in her throat, animalistic sounds of raw pleasure.

She came suddenly, arching up and groaning, holding his head in her hands and pressing him against her. "Stone…oh god, Stone!"

He didn't relent as she came, but increased his pace, licked and suckled and fingered her faster until she pushed him away, gasping and limp in the stream of water. "You're so beautiful," he murmured, rising to his feet. "You're so sexy when you come."

She gazed up at him from beneath hooded eyes. "You make me feel things I didn't know were possible."

"Good."

She reached for him, the tightening at the corner of her eyes revealing the ache of movement. Neither of them would let the pain get the better of them. He stood in front of her, let her touch him. She grasped him in her fist, the water on his back now, and her eyes roamed from his face to his chest, to her hand around him. She took him in both hands, slid her fists around him. A smirk crossed her lips, and then she bent her head and pulled him closer, took him in her mouth. He gasped, groaning as the hot wetness of her mouth surrounded him, the sharp tug of pleasure filling him as she moved her mouth up and down, then licked him, worked the base of him with her hands.

A few moments more, watching her take him in her mouth, and then he pulled her up and carried her out of the shower, set her on the bed, both of them dripping wet. He shut off the water and returned, found her waiting, watching. She reached for him as he crawled across the bed toward her, grasped his aching erection in her fist and guided him into her, curling her arm around his neck and murmuring his name as he slid deep.

He kissed her breasts as he moved slowly inside her, taking his time finding the perfect rhythm. "Wren…" he wasn't sure what he wanted to say, except that he wanted her to know what this meant to him, how incredible this was, but he couldn't find the words.

She put her palm to his cheek and pushed his face up to meet her gaze. "I know." She lifted her hips to meet his, clutching his ass with one hand and pulling him against her. "You don't have to say it. I know. And me too."

How did she know? But she did. He let it come out in his eyes, in the way he refused to look away as they moved together, refused to even blink as they found a rhythm together, faster and faster, their eyes locked, exchanging roiling emotion, letting the pain and the fear and the worry leach away, all of this known and shared between them as they moved together. She saw it, what he wasn't saying, what he wasn't even thinking, but was feeling; what he'd thought impossible. She kissed his chin beneath his lip, the corner of his mouth, her hands on his face, holding him so he couldn't look away.

And then, in a moment that passed out of time, their worlds came apart in a rapture of bliss, a synchronous detonation, something beyond pleasure, a potency neither of them were prepared for.

Wren's eyes watered, tears leaking down her cheeks, and Stone felt something tight in his chest, heat behind his eyes, words stuck in his throat. He kissed the salty liquid away, and she pressed his face to her breasts.

"Don't say it yet, Stone. Not until we're home. No matter how many times we do this until then, don't say it." Wren whispered the words in a fierce growl. "I need that to look forward to. I know it, I see it. But don't say it."

Stone slumped to his side, groaning in pain as the ache he'd denied came to take its due. "I get it, babe. Until we get home."

Wren rolled into him and nestled in the crook of his arm. They both dozed, and Stone was on the verge of sleep when the room phone rang, a shrill, sudden blast. Stone scooped the handset from the cradle and put it to his ear. "Yeah," he mumbled. "Who is it?"

"Dis José, from hotel desk. Some man, dey look for a girl, and a white man. Talk about it, dey lookin' for you, I tink. I don't say nothin' to dem. But dey lookin'. You maybe go away now. Side door, quick-quick."

"You know the guys looking for us?"

"Dey work por *him*. You lib in Manila, you know him. I know what he do. My sister, she neber come home one day, she dead now. For her, I tell you. Go away now, quick-quick."

"Thanks. Check under the mattress, later." Stone tossed the phone into the cradle and slid off the bed. "Come on, babe. Gotta go. They're here. They found us."

Wren didn't waste time with questions. In seconds she was dressed and repacking the little backpack with the bottles of water. Before leaving the room, Stone stuffed one of his few remaining $100 bills under the mattress, tossed another Vicodin into his mouth and swallowed it dry. Then, hand in hand, he and Wren descended the staircase to the ground floor and escaped out the side door, out into the humid Manila midnight.

14

WREN HELD ONTO STONE'S HAND for dear life as he led her in a quick walk through the nighttime bustle of Quezon City. The streets were crowded, cars coming and going, busses and jeepneys and three-wheeled rickshaw things, horns honking, voices shouting and laughing in Filipino and English and dialects and languages unknown.

She hurt, still, and she felt the need, still, but it was fading. She didn't feel as feverish, and the need was distant, manageable. She hoped it would stay that way. She was afraid, deep down, that the need wouldn't ever go away completely, that she'd always feel the hunger in her bones for a drug she'd never willingly taken. Just like she knew she would never forget the darkness, the heady forgetting euphoria, the pain of a fist against her cheek, a foot against her ribs.

Wren pushed those thoughts away as she jogged behind Stone, her bruised ribs aching with every step, hurting with every breath, but she knew she couldn't stop or slow down, no matter how much it hurt.

She distracted herself with pleasant memories, focusing on the way Stone had held her when the nightmares had taken hold of her, the way he'd never let go and never lost his calm. She ran behind him, watching his broad shoulders shifting. She focused on the memory of his close-cropped head delving between her thighs, the stubble of beard on his cheeks scraping her sensitive skin, his hands spreading her legs apart, his tongue doing wicked, delicious things to her core.

She'd never imagined sex could be like that. In the past, it had been pleasant, fun, even hot. But with Stone? It was earth-shaking. Each touch was fire, each kiss was molten, each slide of skin against skin pushed her closer to a volcanic detonation. Her nerve endings seemed hyper-attuned to Stone's every touch and kiss. But yet...it went deeper than mere physical sensation. She felt his emotions radiating off of him. She knew he wasn't a vocal man, he wasn't given to explaining the way he felt, but he didn't need to. The way he felt was obvious in the way he held her, the way he kissed her. His eyes explained for him, his hands communicated what was in his heart. The odd thing was, that despite his claims, when Stone did start talking, he was actually fairly eloquent.

She felt him, felt connected to him. Even now, running for their lives, she could feel him worrying. She knew he was scared for her, worried about her, and that through it all he couldn't help his desire for her, his need for her. And that was the sweetest thing of all. She wasn't unaware of how she looked. The guys she'd dated had made it clear they found her beautiful. But with Stone, she felt more than beautiful. Something in the way he looked at her, touched her, kissed her, made love to her—it was like he needed her in a bone-deep way. Like she was his breath, and he'd been denied it for far too long.

It was how she felt, too. Like she'd never really been alive until now. Like she'd never really taken a breath until his kiss imparted oxygen to her starved lungs.

Stone skidded to a stop, and she smacked into his back, disrupting her thoughts. He pulled her to the side, pressed her back against a wall and buried his face in her neck. She felt the tension coursing off of him, sensed the danger in the air.

"Focus on me. Don't look around." His voice was a barely-audible murmur.

Wren pressed her nose to his scalp; he smelled like hotel shampoo and sweat. She let her hands scrape over the inch-long stubble on his head, soft yet prickly against her palm, trying to broadcast the image of heedless passion.

She saw them out of the corner of her eye, though. Four men with drawn guns, blocky black automatics. They were spread out across the street, peering at each face, ducking into doorways and hopping onto slow-moving jeepneys. "We can't stay here," Wren whispered. "They'll find us. They'll see us. They're coming this way." She hated the panic in her voice.

"Don't move." Stone's lips moved against her skin, and even the imminent threat of discovery couldn't stop her from shivering at the touch of his mouth. "Just kiss me."

She turned her face to his, let her lips meet his. She wanted to get lost, wanted to get carried away, but she knew she couldn't. She tried to keep the kiss light, but her body betrayed her. She felt her hands exploring him, her mouth devouring his eagerly, right there on the street with killers approaching.

Stone pulled his mouth from hers, but only enough to break the kiss and catch his breath. She breathed his breath and waited, holding on to his waist and wishing she could shrink away, wishing they were back in the hotel room, all danger forgotten.

The four men approached steadily, chattering to each other, shoving people out of their way, taking young Filipinas by the shoulders and spinning them around to examine their faces. Stone was completely still, his face against her cheek, one hand on the back of her neck, hips pressed against hers, but Wren felt the hard metal of his gun hidden behind her back in his other hand.

"Be ready," he breathed.

Wren watched the men approach, counting her breaths, her heartbeats. Every muscle tense, she poised to move.

Three feet, now, and their voices were loud, raucous, slurring. Someone shouted in protest, then stuttered what sounded like an apology. Wren held on to Stone's shoulders and trembled as their pursuers neared.

A dark hand clapped onto Stone's shoulder and pulled him around. Wren didn't have to fake the shriek of fear as she frantically buried her face against Stone's chest.

"Hey, what the fuck is this?" Stone growled, grabbing the hand and shoving the man away. "Can't you see I'm busy? Fuck off." Wren clutched his neck and kept her face hidden, not daring to peek.

"I'm lookin' for—"

"I don't give a shit what you're looking for," Stone cut in, "you won't find it here. Fuck off."

"You betta talk nice more dan dat, American, or you find more trouble'an you can deal for." This was punctuated by the distinctive sound of a pistol slide being racked.

Stone twisted in place, keeping Wren hidden behind him, a natural move to protect his frightened girlfriend. He let his own pistol show. "Maybe you should mind your own goddamn business. Don't need trouble, but I'll dish it out if you don't go away." There was a brief standoff, but then Stone's rock-hard muscles relaxed ever so slightly under her hands, and he turned back around to hold Wren against his chest. "That was close," he muttered. "Too fucking close."

Wren only nodded. "Where are we going? Do we have a plan?" She risked a peek over Stone's shoulder, watching the receding back of Cervantes' goon.

"The US Embassy, I'm thinking."

"Is that close by?"

Stone shook his head. "I'm not entirely sure where we even are, honestly. But assuming we're in Quezon City, then no. It's a long way away." He glanced around, then back down to her. "It's west and south of us, I'm pretty sure. We just have to get there without running into anymore of Cervantes' guys." He pulled her into a walk, heading south.

Wren twisted around once more, feeling unsettled, her spine prickling with the sensation of being watched. It was a mistake. She saw a vaguely familiar, dark-featured face contort with surprise and recognition.

"It her!" a voice shouted, pointing with the barrel of his pistol. "Go! Go after dem!"

Stone slewed around, saw approaching bodies, and spurred Wren into a run. "Shit! Move, Wren! Go!"

Wren ran, feeling her fingers slipping out of Stone's grip. She panicked, grabbed at his shirt and tried to run faster, tried to keep up. He was pushing between people, weaving and shoving and stepping around bicycles and mopeds, and Wren tried desperately to keep up with his breakneck pace. Behind them, shouts announced the presence of their pursuers, the curses and angry grunts of bystanders being knocked down. The street was congested, packed even at midnight. Making progress through the crowd of pedestrians and buses and taxis and jeepneys was like trying to run full-speed through hip-deep water.

Wren's lungs burned, her legs ached, and her vision blurred, but Stone kept running, seeming barely winded. A knot of people and cars clustered around a stalled truck spewing gray smoke forced Stone and Wren off of the red-and-yellow brick-paved sidewalk and out into the street, dodging the slow-moving traffic. Stone jerked Wren by the wrist, yanking her out of the way as a panel van roared past, narrowly missing her as she stumbled onto the thin strip of median. Angry voices echoed, tires squealed, horns blared. Wren twisted her upper torso as she ran, making out the forms of the four pursuers slipping through traffic, pistols held out in the open, eliciting screams. Sirens howled in the distance.

Thunder grumbled, and a warm rain settled in the air, misting and drifting in a slow wind, turning the ground underfoot slick. It wasn't a heavy rain, but within minutes Wren was soaked to the skin, her feet squishing in her shoes, and her hair sticking to her neck and drifting into her mouth.

They crossed a bridge, and she caught a glimpse of the river, thick and green and speckled with rain. Onward they ran, slipping between shoppers with bag-laden arms and young men in tank-tops gathered in laughing groups. A truck loaded with crates of produce juddered and honked and squealed protesting brakes as Stone and Wren crossed the street once more, passing through the southbound traffic.

A jeepney trundled past them, yellow and red and orange and green, so crowded that passengers were hanging out of the windows and sitting on the roof. As it passed, Stone grabbed onto a railing bolted to the outside near the back left corner. Wrapping his arm around Wren's waist, he hauled her against his side and clamped down, setting one foot on the rear bumper. They were airborne then, and the jeepney accelerated through another intersection. Stone's arm formed an iron band around her middle, the only thing keeping her aloft. She felt around with her foot, seeking something to step on. She found a lip under her toe, grabbed on to the railing and lifted her weight away from Stone, who sighed in relief, peering through the curtain of warm rain.

"Don't let go." His voice rumbled in her ear.

"I won't." She held tight to him with her other hand, squinting to see if their pursuers had noticed their escape.

Something buzzed past her ear, stinging her earlobe. Milliseconds after the hot, angry buzzing, Wren heard a cracking bark, the report of a pistol. She touched her earlobe, and her finger came away with a smear of red. She felt intellectually detached, in some strange way, from the fact that she'd just been shot, that if the bullet had been a few inches to the right it would have killed her. Stone swung his body away from the jeepney and covered her body with his. She breathed in, smelled him, felt his heat. Another pistol report cracked the night air, and something thunked into the metal next to Wren's knee. A third gunshot, and then a fourth, and then silence.

From within the jeepney came shouts and screams, laced through with a wail of pain. Stone glanced through the window. "Shit, they must have hit someone." He glanced down at Wren. "Are you okay?"

She touched her ear as she rose up to peer into the jeepney. "I'm fine. I think the first one nicked my ear, but that's it." She could just barely make out an older woman leaning against the wall of the jeepney, clutching her upper arm, blood seeping through her fingers. A young man whipped off his shirt and tied it around the woman's arm, cinching it tight. "They could have killed that woman, and she didn't have anything to do with this."

Stone kept his focus on the street behind them. "I think they're still after us. They hijacked a taxi, it looks like."

She tried to follow his gaze, and could just barely make out the shape of a vehicle barreling toward them, weaving recklessly through traffic. "What do we do?"

The jeepney slowed, pulling closer to the curb, and then stopped, disgorging passengers, including the woman who'd been shot and the now-bare chested young man who'd helped her. Stone hopped down, wincing at the jolt. Wren followed suit, and found herself pulled into a run once more, dodging through thick traffic carving in an arc around a mammoth traffic circle. Multicolored lights shone from the center of the circle, the source of the lights blocked by trees. Gasping for breath, she held on to Stone's sweat-slippery hand, hearing his breath going ragged now too. They pushed through knots of tourists all moving in the same general direction, toward the changing lights.

"What is that?" she asked, between breaths.

"I think it's…the Quezon…Memorial…Shrine," Stone responded, panting. "There's some kind of… dancing fountain too. Big…big tourist attraction."

Blue neon tube lettering spelled out words in English: *Circle of Fun*. Shapes hulked, inscrutable, in the darkness beyond, some now-closed attraction.

They passed it by.

Ahead of them, the shrine was visible. They were part of a huge crowd gathered in a wide courtyard, the central attraction of which was a tall three-pronged structure bathed in color-changing lights. As she watched, the lights changed from red to deep blue, paused for a moment, then changed to green, and then each of the three square pillars were bathed in individual colors, one red, one blue, one green. At the very top of the shrine, the three pillars became angels of some sort, it looked to Wren, although it was too far away and too dark to make out anything more specific than that. Between the crowd and the shrine was a circular fountain, surrounded by a thick curb of stone. A plume of water jetted up from the center of the fountain, turning the same shade of purple as the shrine. The plume rose to something like thirty feet, then ceased momentarily, only to rise up once more, joined by thinner, shorter spouts in a circle around it. Wren didn't have a chance to watch any longer as Stone drew her in a stumbling jog around the fountain, closer to the shrine itself.

Behind them, shouts and angry voices reminded her that they were being pursued.

The base of the huge, white-stone shrine was triangular in cross-section, the walls rising several feet in height, the bright-hued lights of the shrine casting shifting shadows. Knots and clusters of people gathered, chattering and laughing as a remix of a popular American song played. Stone led Wren into the crowds, putting his back to the stone and pulling Wren against his chest.

The crowd shifted and changed, but never thinned, providing effective cover. The pursuers were pushing through the crowd, shoving and elbowing, drawing dirty looks and Filipino curses that quickly faded when the offended tourist saw the brandished pistols. Using Wren's body as cover for his actions, Stone checked the loads in his magazine and slammed it home once more, then returned his attention to their pursuers, who were now spread out in pairs. One of the men pulled a cell phone from the hip pocket of his khakis and dialed a number.

Wren tried to regain control of her breathing, tried to suppress the burning in her lungs and the screaming of her injured ribs. Stone had one hand against his side, his face a mask of concentration. When one of the men turned their way, Stone ducked his head, but wasn't quick enough. The man whistled for his nearest friend, who trotted over. The first one pointed at Stone and Wren, the second nodded, and they moved in tandem.

Wren's heart was pounding out of her chest, both from fear and exertion. "They've seen us," she whispered.

"I know. I've gotta even the playing field a little."

"What? What are you going to do?"

Stone stepped in front of Wren, putting his back to her front and pinning her against the base of the shrine. "Buying us time."

Wren felt panic shoot through her. He was going to fight again. Right out in the open, in the middle of a crowded park. People were being hurt, maybe even killed because of her. Stone was tensed in front of her, his stance wide, pistol held by his thigh.

All Wren could see was his back, the flagstones under her feet, the spuming fountain off to the right. She heard Stone pull the slide on his pistol, felt him step away a couple inches.

Shoes scuffed to a stop, dirty white ADIDAS sneakers. Wren wanted to close her eyes, but she couldn't. She peered around Stone. Two men, both armed, less than six feet away.

"You come now. Give us dis girl, Cervantes, he let it all go, let you go home. All he wants is da girl."

Stone laughed, a mirthless bark of disbelief. "Yeah, okay," he said, his voice dripping sarcasm. "How about you two walk away now, while you're still alive."

Wren tasted the tension in the air, felt the danger like palpable waves. The other park-goers had noticed the standoff and were quickly scattering. Wren wanted to run too. She wanted to close her eyes and pretend this wasn't happening. But she forced herself to watch, to pay attention, to be ready. Stone's fist rose, his palm cupping the butt of the pistol.

Seconds passed like hours, drawn out like stretched taffy.

She saw it happening. She watched one of the Filipino men raise his pistol as if in slow-motion, his lips drawing back in a rictus. Before he could get his gun level, Stone's pistol barked—*BLAMBLAM*—and then Stone shifted, just the tip of the barrel twitching slightly, and then—*BLAMBLAM*—and both men dropped to the ground. Screams echoed, shrieks and shouts. Blood pooled like spreading inkblots.

Wren felt herself jerked into a run, and she ran, but she couldn't wrench her gaze away from the dead men, eyes open and staring at the dark sky, holes in foreheads, lives ended. Dead men. Dead men. She tried to breathe, but the sight of the blood glinting purple and blue and red in the shifting technicolor fountain lights stole her breath.

"Don't look. It was us or them." Stone pushed her ahead of him, forcing her look away. His touch on her shoulder vanished momentarily, and she saw him stoop and scoop up a dropped pistol, and then again, and then he was behind her, propelling her, running with her.

She heard sobs break from her chest, slip through her lips. She clacked her teeth together, silencing herself.

A playground, railings and tube slides and empty benches, waving treetops all around them, soughing in the wind. It was still misting, not quite rain, but everything gleamed slickly wet. Sirens howled, the sirens of authority always too far behind. Shouts, a gunshot.

Wren ran on autopilot, guided by Stone's hand on her shoulder, turning her this way and that. Lungs and legs burned, but she ran on. Ribs protested, ached, but she ran on. They came to the other side of the circular park, traffic a thick white-light ribbon in the wet midnight darkness.

Another ribbon of cars, now the red of receding tail lights.

"I think that's Quezon Avenue," Stone said, more to himself than to Wren. "I think that'll take us toward the Embassy."

"Why can't we just take a taxi?" Wren asked, wondering if it was a stupid question.

Stone hauled her through the traffic, following close behind a man on a bike who seemed entirely unafraid of the rushing cars and trucks. "Same reason we can't go to a hospital or the police: because those places are too public and Cervantes has informants everywhere. Bus drivers don't ever really see their passengers, while taxi drivers will. And Cervantes might have enough manpower to question taxi drivers, but not to canvass everyone who rode on a bus." A bus nosed around the traffic circle and onto Quezon Avenue, stopping a few hundred feet away from Stone and Wren. "Get on that bus!" Stone urged.

Wren ran, pushing her exhausted body as fast as she could go. She stumbled, felt herself lifted onto the bus and then into a seat next to Stone, who was panting, pressing a palm to his side.

"Rest for a minute, baby," he muttered into Wren's ear. "We're safe for the moment."

She shut her eyes and rested her head on his shoulder. Would they ever be able to stop running? Hard lumps at his waistband prodded at her hip—his confiscated pistols. He tucked her hair behind her ear with his thumb. Sounds faded to a blur, and Stone's arm around her shoulders was a comforting weight, enough reassurance to let her slip under.

15

Stone didn't dare close his eyes. If he closed his eyes, he would sleep too, and that would get them killed. He had to be alert. He had to watch. No one on the packed bus seemed suspicious, but you never knew. He scanned each face around him, watched the cityscape pass through the window, tried to plan, to distract himself from the heavy weight of exhaustion.

The exhaustion itself was a distraction, though. It kept him from seeing the faces of the men he'd killed.

He blinked, clearing the blur, fighting the sliding, aching, scratchy burn of his eyelids. To keep himself awake, he thought of Wren, of her dark, soft skin pressed against his. Her sighs and moans in his ear, her fingers on his chest as she rode him to mutual climax.

He shifted in his seat and glanced at her. She seemed so innocent, asleep beside him, rocking as the bus jounced, head lolling against his shoulder.

The bus seemed to get darker, quieter. He blinked hard, rubbed his eyes, pinched himself, but the weight was too much.

Starts and stops filtered through his awareness, but couldn't penetrate. He felt a strange desperation inside his chest, the swelling of complete unconsciousness rising up. He fought it.

"Banawe stop!" The voice of the driver, muddy and accented and distant.

Time and silence; Stone clawed at the sleep dragging him down. He heard Wren moan beside him.

More time; more silence.

"Cruz! Vicente Cruz stop!"

He managed to get his eyes open, briefly. An old man sat across from him, staring. The old man nodded, but Stone felt his eyelids falling, fought and lost once more.

Danger. The feeling, the instinct flitted through him, churned in his gut.

The bus stopped yet again. "Quiapo! Quiapo stop!"

Sound altered. The noise of the road, the rumble of tires over concrete became a strange hum, layered over something wide and deep and significant. Stone strained for awareness. He had to wake up. He had to wake up. The dim interior lights of the bus blurred, focused, and he twisted awkwardly to look out the window behind him. He saw moonglow filtering through black clouds, refracting and glinting off of water; rods and rails and crossbars and wires: Quezon Bridge, then, going over the Pasig River.

Close, now.

He shook his head to clear the sleep away, a vain gesture, and the old man across from him only watched, then cut his eyes to the side. Stone followed the old man's gaze to a teenaged boy in rain-soaked cutoff shorts, a clinging yellow tank top and tattered high-top shoes, who was tapping at a cell phone he shouldn't have been able to afford. The boy's eyes shifted from his phone to Stone, and then immediately away.

Danger. The instinct was focused on that boy. Skinny arms and legs, clumsily buzzed hair, dirty clothes, rotting teeth, and a too-new piece of technology.

Stone's brain was sludgy, connecting the dots only with effort.

"Lawton! Lawton stop!" No one moved as the doors whooshed open noisily.

Stone lurched to his feet, bent and lifted Wren in his arms. She moaned, twitched in his arms. Stone tripped over someone's foot, caught himself before he dropped Wren, who was shaking her head and whimpering, caught in a dream or a memory. Solid ground underfoot, and away from the bus, away from the boy with cell phone. The bus stop had a bench, and Stone slumped onto the wet seat.

"Wake up, Wren. You gotta wake up." He shook her gently. "C'mon baby. Wake up for me."

She murmured, mumbled. "No…no. 'Member, gotta…no—no more…"

He kissed her lips softly, touched her cheek. "Wren, wake up sweetheart. It's Stone. You're with me, babe. Wake up, okay?"

Her eyelids fluttered. "Stone?"

"We gotta move. I think someone snitched on us."

"Huh?" She wiggled, stretched, accidentally elbowed Stone in the injured side. He gasped in agony, bending over and stifling curses of pain. "Oh my god! I'm so sorry!" She slid off his lap and onto the bench next to him, hovering anxiously.

He waved her off, wincing as he straightened. "It was an accident. It's fine. We gotta go, though. We gotta move. Someone saw us and reported us to Cervantes."

"Are you sure?"

He shrugged. "Am I one hundred percent positive that's what he was doing? No. But I can't afford to be wrong."

Another bus came, heading south, and he tugged her to her feet, fishing the fare from his pocket of Filipino currency. The bus stopped, and they got on, riding it to the Ayala Avenue stop, then getting off again and crossing the street into Rizal Park. Another lighted fountain played with spumes of red and blue and green and purple water, dancing to the rhythm of a song Stone didn't recognize. The fountain was distant, but loud and highly visible even through the trees and buildings in the way. Wren was stumbling beside him, trying to run but not quite able.

Some internal drive was pushing him. There wasn't any pursuit that he could see, but he felt the need to run anyway. He hauled Wren into a jog.

"Why are we running? Is there someone behind us?" She twisted to look behind.

"We're close to the embassy, I think," Stone said. "I have a bad feeling. We need to move."

Wren didn't argue, just shook her arm free of his hold and moved under her own power. They jogged side by side through the park, cutting through the circular area surrounding the Sentinel of Freedom monument, then crossing a street before finally reaching the central lagoon with the dancing fountain. The park was well-lit by globular streetlights, and it was packed with tourists and locals coming and going, taking photos and milling around the wide, grassy open space. Flagpoles lined the approach to the Rizal monument, the flags horizontal stripes bicolored red and blue with a triangular wedge of white near the hoist, the white marked by a golden sun: the flag of the Philippines.

Stone felt the churning in his gut, the warning sign of impending danger. He led her past the monument and out of the park, across Roxas Boulevard, hustling them between honking cars and rushing taxis. They were near the Embassy, now. Less than a mile, surely, although he wasn't sure. He was operating on a distant memory of Manila's layout, maps memorized long ago, locations to remember in case the mission had gone completely haywire and he' found himself adrift in Manila. Now, those hours spent poring over maps and bus routes were saving his life, and Wren's.

If they could reach the Embassy, they'd be safe. The Embassy would protect them, help them get home. But, Stone's gut warned, Cervantes knew this, and he was sure to have the Embassy watched. Wren was silent beside him, panting, gasping, but keeping pace.

"We're almost there, babe," he told her. "Almost there. The Embassy is just ahead."

Trees blocked their view, but he could see the lights shining through the foliage. His pulse pounded, and his gut screamed.

Tires squealed, horns honked, and then two bright headlights shone, approaching them from the south, barreling toward them the wrong way up the boulevard. Stone stumbled to a halt. He hunted for an escape, any kind of gambit to get them away, but there was nowhere to go. The wall of the embassy stretched away on either side of them. There was only the street in front of them, their way forward blocked by the approaching vehicle, its tires squealing as it skidded and swung sideways—a battered blue van, nondescript and easily forgotten. Stone shoved Wren behind him and racked the slide of his pistol. The van lurched to a stop, the sliding door wrenched open and the dim interior light showed three bodies kneeling on the floor, AK-47s leveled at Stone and Wren.

Twisting to look back the way they'd come, Stone saw four more men with automatic pistols approaching on foot, striding toward them at a leisurely pace, guns held down by their thighs.

"Shit." Stone's gut dropped away. "They've got us cornered, babe."

"No. No. Nononono." Wren shook her head frantically. "You can't let them take me back there."

"I'm sorry, Wren. There's too many of them. If I so much as twitch, they'll kill us both." Guilt and horror rocketed through him; he'd promised Wren he'd get her home.

Wren was choking on her own sobs. "Let them, then. Let them kill me. I won't—I won't—"

"It's not over yet. I'll get us out of this. Okay? Just go along for now, and be ready." He slowly set the pistol on the ground at his feet, then took Wren's hand, lifting her chin so she met his eyes. "I won't let anything happen to you. Okay? I promise. I'll get us out of this."

Wren didn't look very reassured by this promise, especially when one of the assault rifle-wielding men hopped out of the van and scooped up Stone's pistol, then grabbed Wren by the arm and shoved her toward the van. Stone's heart stopped beating. The barrel of the AK turned, trained on him.

They didn't need him. They wouldn't take him with them. They'd just shoot him right here, mere feet from the US Embassy, and Wren would be—

Stone couldn't think like that. He felt time slowing as his executioner shouted something at him, jerking the barrel toward the ground. *Get on your knees!* The message was clear. Stone stayed on his feet, refusing to kneel for his own death.

Not like this. Not like this. Please. He prayed, really prayed, for the first time in a long time. *I have to protect her. Not like this, please!*

He watched the man's trigger finger tighten, squeezing.

One of the other men in the van spoke up. "*Huwag. Mas gusto ni Cervantes na buhay sya.*"

Stone's frantic brain provided the translation: "Not yet. Cervantes wants him alive."

The would-be executioner laughed. "*Si Cervantes ang papatay sa kanya.*" *Only so he can be the one to kill him.*

The stock of the rifle flashed out, slamming into Stone's skull with brutal force, knocking him to one side. He fought to remain upright, but the rifle-butt crashed into his kidney, dropping him to his knees, and then again, to the back of his head. Stone slammed into the ground face-first, tasting blood. Darkness washed over him. He heard Wren screaming somewhere far away. He struggled, wanting to comfort her. *It's okay, babe. I'm fine. I can take it. I'll protect you. No matter what.* The words wouldn't come out. He was cold, and floating. Warm, now. Into deep, deep darkness.

All of Wren's senses were attuned to Stone's limp, bleeding form. Her hands were bound behind her by zip-ties, so she couldn't touch him. She could only watch him bleed and count his breaths.

The van rocked and swayed, jounced over pot-holes and bounced on rutted dirt roads. Wren knew she should pray, or try to think of an escape plan, but she couldn't. A single word repeated itself over and over and over: *Please…please…please…please.*

Please what? She wasn't sure. Please, don't let him die. Please, don't let *me* die. Please, God, anything but this.

After an amount of time she couldn't measure, the van halted. The sliding door flew open and two men grabbed Stone, one his feet and one his hands, carrying him away. Another grabbed Wren's wrist, jerking her out of the van. As she stumbled and fought to regain her balance, hands groped her, cruel fingers digging into the muscle of her ass, pinching her breasts. She wrenched away and kicked out, felt her heel impact flesh. She kicked out again, and again, hitting flesh and bone. She wouldn't go quietly this time. Hands gripped her shoulders, and she wrenched free, twisted, sent her foot flying, hit her captor in the gut, spun and stumbled away, off-balance without her arms free, and kicked at the man holding the syringe. She hit his elbow, and the syringe went flying. Wren lurched toward it, stomped on it, felt it smash under foot. More hands closed around her arms, cruelly strong, and a fist battered against her temple. Another blow, this one to the cheek. She blinked away the tears of pain, slammed her head backward and felt her skull crunch against teeth. The hands fell away, and she tried to run, blurry vision showing only trees and distant streetlights and skyscrapers and rushing cars. She bumped into something, saw green flip-flops and smelled sweat and cigarettes and cologne. Wren looked up to see a familiar face leering down at her, rotten teeth and crescent scar.

"Ha. Now I got you back, huh? Can't run away for long, little American bird." Cervantes grinned, laughed, and his foul breath wafted over her. "Not gonna be so much fun as last time, dat for sure. You better go along easy, or it get bad for you. Let Miguel have you. 'Member him? Wit the knife? Yeah. He get his hands on you, you lose some blood, maybe a finger or two."

Cervantes jerked her upright, spun her around, and shoved her toward a door. Into darkness, low-roofed rooms lit by camping lanterns, almost-blue light shedding long shadows. Men at a table with glass pipes and joints and syringes, playing cards, passing around a bottle of booze. A naked girl sat on one man's lap, writhing her hips slowly. He ignored her, fanning his cards, pulling one free and tossing it on the table. After playing his card, the man gripped the girl's breasts, fondling and rolling, grinding against her. The girl's face was vacant, although she winced when he pinched her nipple and barked something in Filipino, spurring her to move faster. Wren looked away then, glad to move to another room. This one was empty except for a pallet of blankets in one corner. The pile moved at the noise of feet on the floor. Cervantes kicked the blankets, and a tiny girl with dyed-blonde hair and bruised white skin, no more than sixteen, crawled to her feet, completely nude. She cringed away from Cervantes as he spoke to her in Filipino. She didn't answer, just nodded once and vanished through the doorway.

They came to an actual doorway, a slab of wood with chipped red paint, jury-rigged to fit into the space, hinges fastened by bolts to the corrugated metal wall. Cervantes pulled the door open and shoved Wren in. The space was tiny, six feet by six feet, if that. There were no windows, just the dirt under foot and the walls, wood and metal. Cervantes closed the door behind him, pulled the knife from his pocket. He twisted his wrist, and the handle of the knife flipped to reveal the blade, six inches of silvery and serpentine metal glinting in the light of the lantern he held in his other hand.

Wren went still, waiting. Would he kill her? Cut off a finger to punish her? He set the lantern on the floor, casting slanted shadows on the wall. Moving behind her, he cut the zip-tie free, and then traced the tip of the knife lightly up her spine. She didn't dare even breathe. For as much as she imagined she'd rather die than be raped or sold, when a blade was pressed to her skin, self-preservation kicked in.

Cervantes pressed the point into the skin just above the collar of her shirt, beneath her tied-up hair. The tip twisted, and the knife descended, slicing through her shirt. Her skin pinched as he forced the blade beneath the strap of her bra, and then she felt her breasts bounce as the fabric gave under the razor-sharp blade. Down her back, through the thin cotton of her shirt. She bit her lip to keep from crying out. Over her hip, over her buttock, down one leg of her shorts. The fabric hung free around her leg, and then he cut that away. Two more quick slices, through her panties at her hips, and she was naked.

Cervantes stepped back, flicking his wrist so the knife closed, and then opened. Over and over, he flipped the knife closed, open, in an endless circling of his wrist. His eyes perused Wren, taking in her full breasts, generous hips, the bruises on her cheek, the bruises at her ribcage. His gaze finally landed on her privates.

"You need a lesson." His voice was a low slither. His lips curved up.

She shrank away, covering herself with her hands. "Please, no…"

Cervantes reached behind his back and pulled out his gun, leveled it at her. "Shut up. Be still. You been a lot of trouble, little bird. I sometime think it be easier to just kill you." He pressed the barrel to her head. "You don't cause me no more trouble, huh? Or dis be only da beginning."

He closed the knife, pressed the cold metal to the inside of her thigh. She trembled, clamping her thighs closed. Cervantes laughed, a quiet chuckle, and slid the knife upward. Cold metal dug into the soft, sensitive flesh of her core, pressing in painfully. She refused to loosen, to let him violate her.

"No." She shook her head, the hard O of the barrel scraping the skin at her temple. She spoke through clenched teeth. "Kill me. You'll have to kill me."

Cervantes responded by thumbing back the hammer of his pistol. "Don' test me, little bitch. You will die."

She felt steel thread through her veins, cold and ungiving. "Then I'll die."

His eyes narrowed, and he pressed the knife harder. She curled her body inward, closing herself away with all of her strength. Cervantes drew away the gun, and then hit her with the butt, slamming the top of her head so hard she saw flashes and her back slammed against the wall. Blood trickled hot down her scalp. The blow weakened her, and she cried out when the icy metal gouged into her. Screams ripped from her as Cervantes jabbed up, in.

She had no way of comprehending the pain, the raw agony. She couldn't stand up under the brutal onslaught of the pain as he twisted, withdrew, and shoved the closed knife into her again. Something caught, tore. Wren slumped, fought to stay upright. She couldn't even sob, as she had no breath.

Cervantes withdrew his knife, and let her fall. "Maybe next time, the knife will be open, yeah?" He left, taking the lamp.

Wren's lungs screamed from the lack of oxygen, and she gasped in a breath, shuddering, and curled on the floor as if she could curl in on the pain, the throbbing, fiery, excruciating burn inside her.

Beside the pain was something else, something burning just as hot: Rage.

16

REGAINING CONSCIOUSNESS WAS like vomiting, painful and unstoppable. Stone was hot, sweating. His head throbbed, and his body ached. His side was a mass of screaming nerve-endings, something beyond mere pain.

Wren.

Stone opened his eyes, saw nothing. He heard voices, though. Not far away, but muffled. His breathing echoed back to him; he was in a small space, then. His arms were bound behind him by what felt like zip-ties. He flexed his fingers, reaching to see if he could touch the restraints. His fingertips brushed smooth plastic, then the ribbed teeth. He grinned in the darkness.

Levering himself to his feet, Stone clenched his jaw as his side protested the movement. The zip-tie had been pulled so tight his skin was dimpled and throbbing. Perfect. He lifted his arms, bending forward and pressing his shoulder blades together. He raised his arms as far away from his body as he could, tensed against the coming agony, and then slammed his bound wrists against his backside. He ground his teeth as his healing gunshot wound tore open and trickled blood. His wrists were still bound, which meant he had to do it again. He sucked in a breath, tensed, drew his arms up and away, and slammed his wrists against his tailbone, shoving his hips back to maximize the force. This time, the ratchet mechanism of the zip-tie snapped, and his wrists came loose. The plastic had cut into his wrists, drawing blood, and his side was bleeding again, but he was free.

He paused to let the pain subside a bit, then moved toward the closest wall, followed it around with his palms until he found the door. Unlocked—the stupid bastards. He twisted the knob slowly, gingerly. The catch gave, and he pulled the door open a crack and peered through. More darkness, except for a sliver of light. He slipped through the door, moving as silently as he could. The light was just enough to let his darkness-accustomed eyes make out a pile of blankets on the floor of the room, which he avoided. He stopped by the cracked-open door. Beyond, a small fluorescent camping lantern sat in the middle of a table, surrounded by face-up playing cards. Pipes, syringes, joint roaches, and half-empty bottles of booze littered the table. There was only one man in the room, though, sitting on a chair facing away from Stone. His head leaned back, and he was making small groaning noises. A wet sucking sound told Stone what was happening.

Casting his gaze around the room, Stone saw a small folding knife on the table beside a hunk of wood that was being skillfully whittled into the likeness of a bull. He crept into the room, snatched the knife off the table and unfolded it partway, waiting to open it the rest of the way so the *click* didn't give him away. The man in the chair groaned, long and loud, and Stone used the cover of the noise to snap the blade open.

It was a tiny knife, the blade no more than two or three inches wide, but it was better than nothing. He tested the blade against his thumb, and found it razor sharp, probably kept so by the owner. He took small, silent steps until he stood behind the thug. The man's groans were growing louder, and he was starting to move his hands and hips in time with his groans.

Stone could now see over his victim's shoulder. A blonde head bobbed, small, pale, dirty white hands moving below her lips. Her eyes flicked up, saw Stone, and she faltered in her rhythm. He shook his head, displaying the knife, and she only blinked, resumed her attentions. The man began to mumble, repeating a single syllable, *"oo, oo, oo," yes, yes, yes*. He gripped a handful of blond hair in his fist and started shoving down, ignoring the girl's whimper and gag.

Stone brought the knife around, moving slowly, found his target. Drawing a deep breath, he struck just as the man groaned a final time, jabbing the point of the small knife into the thug's windpipe and twisting, sawing. The thug thrashed, and the girl fell backward, semen dripping down her chin. Blood sprayed over her as she cowered, clapping hands over her eyes. Stone sliced again, widening the hole he'd made, then slid the knife point between his victim's ribs and into his heart. The thrashing stopped, but thick ribbons of blood continued to pour from the gaping, ragged throat wound, down over the man's belly and legs and onto the floor. Blood covered Stone's hand, wet and warm and sticky.

He wiped his hand on his shirt, and then knelt beside the cowering girl. "Hey," he whispered. "Stay here, okay?"

"Was? Ich spreche kein Englisch." Her voice was tiny, hesitant.

Stone recognized the German, but didn't speak it. "Stay," he whispered again, moving his flattened palm toward the floor. The girl nodded, scrambling farther away from the dead man, away from his red-painted front and limp, bared manhood.

Stone moved to the next doorway, wondering where Cervantes kept finding these mazes of inter-connected shanties. Maybe he made them, cutting holes in walls and shoring up ceilings, evicting the residents. He peered around the opening, saw an empty room, and another beyond that. Slow, silent steps took him from room to room, following the faint echo of male voices, laughing.

He stopped at doorless entry way, watching shadows move, hearing voices speak. Stone was too keyed up and focused to bother translating, but his brain supplied snatches of words: *she didn't like it... won't hurt her price at all...*

Something gave him away. A shuffled foot, a too-loud breath. Something, it didn't matter what. Cervantes' voice halted, and his face filled the shadows in front of Stone.

"Ah, da American soldier. I wondered if you join us." He grinned wickedly and gestured with the barrel of his pistol for Stone to follow him.

Surreptitiously folding the knife and dropping it in his pocket, Stone followed Cervantes into the room, the largest one yet, lit by several more of the camping lanterns. There were three other men in the room, each armed and sitting at a folding table with several kilo bricks of marijuana in the center, each of them pinching out small amounts into plastic bags, weighing, adding or subtracting until they reached the proper weight.

There were three doors: one led back the way Stone had come, one seemed to lead outside, and another was closed.

"You kill a lot of my guys," Cervantes noted in a conversational voice.

"What did you expect? That I'd just let you take her and get away with it?" Stone kept his hand out of his pocket, but he was planning out his movements: reach into his pocket and unfold the knife while he was lunging, go for the windpipe, or the femoral artery. He'd take a bullet or two, probably, but he didn't see any other way around it. He had to take out Cervantes. He slowed his breathing, tensed and coiled his muscles, readying for the pounce.

Cervantes was eyeing Stone with a speculative look in his eye. "I tink I recognize you. You come after my operation some year or two ago. But I ambush you. Kill many of your stupid American friends. I remember you, yeah." He slid the rack on his pistol and touched the cold O to Stone's cheek. "You got away den. Not dis time, asshole."

Stone smirked, a cold, arrogant smile that was a lie to cover the fear in his gut. "Yeah, probably not. You can try, though."

A fist knocked on the door to the outside, drawing Cervantes' attention for a split second. It was all Stone needed. His hand flashed up, knocking the pistol barrel away. His knee rose to slam into Cervantes' kidney, and then Stone snatched the pistol away. Cervantes stumbled, gasping and clutching his side. The men dividing the marijuana turned to see Stone cupping the pistol in the Weaver Stance; *BLAM— BLAM—BLAM.* Three down, holes in heads; desperation lent Stone unerring accuracy. Cervantes threw himself backward, through the doorway from which Stone had come. Cervantes must have had a spare gun, because gunfire roared and bullets spat, missed, buzzing like bees past Stone's ear. Cervantes scrambled to his feet and lurched to the right, through another doorway, and Stone's answering rounds dug into the dirt at his feet.

Stone followed Cervantes, moving sideways through the door, sacrificing speed for caution. His ears ringing from the deafening gunfire, he heard only his own breathing, muffled huffing as he scuffed from door to door, sweeping corner to corner. He heard a door open somewhere, but he was disoriented and couldn't locate the source. The rooms were all dark, and Stone had no light source. He should have brought a lantern, as unwieldy as it would have been. Better than blind in the darkness, where every shadow could hide Cervantes.

He crept through another room, feeling the tension creep up his spine with every step he took. His instincts jangled, the intangible warning sign that something was about to happen. Just before he'd jumped out of the back of a cargo plane for his first combat mission, his CO had told him to always, always listen to his instincts. *The tighter your asshole puckers, the lower you should duck.*

Stone's asshole was puckered into a knot, so he ducked, dropping to his belly. Muzzle burst flashed overhead, and he rolled, firing upward. A grunt told him he'd hit something, but then gunfire blasted again, and a kiln-hot hammer of pain hit his thigh. He rolled away, hit a wall, then felt something hard against the back of his head.

"Got'chu now." Cervantes' voice was strained. "Stand up. Slowly."

Stone couldn't have stood up quickly even if he'd wanted to. He leaned against the wall and forced himself upright, teeth grinding. Cervantes grabbed him and shoved him toward the dim light a few rooms away. Stone stumbled, caught the door frame in order to remain upright. Back into the room where he'd first encountered Cervantes, the dead men slumped over, bleeding into the piles of green. Cervantes, bleeding from a deep gouge along his cheek, and now missing his left earlobe, kicked a dead man off a chair and shoved Stone into it, then cast around the room for something to tie him up with. Stone's bullet had nearly killed Cervantes, missing his brain by less than half an inch but 'nearly' wasn't close enough.

Two of the dead men wore belts, and Cervantes knelt to unbuckle one, keeping an eye and his pistol trained on Stone. While Cervantes' attention flickered to his attempts to free the belts, Stone fished the small knife out of his pocket and stuffed it into his combat boot. Cervantes wrapped one belt around Stone's midsection and pulled it tight, pinioning his arms against his sides and his body to the chair. The other belt went around his wrists, binding them together. It was sloppy, but effective. It wouldn't hold him long, but it would slow him down enough now that Cervantes had more of an upper-hand.

"And now, I kill you slowly. Before dat, I tink I fuck your girlfriend while you watch." Cervantes went to the closed door that led into the shanty-maze. Stone felt panic turn his blood to ice as Cervantes strode into the next room.

A moment later, Cervantes screamed, "Where da fuck she go?"

Hope swelled in Stone's belly, but he kept his expression neutral as Cervantes stormed past him.

Stone scanned the room. Each of the dead men had had a gun of some sort. But now, upon closer examination, he realized there were only two firearms left.

17

WREN HELD THE HEAVY GUN in both hands as she tiptoed through the darkness. Every sound startled her, forced her to fight to keep her breathing quiet and her step light.

She'd heard several gunshots, and then silence. She'd emerged from the darkened room expecting to find Cervantes waiting or Stone dead. Instead, she found three men with holes in their head, the accuracy a trademark of Stone's skill. She'd snatched the first weapon she saw, a blocky, black thing sitting on the table. It was heavier than it looked, and merely holding it made her shiver in terror at the thought of using it. She'd never fired a pistol before. She'd used a rifle once, with her father, and a shotgun a few times with Jon, out in the Virginia countryside. They'd only shot at targets. This was for real.

The part that scared her, more than holding the gun, more than being naked and alone in the darkness, more than knowing Cervantes and his men were somewhere close by, looking for her, was the knowledge that she was absolutely prepared to pull the trigger, if she got Cervantes in her sights. As prepared as she could be, at any rate.

A gunshot from off to her left. Wren huddled against a wall until a second shot rang, and then silence. Her toes touched some kind of fabric, and she felt around with her hands, the dim light revealing only vague shapes. A blanket. Something hard underneath it. Cold flesh. A leg. Alive? Dead? She couldn't tell. She followed the leg up to hard ribs, felt a faint heartbeat, thready and slow. Pulling away the blankets, she found a small pile of clothing, what felt to her touch like a minidress of some kind. She found the opening and pulled it on, tugged it on. It was far too small, constricting her chest and not even completely covering her ass, but it was better than being naked. She tugged it down farther, feeling her breasts squeeze up and out of the too-small bodice, and her backside hanging out beneath. She wished for proper clothing, knowing she wouldn't find it here.

Her violated privates throbbed, ached, and that only fueled her rage. It was cruelty for the sake of cruelty, inflicting agony simply for the joy of hurting someone else.

Wren had had enough.

She turned around and went toward the direction where she'd last heard gunfire. She crept through the darkness, straining her ears.

"Where da fuck she go?" Cervantes, discovering her absence. He wasn't far away, and was moving toward her.

Wren spun in place, found a corner, and crouched in it, making herself as small as she could. Feet scraped on dirt, a darker shadow filled the doorway to her left.

"I know you're here somewhere, little bird," Cervantes said. "Give up, and I may let your man live. He gonna bleed out soon. You can help him."

Wren didn't breathe, didn't move. Cervantes moved on, into another room. She slid into the doorway he'd come through, following the bluish-white light of the lantern. She had to save Stone. She knew better than to believe Cervantes would let either of them go, at this point.

The shadows grew lighter as she moved toward the lit room. Looking down, she could see her dress was jade green, and didn't do anything to hide her body. It displayed it, if anything. Which was the point, really, she supposed. Her heartbeat ratcheted into a pounding crescendo, her gut roiled, but she kept going. She couldn't afford to let her fear stop her now. Stone was just through that door. She knew it.

She saw him, then. He was covered in blood. His thigh was gushing crimson, his face and shoulders were crusted with dried blood from a gash on his head, and the wound on his side had reopened. Knotted belts tied him to a chair, and he thrashed, struggling against them, trying to wiggle loose.

"Stone…" She stepped into the room, the same room she'd come from, with the dead men and the drugs, and realized she had gone in a very short circle.

Four rooms, all connected at two walls. Which meant…

"Stupid. Think you get away?" Cervantes, behind her. "I like da dress on you. It fit you much better dan ugly little Liesel. You gonna make me a lotta money, I tink. Come here, or I shoot you, and him."

Wren was facing away from him, and had the gun in front of her, so she didn't think he'd seen it yet. Stone was still wiggling, less noticeably though. She could tell he had his hands free, and was reaching for his boot. Something hidden in his boot, she thought. She had to buy time. Stone's eyes were grim, hard, desperate.

She wanted to tell him she loved him. Maybe it was just the danger speaking, the memory of incredible sex. She didn't know, or care. He'd come for her, and now she had to give him time to make a play.

She turned around, lifting the gun, planting her feet in a wide triangle, holding the heavy pistol in both hands. She didn't try to aim it, just pointed the barrel at Cervantes. He looked shocked, his own gun held down at his side.

"Put it down, little bird. You ain't gonna shoot nobody." Cervantes slowly lifted his pistol, never taking his eyes from her.

"Shoot him, Wren." Stone's voice, low and calm.

"You won't, *Wren*." Cervantes laughed. "Funny, I call you 'little bird' all da time, and you really are a little bird. Put it down, I won't kill him. I sell you to a nice guy."

That was the wrong thing to say.

BLAM! Cervantes stumbled backward, a hole in his chest blooming scarlet.

Wren remembered timeless time in a dark hole, needles in her skin. *BLAM!* Fingers touching and pinching, fists hitting, feet kicking in her ribs. *BLAM!* Eyes, hungry eyes. Girls, naked and starving and drug-addled. Miguel, with his knife and brutal hands and killer's eyes. *BLAM!BLAMBLAM!* She advanced a step, toward Cervantes, who looked stunned, staring at her as multiple holes opened in his chest and poured his blood down his chest. She raised the gun slightly. *BLAMBLAMBLAM!* She remembered being bartered for, sold, like produce. Hungry, scared, hurt, exhausted, drug-addicted.

BLAM! The folding silver knife he liked so much, jammed inside her. *BLAM!* She pulled the trigger twice, but the gun only fired once, clicking empty on the second pull.

Stone was beside her. "You got him." He pulled the gun from her hand. "He's dead, babe." He hopped closer to her, tossed the empty pistol onto the table.

Wren couldn't take her eyes from Cervantes, his chest a mess of red. His eyes were glazed and shifting, his mouth working like a fish out of water. "He's not dead."

"He will be."

Nausea hit her like a fist. She'd just killed a man. She'd pulled the trigger, fired bullets into him. "I killed him." Acid burned her throat, and her stomach rebelled, lurched, and puke jetted from her in wave after wave.

Stone held her as she vomited. When she finally stopped, her stomach still lurching and dry-heaving, he pulled her against his chest. He was balanced on one leg. "I know, babe. You had to. He deserved it. I know that doesn't really help right now, though."

She felt tears start, and blinked them away. "I... oh God. Oh God, I killed him." She looked up at Stone, whose eyes were soft with sympathy. "Does it...how will I ever sleep again?"

Stone pressed a kiss to her forehead. "Time. Therapy, maybe. You'll have bad dreams, but...with everything you've been through, I think that was a given." He looked down at her, looking her over for fresh injuries. "Are you hurt anywhere? Did he hurt you?"

Wren nodded against his chest. "He...God, oh God. He hurt me. Inside. With the handle of his knife." She didn't know how to say it, how to make him understand that the knowledge of what he'd done was almost as bad as the pain of it. "He used that knife, the flippy thing—"

"A balisong. Butterfly knife." His voice was hesitant, as if he understood what she was getting at but didn't want to believe it. "What did he do to you?"

She closed her eyes tight, clutched his shirt. "He used it...shoved it in—inside—inside me. It hurts. I think he cut me open, in there."

"Shit." He spoke through grinding teeth.

"I know—I know it's better than being raped, or sold, but...I tried to stop him, I fought him, but he... *fuck*." She sobbed, went limp into his arms. "It hurts. I feel it, over and over. That cold hard thing, edges, forced into me. Scraping, cutting. It was closed, but it still...it hurts."

Stone was silent, his arms tight, almost too tight. Then, he swayed. "I...I gotta stop this bleeding." He stumbled backward, back into the chair he'd been tied to.

She watched as Stone leaned forward and used his knife to cut away the shirt from one of the dead men, folded the cotton lengthwise into a bandage and wrapped it around his thigh, then tied it in a knot. He cursed under his breath the whole time, a constant stream of florid expressions. Next, he wrapped one of the belts he'd been tied up with around his thigh, over the shirt, and cinched it as tight as it would go, just above the wound. When he had it pulled tight, he slipped the bitter end of the belt between his leg and the leather, leaving a loop through which he passed the end again, creating a makeshift knot. When he was done with this, he was sweating and out of breath.

"We have to move. Get back to the Embassy."

"But he's...he's dead."

"His goons don't know that yet. We might still run into trouble. Plus, with Cervantes out of the picture, there'll be a power vacuum, and a fight to fill it. We don't want to be around when that shit goes down."

"Power vacuum?" Wren asked. She felt limp, numb, shocked, unable to process thoughts or emotions.

Stone worked himself to his feet, hopping on his good leg to stay balanced. "He was the big dog in Manila. Now he's gone, and someone else is going to want to take his place, and it'll mean an underground war in the process. Don't worry about it. Our only concern is getting home."

Wren slid under his arm and took as much of his weight as she could. "Home. I want...I want to go home." She tried to summon thoughts of home, but nothing came.

She had trouble remembering what her dorm room looked like. Had she ever sat in a classroom, listened to lectures? Sipped coffee and laughed with friends? Gone to sorority parties and had too much cheap beer? She had memories of those things, but they felt more like a movie watched in years past, snapshots and vague notions of things that had happened. It felt like she'd been in Manila forever. Like the person she'd been was gone, and someone else had taken that place. She was still Wren Morgan, still had the same brain and body and soul, but the fabric and substance and content of who she was had been irrevocably altered.

They emerged onto the narrow street in the dim gray of onrushing dawn. Stone peered around, twisting awkwardly to try and find some visual cue as to where they were. He must have seen something he recognized behind them, because he laboriously twisted around and began limping in that direction. He couldn't put much weight on his leg, but Wren was simply not strong enough to support his weight, so he had to hop.

It would be a long walk back to the Embassy.

18

IT SEEMED ALMOST ANTICLIMACTIC, in a way. The last several days of chase, hunting for Wren, rescuing her, fleeing Cervantes and his men, only to have it all end with a few bullets in a back room. Now they were adrift in Manila again, alone, and still hurt, still hungry, still exhausted. More so than ever. The question remained, though: were Cervantes' men still after them? Stone didn't dare relax his guard, didn't dare take even a single moment to relax until he knew they were safe.

And the streets of urban Manila were anything but safe, even under the best of circumstances.

It took over two hours for them to find their way to a major road, where they happened upon a taxi disgorging a young couple. Stone pushed Wren into a hustle, hobbling after her, putting more weight on his leg than was really advisable. Wren slid across the ripped upholstery, holding on to Stone's hand as he clutched the roof of the car and lowered himself in.

The cabbie turned his head slightly, the international unspoken gesture meaning "where to?"

"The US Embassy, please," Stone said.

"No, no," the cabby said. "I don' go dat par. Only Pasay City. Tapt Abenue? LRT EDSA? Go nort', get dere easy-easy."

Stone had to work through the scruffy, gray-bearded old man's thick accent. Tapt? Taft, Taft Avenue. A pretty major thoroughfare in the Pasay City area, and one that would take them, as the man had said, pretty close to the embassy. "That's fine," Stone said. "Take us to the station, then."

"Okay-okay. Comin' up, quick. Not par." He slewed the wheel to the right and into traffic, cutting off a rumbling old half-ton truck.

Wren clutched Stone's hand with panicked strength as the cabby swung the car through traffic, stopping with inches to spare between their car and the one ahead of them, jamming the accelerator so hard the car jolted forward, slamming them both into the seat. After a few minutes of this, the traffic congealed to a standstill, and their forward progress was halted. A raised roadway or train platform ran between the north and south traffic, and through the cracked-open windows Stone could hear the incessant honks of cars, the squeal of brakes and the rumble of diesel engines, motorcycles buzzing, voices raised above the din, a traffic policeman's whistle shrilling. He found his eyes growing heavy, despite the throbbing in his leg and the constant ache in his side.

Stone rolled down the window farther and sucked in deep breath of the humid air, hot already despite the early morning hour. Beside him, Wren rubbed her eyes.

"I can't keep going much longer," she said. "I feel like I've been awake and running for a week straight. I don't even know what day it is, or the last time I ate something. I'm dizzy, and shaky."

Stone fought a yawn and pulled her shoulder against his side, wrapping his arm around her. "I know, baby. I know. Me too. We're almost there. A train ride, and we're there. Stay with me, okay?"

She nodded, jerking as the cabby rocketed the car forward, slipping between two buses and a jeepney to cut through to the far right lane. "I'm with you." She blinked hard, then sat up, shaking her head as if to shake away sleepiness. "Will anyone else come after us?"

Stone could only shrug.

A few more minutes of start-stop-start-stop, and the cabby jerked the wheel to bring them to the curb. "Out here, station across street."

Stone dug the correct amount in Pesos out of his pocket, along with a tip, and then shoved the door open and hopped away from the car, balanced on one foot. He extended a hand to help Wren out.

MRT Taft was a madhouse. Even MRT Shaw in all its insanity couldn't compete with the sheer crush of humanity flooding into and out of the Taft transit station. People flowed in every direction, holding briefcases over their heads, lugging babies on their backs, bags of groceries in their hands, moving in ones and twos and larger groups. A voice squawked in distorted Filipino over the PA, then again in what sounded like barely intelligible English, announcing arrivals and warnings to stay away from the tracks. A set of stairs led up to the platform, and a sluggish knot of people were traffic-jammed around this stairway, arrivals and departures mixing until there was simply no way to move, except with the mass of bodies.

Stone felt his stomach drop at the sight of what he had to navigate, with a reopened bullet hole in his side and another fresh one in his thigh, a gash on his head and a mouth that hadn't tasted water in hours and an empty stomach. He'd be elbowed, his leg bumped and kicked, and it would take forever to get into the station.

"Let's get this over with," he sighed, adjusting his grip on Wren's shoulders, forcing himself to use his injured leg as much possible to save the strength in his good one.

Together they entered the press of travelers waiting to ascend to the elevated train station. Within minutes, Stone had been elbowed or bumped so many times he was sure his wounds would be bleeding again, but there was nothing he could do, except deal with it and hope.

Getting up the stairs was hell. He had to use his wounded leg to push up, and nearly screamed with the pain of the effort at each step. Behind him, people were shouting their frustration at his torturous progress. Wren set her shoulder under his armpit and helped him lift up to each step, groaning and using every ounce of strength she had.

It took them nearly ten minutes to ascend the steps. They found a pillar and Stone slumped down to his ass, heedless of the stares he drew. He spotted a vending machine across the station, and pointed to it, handing Wren the last of his Philippines Pesos. "Get us some water, huh?"

She returned after a moment with two liter-bottles of water, and a panicked expression. "I think there's someone here looking for us. I think I recognized him from the first place Cervantes held me. He was looking around like he was waiting for someone."

Stone uncapped the water and drew slow, short sips, swishing the icy liquid to get rid of the cotton mouth. "Shit. I don't have a gun anymore, either. I lost mine in the fight with Cervantes, and never replaced it."

Wren drank her own water in long gulps, then paused. "What do we do?"

Stone shrugged. "Get on the train. Hope he doesn't see us."

"What if he does?"

Stone gathered his good leg beneath him and held on to Wren's outstretched hand, climbed laboriously to his feet. "I'll deal with that if we come to it."

He realized as he spoke that he still had the knife in his pocket. He withdrew it and held it in his palm. Stone was ready to be done with violence. He wanted to be home, to lay in his bed and watch ESPN. Work on his Monte Carlo. Take Wren out for ice cream, find an empty meadow in the countryside and make slow love to her on a blanket beneath the stars.

He stuffed the water bottle in the cargo pocket of his shorts and held on to Wren as they moved toward the northbound train rails. Stone spotted the man Wren had seen. He was thick and brawny, but on the short side, with bare, tattooed arms and low-hanging shorts. He was turning in slow circles, scanning the crowd like a man looking for someone in particular. He let the crowd slurry around him while he stood on his toes and consulted a cell phone every once in awhile. Stone halted behind a pillar, hiding from view in a place where they could still wait for the train to show up.

Wren buried her head against his chest and breathed in, breathed out, fighting panic.

A deafening roar and the shrill squealing of grinding brakes announced the northbound train's arriving from the Baclaran end of the line. The announcer squawked, and Stone found it easier to translate the Filipino than to understand the garbled, accented English: *"Pahilaga sa Monumento… susunod na hinto, Libertad…"* Northbound to Monumento…next stop, Libertad. *"Iwasan ang pagtayo malapit sa pinto…"* Stand clear of the doors…

The blue, white, and red train ground to a stop, and the knotted mass of people waiting to board shifted forward. Stone hobbled forward as fast as he could, letting the crowd guide him while he kept an eye on the man looking for them. Wren was hidden in the crowd, blending as well as she could considering her skimpy garb. Stone, however, towered head and shoulders above most of the crowd, and his face, neck and shoulders were covered in blood. He stood out like he was wearing a flashing neon sign.

The man saw him, glanced at his cell phone and frowned in clear confusion, then followed the crowd onto the train, shoving through to make headway.

Stone pushed Wren through the crowd to the end of the car, put her back to the wall and stood in front of her, watching as their pursuer pushed and shoved toward them through the jam-packed car.

A warning burbled on the overhead PA, and the doors closed with a hiss. The car jerked, and lurched into motion, quickly picking up speed as it left the station and moved out into the daylight. It was well past dawn now, with the sun washing over the landscape, shedding long shadows. Riders exchanged desultory conversation, listened to iPods, spoke on phones, swayed in silence, stared out the window, all unaware of the unfolding danger.

Stone held the folding knife in his palm, pressed his thumb to the nocked edge, ready to snap it open. The other man kept his hand in his shorts pocket, which Stone realized was hanging low, misshapen by the weight of must be a small handgun of some sort, a Walther PPK or similar.

Adrenaline rifled through him, making his blood sing. He planned out his movements. In close quarters like this, with such a small blade, his best bet was the femoral artery. It would be quick, low-profile.

The two men were face to face now.

"Where you gonna go?" The man had a soft voice, contrasting oddly with his brawny, tattooed physique.

"Let it go," Stone warned. "Let us go."

"You come now. Be easy. Or dere be trouble." The man lifted his fist from his pocket, letting silver flash.

Stone readied himself, unfolding the blade slightly. "You haven't heard from your boss in awhile, have you?" The thug narrowed his eyes. "No, you haven't. Know why? He's dead."

"Kalokohan." Bullshit.

"Call him. Right now." Stone lifted an eyebrow. "See if he answers."

"You try pool me. Shut up now."

Stone forced a laugh. "Would I joke about something like that? Cervantes is gone, man. I pumped an entire clip into his sorry ass. Give him a call. See what happens."

"Maybe he dead, maybe not." The gun came out entirely, held flat against the man's thigh, mostly disguised by his hamhock-fist. "Maybe I kill you, take her."

"Maybe you can try. You'll die like all the rest who've tried."

People around them shifted, hearing the tension in the voices, some understanding the words. Stone held his palm against his thigh and unfolded the knife. The soft *click* of the blade snapping into place was lost in the noise of the rushing train.

Stone was a heartbeat from pouncing when the train jerked and slowed, the PA announcing, "Libertad!"

Bodies pressed and crushed and jostled, shoving and ducking. He caught a glimpse of the man holding on to a rail, fighting the motion of the crowd like a leaf stuck against a rock in a rushing river. Then the crowds waiting at the Libertad stop boarded, and the rush began in reverse, the two bunches of travelers mixing and merging like meeting waves, congealing momentarily and then parting. The door closed, and Stone held his ground while the tattooed thug pushed toward him, his eyes hard, glittering with the threat of violence.

"Why are we doing this, man?" Stone asked. "Cervantes is gone. You have to know how many of your friends I've taken out at this point." Stone murmured the words, pitched just loud enough to be heard. "Put it away and get off at the next stop. Nothing has to happen. Just let us go. We just want to go home."

"I don' tink so. Not so easy. Many of prends, yes. For dem, you die."

Gunfire would result in injured bystanders. Stone had to hit first, and hit hard, so that wouldn't happen. Some men just thrived on the violence, the conflict. When those kind of men had the promise of bloodshed in their teeth, they wouldn't let it go, wouldn't back down, logic be damned.

A breath, a pause, time slowed to treacle as Stone shifted his weight with the motion of the train, ignoring the screaming in his thigh as he forced his weight on the muscle. Another breath, and he lashed out, blade held low, hammer-style, extended from the bottom of his fist with the blade toward his body. Strike into the thigh, high on the leg, near the crotch, drag the blade through meat. Withdraw. Step back.

The pistol clattered as it fell from surprised, limp fingers. Stone bent and scooped up the dropped weapon and shoved it into his waistband, watched as the man sagged back into the crowd. No one screamed, no one saw. The man's eyes glazed, fluttered, his mouth worked vacantly, silently, voice leached by agony. Pants leg darkened by blood, the liquid sliding underfoot, pooling unnoticed. Someone shoved, and the tattooed man stumbled, lurched, fell into someone else, who shoved him as well, thinking he was drunk.

The train stopped again, and Stone grabbed Wren's wrist, pulled her with him into the exodus. The crowd dispersed outside the train, and others boarded. The doors closed, and the train chuffed as it began drawing away. Now a scream rent the air, audible even over the noise of the crowd and the roar of the train. The human body held a lot of blood, and the femoral artery carried much of it, especially in the Scarpa's triangle, where Stone had sliced him open.

It was peak morning hours, so another train arrived within three minutes, and Stone and Wren followed the crowd on board. Adrenaline still ran rampant through Stone, who noted that security guards were already swarming through the station, walkie-talkies held to mouths. The transit authority security guards had a much quicker response time than the city's police, it seemed.

The map of stops printed on the wall of the train informed Stone that they had only two more stops before the United Nations stop, which was where he was planning on exiting, since it was closest to the Embassy. Wren held on to his arm, both supporting him and herself.

"Is it easy for you?" she murmured up to him, her liquid brown eyes conflicted.

"Is what easy? Killing someone?" Stone rubbed his hand on his shorts, feeling the blade in his pocket. "No. It's never easy. I do what I have to, to keep you and me alive, but it's never easy."

"Will you have nightmares about it?"

Stone sighed. "I already do, sweetheart."

"I keep...I keep seeing his eyes. He looked so—so surprised." Wren's voice shook. "Every time I blink, I see it. Red...so much blood."

"I wish I could have done that for you, Wren." He buried his nose in her hair. "I would have. I should have."

Wren didn't answer, just pressed her face to his chest and breathed, shaky, feeble breaths.

Two stops later, they debarked the train, just as a vague announcement went over the PA about a delay in the schedule. Stone clenched his teeth and hustled them through the crowd, weaving to avoid contact with the security guards. He doubted anyone had seen enough to even identify the perpetrator as American, much less describe him, but he was covered in blood from his wounds and the earlier fights. It was best to get clear, just in case.

Descending to street level was easier than ascending, fortunately, as Stone could hold the rail and hop down each step. They found themselves on United Nations Avenue, heading west. Sirens howled somewhere far away.

He hobbled slowly, glancing behind him at the oncoming traffic, waiting for a taxi. He couldn't make it on foot to the Embassy. He just couldn't. The adrenaline was flooding away, leaving him shaky and tired and numb, as well as dizzy from blood loss.

An ancient white Toyota slid to a stop in front of them, hailed by Stone's waving hand. Wren slid in first, and Stone next, lowering himself with a trembling arm.

"US Embassy, please." He barely recognized his own voice.

"Maybe hospital betta?" The cabbie was a young man with long hair and a scraggly beard.

"No, just the Embassy."

"Okay-sure."

Fortunately the cab ride was gentler than the last one, and it was a matter of minutes before the cab bumped to a halt in front of the white stone and black iron gates of the Embassy of the United States of America. Stone dug in his pocket, found it empty.

"I don't—don't have any Pesos," he mumbled, feeling himself fading quickly.

Wren shoved a pile of bills over the seat, not bothering to count. "Come on, Stone. I've got it covered. Get out for me, okay?"

He was dizzy, weak, but he shoved the door open and hopped away, nearly falling. Wren was there in moments, her skimpy, stolen dress hiked up and baring most of her flesh. "You need some clothes," he said.

"That's the last thing I care about right now." Wren glanced toward the gate. "Will they let us in? I don't have a passport. I don't even know where it is. In my purse? That was gone a long time ago. When they first took me, I think."

"They'll let us in," Stone growled.

A blue-uniformed guard wielding an assault rifle approached them, young and hard-eyed and intense. "State your business."

"I'm Lieutenant Stone Pressfield. I'm a retired Navy SEAL. My girlfriend was kidnapped." Stone couldn't get all the words out right. "I got her back. We need…we need help. Let us in." She wasn't his girlfriend, but it just came out, slipped out.

The guard's eyes raked up and down Stone's body, taking in the numerous injuries. "I'd say you need medical attention, sir. You look—"

"I know, dammit!" Stone snapped, reverting to military posture, ramrod straight, glaring down at the young man. "But first, we need to get off the street. I need to brief someone about what happened. Goddamn it, I just—I need to sit down." He felt himself stumbling, falling.

Wren tried to catch him, but he was too heavy. He felt hard arms go under his armpits, dragging him. He fought to get his feet underneath him, to walk, but darkness was encroaching, weakness and exhaustion and blood-loss and hunger dragging him down. Radios squawked, garbled. He felt himself laid down on a cold floor, and then Wren's soft, warm hand touched his face.

"Stone? Are you okay?" Her voice was afraid.

He blinked, fluorescent lights overhead blinding him. "I'm okay," he mumbled. "Just tired. Stay with me, okay? Don't leave my side, no matter what." He had to stay awake, had to make sure she was safe. He'd gotten her this far, he couldn't let go now.

But he was so tired, so weak. It hurt, it all hurt. His whole body throbbed like fire.

Voices around him, English, both native and accented. He was lifted up, jostled, eliciting a groan, set on a stretcher. "Wren?"

"I'm here. We've got an escort of soldiers. They're taking us to a hospital." More movement, vehicle doors closing, engines rumbling.

"Americans? Don't trust anyone."

"Lieutenant Pressfield." The voice was gravelly, the voice of someone used to shouting. Stone opened his eyes to see an older American man, lean and weathered. "I'm Commander Daniel Stanton. Your friend Nick alerted us to the situation. We've had people looking, but all we've found is your... handiwork. You don't have to worry anymore. We'll take care of everything from here"

"Commander...Wren lost her passport. She needs medical attention too."

"It's all covered, Pressfield. Relax. You brought it in, son. Well done."

The sound of a confident military voice did something to Stone, sent him back. He should salute, but he couldn't move his arm. "Sir."

"I'll debrief you after you've been looked at, but I have to know. Did you ever make contact with someone named Cervantes?"

Stone fought to keep his eyes open. "Cervantes… he's dead, sir."

"You know this for sure?"

Stone met Wren's eyes. "Yes. 100% positive. I saw him die."

Commander Stanton leaned back against the ambulance wall. "Good. About time someone offed that fucker." He glanced at Wren. "Apologies, ma'am."

Wren's expression didn't change. "Don't apologize. I'm the one who killed him."

Stanton's voice reflected his shock. "You?"

Wren flinched. "Yes. You don't know…you don't know what he did to me."

Stanton's eyes hardened. "I've been tracking him for years, Miss Morgan. I believe I can guess what you've been through." He leaned forward. "You don't have to worry about a thing, from now on. You did the human race a favor, ma'am. I'll have you two home on a private charter as soon as I can work out the logistics. No press, no mess."

Stone's eyes fell shut again, but before he passed out, he felt Wren's fingers thread through his.

"As long as we're together," she murmured.

Stone wanted to agree to that, but unconsciousness overtook him.

19

—Two weeks later—

WREN TOSSED THE TEAL MAXI DRESS onto her dorm room bed in frustration. Nothing fit right. Nothing looked right. Nothing felt right. She'd tried on a dozen outfits, but none of them were right. Her hair wasn't right. Her makeup wasn't right.

She wasn't right.

Nothing was right.

She'd been back in her dorm for a week, and she should be relieved, overjoyed, happy, excited. She should feel like she had a new lease on life.

She was healthy once more, for the most part. Her ribs only ached a little bit if she moved wrong, her privates were healed. She still felt the chemical need every once in a while, in random spurts. She would wake up from an already fitful sleep feeling the crawling under her skin, the itchy veins and hot-then-cold need for the euphoric drift of the heroin.

Nightmares hounded her. She had to have lights on, all the time. She'd tried sleeping with the lights off the first night she'd been home. She'd spent the first few days back Stateside with her parents, and she'd woken up screaming, thrashing, sobbing. The darkness had been alive. Waiting. Hungry. The darkness had been waiting to take her back, to drag her into the hole with the scratching, crawling things and the beatings and the needles.

She hadn't been able to sleep again that night at all. Even with the light on, she hadn't been able to sleep. Even after being taken to the doctor and prescribed sleeping pills, she couldn't find any rest. The sleeping pills were worse, really. They would trap her in the nightmares, keep her under so she couldn't escape them by waking up. She'd be trapped in that black pit, waiting to be punched and kicked, waiting for the needle in her vein. She would start to drift off, and then she would jerk awake, hand clapped over her forearm, huddled against the headboard.

Her parents hadn't known how to cope, how to help. Therapy, talking through it, only forced her to relive the horror. She'd stopped going, against her parents' insistence. So, she'd taken a bus back to her dorm room, to hide. The start of the semester helped, nominally. Going to classes let her pretend she was fine. She could forget while listening to an anthropology lecture, or while doing calculus.

It hadn't been an easy transition back home. There had been news stories, interview requests— which she'd turned down—reunions with her friends and family. She'd spent days in the hospital in Manila, and then more in a hospital Stateside. Psychological evaluations, police reports. Follow-up appointments with her family's doctor. Visits from just about everyone from LifeBride. Apologies from Nick and Pastor Len and the staff. She accepted the apologies, but didn't think she'd be going back to LifeBridge any time soon.

She'd had visits from just about everyone.

Except the one person she wanted to see: Stone.

She hadn't seen or heard from Stone since they'd parted at the airport. He'd hugged her, kissed her, promised he come see her, and now a week had passed, and she hadn't heard a word.

Until today. He'd called her, asked her if she wanted to have dinner with him. Like, on a date. It seemed strange, unnecessary. They'd witnessed death together. They'd run for their lives together. They'd had mind-blowing sex together. And now he wanted to sit in some noisy restaurant and chat about…what? The weather? Sports? The latest episode of *The Big Bang Theory*?

He knew where she lived; why hadn't he come to see her? Did he regret sleeping with her? Did he just want to forget everything?

Wren shuddered, let the blouse she'd just pulled off the hanger slip through her fingers as she slumped to the floor, choking on sobs that wouldn't come out. She gasped, dry-heaving as the sobs caught in her throat. She hadn't cried. Not once. Not alone, not in therapy, not with her Mom. She wasn't okay, and she knew it, but she couldn't cry. She wished she could. She felt the sobs pent up inside her, pressure building within like a shaken bottle of soda with the lid screwed on tight.

A soft knock on her door startled her, but she couldn't get to her feet. She tried, but she couldn't. Everything was spinning, but she was weighed down by the hundred tons of nightmare-memories and lack of sleep and shock she couldn't deal with. And she missed Stone—she missed him so bad she couldn't breathe. He'd rescued her and fought for her and killed for her and bled for her and comforted her without having to speak and he was gone, he wasn't here and she missed him.

She was huddled on the floor of her bedroom, in the corner by her dresser, wearing nothing but a pair of barely-there lacy panties.

And then he was in front of her, huge and warm and comforting.

"Someone let me in when I told them I was picking you up," he said by way of explanation. "Hey. Talk to me, babe."

Wren didn't have any words. She blinked, peered up at him, saw his tan face and rugged features, close-cropped dark blond hair, soft brown eyes tender with compassion.

"I—" What was she supposed to say?

Stone seemed to understand. He scooped her up, one arm beneath her knees, the other around her shoulders, and lifted her as if she weighed nothing. He favored his leg a little, but that was the only sign of having two bullet holes in his body. He slid onto the bed, his long legs crumpling her discarded clothes.

He smelled clean, like soap and faint, spicy cologne. His shirt smelled like fabric softener, warm and soft. She burrowed against his hard chest, wrapped her arms around his neck and held on.

"I can't—can't sleep. Can't eat. I still feel the craving for that drug. I can't even say the word. Heroin. Part of me wants, *needs* the heroin, and it's eating me up inside. Not all the time. The dreams. Stone, the dreams…they—they're inside me. Like, I held it together when I was going through it. I just wanted to live, to not be sold. You rescued me. Saved me. Stayed with me. And now I'm back home and it's all wrong. I'm wrong. It's like I'm not here." She was speaking in a stumbling rush, the words suddenly pouring out, because it was Stone, and he *knew*. "I'm not here. Does that sound crazy? Like I got left behind, somehow. Part of me is still over there. Still in Manila, in that hole, that fucking black hole with the bugs and the drugs and the darkness and *him*, Cervantes, hitting me. Holding me down and sticking that needle into me. I'm still there, and this…this body, *this* me is some other Wren. Who am I, now, Stone? How am I supposed to be here? Those other girls? What happens to them? They don't get to go home. They didn't have Stone to rescue them."

Stone grimaced. "That's what I have nightmares about. Those other girls. After that first mission, the one that went wrong? It was Cervantes then, too. The innocent girls, no more than children. They haunted my dreams for…months. And now they're back, with different faces. The same faces. I see Lisa, too. Over and over again. Lisa Johnson, naked and starving, track marks on her skin, bruises and scabs and matted hair and eyes that said she'd never really be whole again. And I see you, in that room." His voice was low, a murmur like thunder rolling somewhere beyond a midnight horizon.

"I pray…" Wren wiped at her eye with a thumb, at the wetness leaking down that still refused to be the tears she needed to shed. "I pray, Stone. But

God doesn't do anything. He doesn't take away the memories."

"You know how many nights I laid awake in bed, unable to sleep for the dreams? Unable to focus on anything because the nightmares didn't stop when I was awake. They didn't stop, you know? They just became memories. I'd lay in bed and watch the moon move over the horizon, praying, begging to God to take the memories and give me five *fucking* seconds of peace. Sometimes I think I believe in God because I've seen His presence, but I don't always *believe* like other people at church, like Nick believes. I've seen good things. I've seen the sunrise on the wide open ocean from the deck of an aircraft carrier, and that… that's glorious. Sunsets in the Alps. A full moon on fresh snow. People banding together to help each other, doing selfless things, acts of courage and heroism. I've seen men who should be dead get up and walk away and kiss their wives and kids, and the only explanation is that God protected them. I'm still alive, and I've had some ridiculously close calls. Felt like God protected me when I should have died. So I believe in God, I believe in His existence. He's real. That's a fact as immutable as sunrise and sunset and the basic physics of the universe. But sometimes, I don't understand Him. I don't get why He lets such horrible shit go on in this world He created. Why good things happen to bad people, and vice-versa. Those questions people struggle with all the time, you know? I struggle with them, too, just like everyone else.

"Except…for guys like me, who've seen the most vile things humanity can offer…those questions are worse. And I don't have any answers, Wren. I've never found any answers. I learned to sleep at night, over time. I try to accept that what happened, happened, and nothing I do can change it. I accept that I saw what I saw. I did what I did. I pulled the trigger. I have to own that. I have blood on my hands, Wren. So much. I can't ever escape that. Even though the men I killed were all awful, evil men, drug dealers and killers and rapists—bad guys—they were still people. They may have had wives or kids, a mother. A father. Someone who would miss them. I ended them, ended that. And I have to live with it. The times I failed, the missions we fucked up, the bad guys who got away, I have to live with that too." Stone's voice quavered, and Wren didn't dare look at him. The torment in his voice was too raw and personal. "I helped people. That leavens the guilt. I saved people. I saved entire fucking villages. Towns. Killed the cartel kingpin and freed them from his tyranny. Stopped the terrorist from making more car-bombs and killing innocent people. But…it's all there. And you have to get up every day and live your life and not let it define you, not let it drag you down.

"Does belief in God help, all the time? No. Not really. He won't take the memories away, in my experience. But it helps to believe that there's a plan I'm too small to see. A plan I can't understand. A purpose to things. Maybe that's just blind, a salve to my conscience like the bitter, jaded nonbelievers say. But it helps, and I'll take all the help I can get. It helps to believe in something bigger and stronger and smarter and more powerful than me, that there's purpose in the death of guys I cared about. Brothers, men I loved like family. Dozens, Zane, Benny, Hector, Billy, Connor." He spoke the names like a litany. "Adam. Shiny. Bradshaw. Sue. Fucking Sue, a boy named Sue. His dad named him after the Johnny Cash song, for real. Sue was a nasty ass bastard, mean as a snake. But he was loyal to a fault. Acted like he didn't like anyone, but he loved us all. Got killed saving us all. A grenade landed at our feet, and Sue? He didn't even hesitate. Picked it up and threw it, but it was too late. It went off a foot from his head. Blew him to fucking pieces. There's got to be a greater purpose to that, right?"

Wren heard him swallow hard, breathe in and out deeply, deliberately. She still didn't look up at him, kept her eyes on the wall, on his hand clenched into a fist beside her. She reached up and felt his jaw, smooth and freshly-shaven, felt his cheek. Wet.

And that broke something open inside her. Let the dam open. It was a hiccup at first, a tear down her cheek. The hiccup turned to a sob, her lip sucking into her mouth, her throat scraping.

"Yeah, babe. I know." Stone brushed her cheek with his thumb in small, slow circles.

Her eyes burned, her chest ached, her throat hurt. Everything came apart, then. Opened up, somehow, a geyser of everything she'd held in, trapped inside her for days and weeks. The tears she refused to cry for herself in the darkness. While she was running, dodging Cervantes and his men. All of it came up and out.

Sobbing wasn't really the word for it. It was something beyond sobbing. It was the sound of a soul being shattered, of terror and pain finally being given true vent. Wren couldn't breathe for the wracking, wrenching sobs being torn up from within her. It was physically painful to let it out, to feel the horror. She delved deep, felt it all over again. Felt the hard fists bashing against her cheek, the kick to her ribs. The examination, being sold. Watching that girl being gagged as she went down on Miguel. The apathy in her eyes.

Death. So much death. The crack of pistols, the chainsaw ripping of AK-47s. The wet *thunk* of bullets hitting flesh, ending lives. So much blood. Cut throats, pierced skulls.

The kick of the gun in her fist, over and over. Watching, almost from outside of herself, as she blasted Cervantes again and again. Rage taking over, but unable to banish the guilt, the horror. His eyes, she saw his eyes, over and over. Every night, she saw Cervantes' eyes as he died, the confusion as he felt himself dying, the way his mouth gaped and worked like a fish out of water. The pool of blood spreading, spreading.

"Am I—am I a bad person? For killing Cervantes?" The question had haunted her for days. "Am I going to hell? I killed him, Stone. I shot him, so many times. I couldn't stop. It was like watching someone else. I know he deserved it, but does it make me like him, for killing him?"

"No, babe. It doesn't make you like him. It doesn't make you a bad person." He leaned away and met her eyes. "Am I a bad person? I've killed more people than you can imagine. All of them were bad guys, but I still killed them. How do you justify that? You can't dwell on it. You have to just—I don't know… accept it, I guess. He was evil, Wren. You know he was. And really, it was self-defense, and defending me. That's the best justification I can give you. I can't deal with the guilt for you, but I'll be with you the whole way."

"Where were you?" Wren demanded. "Why didn't you come for so long? I can't sleep, Stone. I can't eat. I can't do anything. I need you. You make it so I can breathe."

Stone sighed. "I'm sorry. I just...I needed my own time to—to deal. I'm no good to you if I'm a mess too. I needed some space to figure my own shit out. I'm here now, and I'm not going anywhere."

Wren cried silently, then. She held onto Stone and felt his shirt growing damp beneath her cheek. When she was finally able to stop the flood, she was wrung out and limp.

"I don't think I can move," she mumbled.

"So don't. Let's just stay here, like this." He sounded sleepy himself. "Will you get in trouble if I stay here with you?"

Wren managed a shrug. "Class...in the morning. Nine."

"No problem."

Stone helped her into bed and she drifted, slept without dreams. At some point, she felt Stone kick the blankets from underneath their bodies and pull them up, and she burrowed closer against him.

She woke up in the dim gray pre-dawn with Stone spooned against her. She felt lighter, cleaner, rested. Not totally okay, but better. And Stone was there with her, holding her. His palm was flat on her belly, just beneath her breasts. She felt something hard against her spine, and she felt her heart lurch and her body tighten at the knowledge of what it was. She placed her hand on his, threaded her fingers through hers, and listened to him breathe, wondering how to classify her relationship with Stone. Were they together? Would he make love to her? Would he bring her to his place and show her more of who he was, tell her more about himself, share his life with her?

"You're thinking too hard, babe," he mumbled.

"You and me…what are we?"

Stone shifted his hips, stretching, then seemed to realize that he was pressing himself against her and pulled away. "Sorry, I—"

Wren wriggled against him. "Don't be sorry. I didn't mind."

"What are we?" Stone's fingers flexed against her belly, then slid upward, just slightly, brushing the underside of her breasts. "We're us. We're together. If that's what you want, that is."

"Of course I do." She moved his hand higher, cupping her breast with. "I want this."

"Wren…" he groaned, clutching her gently, moving his hand so his palm scraped over her nipple. "What about your roommate? I'm not sure a dorm room is the best place, or that now is the best time. But I want it too."

"My roommate is never here. Her boyfriend has an apartment, and she's there pretty much all the time. She only comes here to study sometimes in the afternoon between classes." She shifted her body, pressing her ass up his hardness. "Stone...please."

He writhed with her, groaning and breathing against her bare shoulder. "I want it to be right. To be perfect. I want to go on a date with you. Take you home to my place and take all night with you. I don't want to be rushed, or have to worry about being interrupted."

"I feel like I'm going to explode," Wren said, breathless. "Like everything is...on fire inside me. Building up and ready to go off. Crying last night helped, but I need this with you too. I don't want to wait. I can't wait." She moved rhythmically against him, sliding her lace-clad backside against the rough fabric of his jeans.

Stone massaged her breast, even as he protested. His fingers twisted her nipple, gently pinched it, then his whole hand engulfed the weight of her breast. His hips moved with hers, and his lips pressed helpless kisses to her shoulder. Each time his lips touched her skin, Wren shivered, gasped. She took his hand again and guided it down, down, between her legs.

"Just touch me. Give me something." She slid his fingers under the elastic of her panties.

Stone kissed her neck, under one ear, then her jaw. He took long, slow, deep breaths, growling slightly on the outbreath. He traced circles on her inner thigh, then pushed his fingers between her legs, found her entrance and slid his touch inside her, then stopped. "What about—"

She put her hand over his. "I'm fine," she assured him. "I promise. Totally fine. I won't be fine if you stop, though."

"You make it hard to do the right thing," Stone said, stroking her with gentle, probing fingers.

"The right thing is us. The right thing is to be with me, to make me happy. *This* makes me happy." She tilted her head back against his shoulder, turned her face to kiss his jaw. "We'll do all that. We'll have romantic dates and we'll make love by candlelight or moonlight or whatever, wherever. But nothing about us is normal. And I need this with you, right now. Make me feel good."

"Wren...Jesus help me. I can't resist you."

"Don't. If we're together, then why do you have to resist me?" She twisted in his arms. "Everything we went through together...what did it all mean if you're back to trying to stick to some preconceived notion of the right thing, regardless of what I want? Just be with me, take me. Don't make me beg you. Show me you want me as much as I want you."

"God, do I want you." Stone brushed her flyaway, tangled black hair to either side of her face. "I just— you deserve more than rushed, desperate moments. You deserve time and attention and perfection."

Wren slipped out of bed, locked the door, and then stood in front of Stone, staring down at him. "Then give that to me. Nothing else matters to me, right now." She pushed her underwear down and stepped out of them, crawled over the bed and lay down on her back beside him. "Just this matters."

Stone's eyes raked over her, and then she watched as the last vestige of hesitation fled from his features. He rolled to his side, leaning on one elbow, and kissed her lips. Tentatively at first, slow and tasting. Wren pulled at his neck, lifted up to deepen the kiss. She peeled his shirt up over his abs, and he shifted to let her tug it away, and then he dipped in to kiss her once more. Aggression tinged this kiss, finally. She moaned in relief as he began to devour her lips, and his hand scoured her ribs, drifted up over her breasts and nudged her erect nipples with his thumb, one and then the other.

His tongue slid between her lips and touched her teeth, found her tongue.

Now her hands explored, traced the lines of his abdominal muscles, the scars of his still-healing gunshot wounds on his side and thigh. This all felt so familiar, yet not. That one night in the hotel in Manila seemed like a distant dream, with so many nightmares rampaging between that one sweet night and this morning. She found the button of his jeans, and slipped the cold circle of metal through the loop.

The engorged hardness of his manhood spread the zipper apart, and she lowered it the rest of the way, then slid her fingers around the waist of his pants, pushing them down. He lifted hips, and she pushed the denim over his knees, and they used their toes together to shed them the rest of the way, kicking them off the bed from beneath the blankets. Now, only a thin barrier of cotton separated Wren from what she wanted. She made short work of his underwear, and now he was naked with her.

Sunlight streamed through the fourth floor window, showing a blue, cloud-free sky. Warmth suffused Wren as Stone's hand roamed her body, sliding over her hips, down to her knees, over her thighs and up between her legs, which she spread apart for him, welcoming his touch eagerly.

She shrugged the blankets away, letting them fall to their hips, and then pushed them down farther, baring Stone's huge, rigid cock to the air. She marveled at it, then wriggled, remembering how it had felt inside her. She wrapped her hands around him, squeezed gently, then slid her palms up and down his length.

"I love how your hands feel on me. You touching me like that…it makes me crazy. Like I'm drunk on how amazing you make me feel." Stone's voice was pitched low, a rumble in the space between gasps.

Wren didn't know what to say to that. All she knew to do was kiss him and keep touching him, rub her thumb over his tip and spread the moisture that leaked all over him, twist her hand around him as she plunged her fist down. He groaned, and she did it again, this time tasting his moan, devouring the sound of his pleasure with her mouth over his.

He touched her too, gave her pleasure even as he seemed out of his mind with his own ecstasy. Two thick fingers scissored inside her wet warmth, finding her perfect spot and rubbing there, then ascending to circle her clit.

"Kiss me there," she breathed. "I want that again."

Stone slid down her body, hands trailing fire on her skin. He lay on his stomach, his head between her thighs, weight on his elbows, and she felt his lips kiss her inner thigh, then inward. She let her thighs fall apart and gasped as his tongue speared into her. She curled her legs around his shoulders, and he shifted so her knees hung over his shoulders.

"You taste so good," Stone murmured. "Your pussy is so sweet."

She felt herself blush. "Stone...God." She forgot her embarrassment as he did something with his lips, tongue and fingers all at once that had her moaning.

He laughed. "What? It's true." He lifted his head to meet her bliss-heavy eyes. His mouth was slick, glistening with her essence. He licked his lips, grinning as she writhed in embarrassment.

"Really?" She gasped again as he slid his fingers inside her and moved them, rubbing that spot high inside so she couldn't breathe for the ache of building ecstasy. "You really think my...my pussy tastes good?" She'd never called it that before. It didn't sound the same as when he said it. His deep, growling voice gave the word a dirty edge.

Stone took a breath to answer, then just grinned and bent his head to lick up her opening, used the tip of his tongue to circle her clit, slowly at first, then with increasing speed. He matched the speed of his tongue with his fingers, and then, just when she felt the edge approaching, he slowed, and she bucked her hips against him, hearing a tiny, feminine growl of frustration escape her.

Stone laughed at her growl and gave her what she wanted, the speed and intensity that brought her to the cusp of orgasm. When she wavered on the edge but couldn't fall over, she tugged with her legs, pushed his head harder against her. He suckled her clit into his mouth and flattened it with suction, reached up with one hand to pinch her nipple, his other hand working inside her.

She felt it break over her, then, a blinding wave shaking her entire body, clenching her insides in a vise. She twisted her head to bite the pillow, muffling her scream of release. He didn't relent when she came, but continued his frenzied assault on her until she was writhing, unable to take anymore but unable to not take it. Wave after wave hit her, stealing her breath, making her already erect nipples go diamond-hard. Her pussy clenched and clamped and pulsed, and still he devoured her, licked her, fingered her.

Finally, she couldn't take it anymore. "No more..." She pulled him up, taking his erection in her hand. "Your turn, now."

She slid out from beneath him, pushed him to his back and pressed her cheek to his belly, sliding toward his cock. She wrapped her lips around his tip, flicked him with her tongue. "Your cock tastes good," she said. "Maybe I'll just make you come like this."

"I thought we were—"

"We're doing whatever we want. And right now, I want to make you feel as good as you just made me feel." She circled his thickness with her fingers, twisting his base as she sucked the springy, broad head of his cock into her mouth. "Does this feel good?"

Stone laughed, a disbelieving bark. "Good? It feels fucking amazing. But you don't have to—"

"I *want* to."

"Would you let me finish a sentence, woman?" He said it with a laugh.

"I don't need to let you finish a sentence, because I know what you're going to say. And it's stupid. You really think I'd do this if I didn't want to?" She kissed the very tip, then focused on the rhythm of her hand around him, slow, pulsing strokes, shallow at the base, squeezing gently.

"I just want you to know it doesn't have to be equal. Besides, if you make me come like this, we'll have to wait for me to be inside you."

"The more time I spend talking to you, the less time I spend doing this." She took him deeper into her mouth, working him with her tongue and sucking hard.

"Oh God...then don't talk."

She didn't. She squeezed and twisted with her hands, sucked with her mouth, and Stone gasped, groaned, and swore. He began to move his hips into the rhythm of her mouth on him. Slow bobs of her head, taking him into her mouth, then backing away, never taking him very deep, but sucking so hard he groaned. She moved her hands with increasing speed, but kept going slow with her mouth, and Stone's groans grew frantic, needy, breathless, and his hips moved faster and faster.

"Wren..." Stone growled. "Fuck, I'm so close—"
He tangled his fingers in her hair, and then with a muttered curse, hooked his hands under her arms and pulled her up, twisted her onto her back and

was kneeling over her before she could respond. His cock left her mouth with a pop, and she squealed in protest as he manhandled her into place.

He was there, at her entrance, huge and thick and leaking moisture. "I need this." He spoke with clenched teeth, and her palms on his back touched iron-hard muscles.

"I wasn't done with you," Wren muttered. "I wanted to feel you come like that."

"I need this. You need this." He pushed with his hips, and the tip of his cock probed into her damp core.

"Yes…" she gasped. "Please. I do need that." She curled her legs around his hips, lifting her ass off the bed, her arms on his back, her hands clawed against his shoulders.

In, then. Deeper. Wren moaned in bliss as he rocked into her, filling her. Stone growled in his throat, a primal noise of pleasure. She moved with him, rolled her hips so he sunk deeper. Her lips touched his shoulder, and she sucked his skin, tasting his salt, then kissed his throat, his chin, his mouth. The kiss went from zero to sixty in an instant, immediately desperate, frantic, needful. He thrust deep, and matched the thrust with his tongue.

Rhythm together became panting, tangled moans, her arms around his neck, his fist beside her face, one hand caressing her breasts.

Already on the edge from having just come, Wren felt an orgasm stealing over her, creeping up with insatiable speed. She welcomed it, arched her back and ground her pussy against him, searching for the right angle. He seemed to sense her need without having to be told, and adjusted the angle of his hips, moving shallowly, thrusting quickly.

When he did that, she whimpered and felt herself burst apart. "You...now."

She pushed at his shoulder, rolling to one side, keeping him seated deep inside her. He moved with her, and she straddled him, found her balance, her palms on his chest and her weight on her shins and knees. Her hair cascaded around their faces like a black waterfall. Wren held still, letting him fall away from the edge so she could take him there once more. Their eyes met in a moment of stillness and silence.

"I love you, Wren." Stone whispered the words into the dawn glow.

Wren blinked twice, surprised, and then the weight of what he'd just said hit her. She gave a sound that was half-laugh, half-sob of joy. She lifted up and plunged him deep, letting the love she felt for him seep into her gaze. Once more she lifted up so he slipped almost out, and then sank down, her mouth wide and trembling, her eyes shimmering with unshed tears of need and ecstasy and joy and love.

"I love you." She breathed it on a down-thrust. "I love you," she whispered it as she drew him out. "I love you, oh God I love you." She spoke it out loud as she sank down on him and lifted up, setting a rhythm, slow and deep. She felt his stomach muscles tense, and she quickened her rhythm, made her strokes more forceful, deeper. "No. Don't hold it back. Give it to me. God, Stone…I love you so much. Give it to me, give me it all, right now. Come, Stone. Come now, and come hard."

Stone lifted up and took her nipple in her mouth, thrusting in time with her, meeting her down-stroke with lifted hips, rolling inside her and suckling her breasts and moaning as she rode him. He fell back against the bed, took her hips in his hands, his thumbs in the indents, pulling her down onto him and groaning her name. "Wren…Wren…shit, Wren…God, I love you…oh God, I'm—I'm coming…"

Wren leaned back and moved with her hips alone, balanced so he was deep, buried skin to skin, rolling and rolling with aching and tender ferocity, unrelenting desperation. She was there too, a third detonation erupting within her, brought on by the throbbing of his cock inside her, the press of his hands on her hips, the knowledge of love and safety making each breath she took erotic, each thrust pulsing with fervor and the coiling blasting heat of impending release for both of them.

Soul-to-soul, they moved together, loving each other.

She felt Stone come apart beneath her, felt the hot flood of his release inside her. He juddered, pushing into her desperately, eyes open and locked on hers, and she came with him. Time slowed, stopped, froze mid-stream as Wren felt her body shake and tremor and spasm, heat and pressure unfolding inside her and making her brain go blank, ripping tears from her eyes and whimpers from her throat.

Stone seemed possessed, wordless, fraught with emotions of such potency he had no way of expressing them. "Wren. Tell me…again…say it again," he gasped.

Wren saw him, saw into him, felt the same intensity inside herself, and how impossible it was to express such love, such wild and heart-pounding, stomach-lurching emotion.

She rode him, leaning forward now, collapsed on his chest, her mouth against his throat, sliding down against him, milking him with each pulsation of her hips. "I love you, Stone. I love you, George Alexander Pressfield."

"The third," he muttered. "Don't forget that part."

"The third," she agreed, smiling into his mouth as she kissed him.

Stone watched Wren sleep. Black hair wafted across her face, blown by the oscillating fan in the corner of her dorm room. The sheet had slipped down while she slumbered, and was now bunched around her naked hips, leaving her upper torso bare in the near-black of midnight. Moonlight shone through the window, a sliver crescent shedding silver across her tan skin. Her mouth pursed, her eyes scrunched tighter, her fists clenched beside her cheek, and she shook her head, moaning, whimpering, emitting tiny, fearful noises.

"No, no…don't, please!" The terror in her voice ripped a hole in Stone's heart. "No more…please no more…"

He reached over and touched her shoulder, skating his fingertips over her warm skin. He nuzzled her cheek with his lips. "Wren. Wake up, baby. It's a dream. It's not real." Wren shook her head violently, then her eyes flickered open, locking on his. At first, all he saw in her eyes was disorientation and fear. He brushed her cheekbone with his thumb, smiling at her. "You're fine, babe. Just a bad dream."

She closed her eyes and shuddered. "It wasn't… wasn't a dream. It was a memory. I saw…the naked girls, locked in tiny rooms. Never getting out. Never getting away. Never being free. I saw him, saw him in the darkness, coming for me, with the drugs. The needle, it erased me. Made me forget who I was."

Stone gathered her in his arms. "I know." His heart broke for the agony in her voice.

"We have to do something. I can't—I have to help them. I have to do something to stop it. At least try. Raise money, or awareness. Something." She pressed her face to his bare chest, and he felt the warmth of her skin and the wetness of tears. "Stone, we have to do something."

"We will. I promise. We'll do something. We'll get everyone we know in on it."

She nodded, and began to drift once more. Stone held her and watched her sleep, his own nightmares keeping him awake, his mind whirling with ideas.

20

—Six months later—

STONE TUGGED ON THE CUFF OF HIS SLEEVE and took a deep breath. He'd never been comfortable in the full dress uniform, with all the ribbons and medals and all the other official bullshit. It was hot and stuffy and uncomfortable. He preferred BDUs, or shorts and T-shirt. Anything, really, other than the full dress uniform. He'd even take a suit and tie, which he didn't own. But here he was, in full dress, hair freshly cut to regulation length, about to step into a ballroom packed with hundreds of people. It was worth it, though.

Wren had campaigned tirelessly over the last six months, organizing a fundraising dinner to benefit the victims of sexual slavery and human trafficking. She'd pulled in organizations from all over the world, non-profits, charities, political groups from both sides of the aisle. Stone had used his few connections into the political world to get more people involved. Senator Johnson had been the first person to donate money, and he'd also used his enormous amount of political clout to bring attention to Wren's efforts. His daughter Lisa—whom Stone and his men had rescued from Cervantes' operation—was a keynote speaker, along with Wren and several others. There were senators and congressmen, ambassadors from all over the world, lobbyists, mayors, governors, movie stars, sports stars, and a host of ordinary citizens.

Stone had worked alongside her to get this event off the ground, and to make it as visible as possible, but Wren had been the driving force. She'd continued her classes at the university, but her life had become focused on this event, on raising awareness and gathering funds to benefit those who had survived experiences like hers and Lisa's.

It was astonishing what she had accomplished, really. Even before the fundraising dinner, she'd raised tens of thousands of dollars. She was planning on using the money this event raised to establish her own non-profit organization, which would work hand in hand with governments all over the world to crack down on human trafficking and sexual slavery, as well as providing aftercare to survivors.

Now, it was all coming to fruition. Wren was in another room, having her hair and makeup attended to by a team of professionals, a service contributed by a high profile film actress. In just a few minutes, she would enter the ballroom and make her presentation, beginning the dinner event and sharing her story.

Stone was nervous for her, although she claimed to be more excited than nervous.

A knock sounded at the door and Stone spun on his heel. Wren stood in the doorway, clothed in a custom-made gown contributed by some designer Stone had never heard of. When the event was over, the gown would be auctioned. She was also wearing earrings which would be auctioned as well.

Stone couldn't breathe as he stared at her. The gown was sapphirine, made of some kind of silky, slinky material that hugged her every curve. The neckline was high, circling the base of her throat, but the back was open to just above her waist, and the hemline brushed the floor. She held a clutch purse in both hands and her ears sparkled with teardrop sapphire earrings.

Wren ducked her head. "Say something. Do I look okay?"

Stone took three long steps to cross the room. "I—I'm speechless. You're so beautiful I don't even know what to say."

She grinned, tilting her head up to meet his eyes. "I feel...silly. I don't know. I've never worn anything like this."

Stone took her hand in his and kissed her knuckles. "I know what you're saying. I hate wearing this uniform too. But you honestly look stunning. That's not even a good enough word." He pulled her flush against him. "You're beyond beautiful. Just... breathtaking."

"Really?" She took a deep breath, and Stone couldn't keep his eyes from the swell of her breasts stretching the material of her dress.

"Really." He grinned. "If we weren't supposed to be out there in a few minutes, I'd lock this door and show you how beautiful you are."

Wren grinned wickedly. "We have time, don't we?"

Stone was instantly hard. "Don't tempt me. There's no way I can do what I want to you without effing up your hair and makeup."

Wren's mouth twisted into a dissatisfied moue. "I hate that you're right. You look delicious in that uniform. Keeping my hands to myself tonight will be difficult."

"Ain't that the truth." Stone lifting her face to his, touched his lips to hers. "Now, let's go raise some money."

Wren nodded and took his hand, threading their fingers together. They strode through a pair of double doors and out into the ballroom. As they entered, the gathered crowd took notice and parted, clapping as Wren and Stone made their way to the dais at one end of the ballroom.

Wren took her place behind a podium, adjusted the microphone, and smiled at the crowd. Stone stood behind her and to the left, automatically assuming the "at ease" stance.

"Hi everybody," Wren began. "I'm Wren Morgan. Six months ago, I was kidnapped by a sex slaver. His name was Cervantes. He wore green flip-flops. He had rotten teeth and a scar on his face. He clapped his hand over my mouth and dragged me into the back of van, shoved a needle full of heroin into my arm, and drove away with me. It was broad daylight, half a block from my hotel. He—Cervantes—locked me in a hole in the ground that was pitch black. Bugs and rats crawled all over me. Bit me. He fed me food with worms in it. He brought men down into the hole and showed me off like I was a cow at market. They touched me, ripped my clothes off…

"Cervantes wouldn't let them rape me, though. He wanted me…intact, I think. So he could get a better price. He beat me. Hit me. Kicked me. Shot me full of heroin several times a day so I wouldn't try to escape. When I was high, I couldn't remember who I was, or where I was, or why I was alone. All I knew was that I was alone in the darkness, with insects crawling on me."

Wren paused, her voice shaking. She closed her eyes and gathered herself. The room was silent.

"They brought me to a hotel room. Somewhere far away from where they kept me. Men stood around in the room, haggling over me. I was being sold. I was being bartered away to a man who would use my body for sex, to make a profit off of me. I saw…I saw girls no more than ten, twelve, sixteen years old, naked and bruised and beaten, half-starved, being forced to perform sexual acts. Sometimes at gun or knife-point. Their eyes, those girls…they knew they'd never be free again. They knew they would be forced to…to be *fucked*…like animals, worse than animals—all day, every day, until they died. Excuse my language, but there's just no other word for it. For what those girls endured. There was no one to save them. No one cared. Some of them had been sold into that by their own parents. Others were kidnapped like me. Stolen. Lied to. Coerced. There were so many of them. Not just local Filipina girls either. Americans like me. Germans. French, Italian. Girls on vacation, kidnapped. I was lucky." She blinked hard and glanced adoringly back at Stone, then returned her gaze to the rapt audience. "So, so lucky. I was never forced to have to sex. Because I—I had—I was rescued. By a courageous, selfless man named Lieutenant Stone Pressfield. When I went missing, he came after me. He...he shed blood to save me. By himself, he got me out and brought me home.

"Thousands...*millions* of other girls all over the world aren't anywhere near so fortunate. So blessed." She paused again, gathering her thoughts, then continued. "This isn't just in Manila. It's not just Thailand and Taiwan and Russia. It's *here*. In America. As I arranged this event, sought out donors and contributors and speakers, I met so many girls, and some boys too, who grew up just like me, going to school and church and playing kickball, average suburban American kids, who through one way or another, ended up sex slaves. No one talks about it. You hear about cyber-bullying, and suicide. You hear about hashtags and YOLO and Facebook and Twitter and hipsters and who got a boob job and who's breaking up with whom...you hear about all that. There have been gay rights marches and elections and political campaigns...and there's nothing inherently wrong with any of that. Some of that is important, things we *should* be talking about. But it's time someone spoke up about *this*.

"Slavery didn't end when Lincoln issued the Emancipation Proclamation. Slavery still happens. Right now, today, this very second, there's someone in chains, locked away until the next time someone pays to have involuntary sex with them. They're drugged, starving, naked, and alone. No one is going to rescue them. This event, as incredible as it is, as many people are here donating their time and their money and their talent, isn't even a drop in the bucket. It doesn't even begin to touch the problem. But it's a start."

She closed her eyes, blinking away tears, swiping under her eyes with a finger. "There's someone else here that's going to tell you her story." Wren stepped away, turned to take the arm of thin, fragile-looking blond girl with frightened eyes.

Lisa stepped up to the podium, visibly terrified and shaking. She had a piece of paper crumpled in her fist, and she unfolded it, smoothed it against the podium and read from it without looking out at the audience. "My name is Lisa Johnson. I grew up privileged. My father was a politician, a successful and important senator. I lived in a big house, drove a nice car, went on fancy vacations. I went skiing in the Alps, had dinner beneath the Eiffel Tower, and drank wine in Tuscany. When I finished my second year of college, I spent the summer backpacking around Europe and Asia. We went to Germany and France and the UK, Italy, Greece, Egypt, Spain, Thailand. And the Philippines. Manila. And just like Wren, I was kidnapped in broad daylight. I never even saw them. I was jerked from behind into an alley. A cloth bag was put over my head and a needle poked into my arm. When I woke up, I was in a locked room with no window. I was naked. I hurt, all over. I'd been…raped…while I was unconscious. Hours and hours went by, without a sound, without light or water or food. And then the door opened, and a man came in. He left the door open, and another man came in. The second man unbuckled his belt, took it off. He hit me across the face with it. I cried and screamed and begged him to stop, but he didn't. When I was too hurt to move, he raped me. And then another man came in, and he raped me too. This…this went on so long I stopped counting how many times I was raped. They left me there, bleeding. I passed out, and when I woke there was a bowl of water and a bowl of dog food on the ground. Actual dog food. I was so hungry that I—I ate it.

"Some version of this happened every day. Really, there wasn't day or night. Just…the time between." Lisa paused to compose herself, and it took visible effort. "I have no way of knowing from my own personal experience how long I was in that room, but my family says I was missing for four months. No contraceptive was ever used. I got pregnant, and it was…rip-ripped from me. With a coat hanger. There in the room, just…dug out of me. I was raped again within hours. No one cared how loud I screamed.

"I'll never be able to look at a man again, not the same way. I'm terrified of…of everything. I still sleep on the floor sometimes. I go to sleep in my bed, and wake up on the floor, in the corner, crying."

She broke, then, crumpled. Wren caught her and helped her from the stage. Lisa's father, Senator Johnson, took the podium, his face grave.

"What happened to my daughter…it can happen to anyone. It *does* happen, all the time. It's probably happening to someone right now. I've helmed a lot of projects in my career. I've served on numerous committees and oversight panels. I've campaigned based on any number of social and economic and political issues. I still stand by all those things. But this? This is personal. This isn't about my career as a senator. I'm not using this to get votes, or to get into the Oval Office. This is purely about stopping this evil from occurring any longer. It's about making sure that what happened to…to Lisa—" his voice broke, and he paused for a long minute, breathing hard and blinking, before he could continue, "—that what happened to Lisa doesn't happen to anyone else. It's about helping those who have been through it and survived. Lisa was hospitalized for two months when we got her back. She went through dozens of rounds of surgeries to repair the damage done inside her. She'll never have children. And psychologically? I can't touch her. She freaks out if I try to hug her.

My own—my own daughter, and I can't even comfort her when she's upset. It's been more than two years, and she's been in therapy twice a week ever since. The medical bills from all this are staggering. For someone less economically secure than I, the bills would be ruinous.

"To this end, I'm proud to announce the formation of the International Abolition Coalition. This is a multi-government cooperative. It spans forty countries all around the world, with more signing on every day. It encompasses police forces and national military forces, investigative agencies, aid relief organizations, the Red Cross, hospitals, half-way-houses, insurance agencies…the list goes on. The singular goal of the IAC is to halt human trafficking in its steps, to prosecute on an international level anyone found engaging in this vile practice, and to provide free, professional aid to victims of trafficking and sexual slavery.

"Miss Wren Morgan was absolutely instrumental in getting this Coalition off the ground. Her passion, her willingness to use her story, her personal engagement and tireless working has made this possible. She's been one of the few people outside of my wife Annette and I that Lisa has opened up to.

"And as for Lieutenant Pressfield? I've already thanked him in person. He received a Silver Star for his part in rescuing my daughter, which he and his men accomplished at great personal cost. Four men died saving her. But a mere thank you, even a military medal…it's not anywhere near enough." Senator Johnson met Stone's eyes, and the message Stone saw there was clear.

After a moment, the senator continued. "Ladies, gentlemen. Don't just write a check and go about your lives. This affects us all. I know for a fact that there is a person in this room whose teenaged daughter is a victim of domestic human trafficking. This person…I won't name them or provide any identifying information, but…this person's daughter suffered from depression. She turned to drugs, and through a tragic concatenation of events, she ended up on the streets of Los Angeles, homeless and addicted to heroin, starving to death. She was forced into sexual slavery in return for food and drugs. This was in suburban *Los Angeles, people*. LA. Not Thailand or the Philippines. She was arrested for solicitation by the LAPD, and her story came out. She was returned to her home, to her parents, and now she's living in a halfway house in Delaware, with seven others like her. This is our nation, ladies and gentlemen. It's the country we've fought and died for. We're supposed to stand for freedom and opportunity. But things like this are happening, just down the street from where we stand. People you know, their kids, their friends.

"Don't ignore this. Don't bury your heads and go back to your lives and your iPhones and Facebook updates. Make a difference. Every dollar donated, every second spent volunteering at any one of the IAC shelters that will be opening all across the nation in the coming months...it all helps."

Senator Johnson stepped away, and the gathered crowd clapped and cheered. They quieted when Wren re-took the stage.

"Next up is a young woman named Irena Bulova. She's originally from Russia, but she came to the US five years ago to pursue her dream of becoming a dancer. She was forced into prostitution, and only recently escaped. It's her story to tell, and I'll let her tell it, her way."

Irena was a beautiful, petite woman of twenty-five or so with brown hair hanging in thick dreadlocks to her mid-back, a ring through the center of her lower lip and thin white scars criss-crossing her wrists and forearms. Two men took the podium away and another set a microphone and stand in front of a chair. Irene sat down in the chair, settled a battered, shiny black guitar on her crossed legs, and set about strumming and adjusting the tuning of her guitar.

"Hello. I met Wren three months ago, on the street of Washington D.C." Irena had a soft voice touched by a Russian accent. "She seemed to see something in me, a thing she recognized, perhaps. It is in our eyes, what we have been through. She got me to tell her my story, and she convinced me to come here, and do this thing." Irena breathed deeply, and then began strumming her guitar in a simple rhythm. "Out of hunger and desperation, I was made to be a prostitute. I nearly starved to my death before this happened, and from desperation and fear I continued to sell myself, not for money or for drugs, but for bread, and water. Often, this was moldy bread and dirty water. And I had to do much, turn many johns to get it. Only through the kindness of a police officer named Daniel Harris was I able to escape this and learn to become something else. During my time as a prostitute, my knee was broken. It was so that I could not run away. It was done on purpose. I will never dance, now. But I have fingers to play this guitar, which Daniel taught me to play. And I have a voice, with which I can sing."

She picked a melody on the higher strings, eyes closed, and sang.

"Only one breath, and then another,
Only one day, and then the another.
I cannot hope, I can only breathe.
I am here, and I cannot leave.
The streets are empty in the dawn, and cold.
Buildings around me are gray, and old.

A sparrow hops from square to square just beyond me,
Brown and small, and free.
My arms have scars,
My window has bars,
A knife to free me made the scars,
A man who owns me made the bars.
The sparrow flies away, and I return.
Someone is waiting for me, watching,
And inside I burn.
My soul is dying, weeping without stopping.
And then one day, in the cold and swirling snow,
I meet a man, with a heart that is kind, and eyes that glow.
He heard me, listened to the pleading in my silent eyes.
Ignored the 'I am fine' lies.
Now, my window has no bars,
But always will I have the scars."

Irena let the last note hang, quavering. She glanced off to the side, and a man in a policeman's dress uniform watched her, his loving expression telling as much of a story as her song. Irena bowed over her guitar as the crowd cheered. She strummed her guitar once more, and then began playing again, but Stone's attention was drawn away by the sight of Wren, hand clapped over her mouth, fleeing the room.

Stone followed, and found her in a darkened office, sitting in a visitor's chair, slumped over and weeping. He knelt in front of her, and she leaned forward, wrapping her arms around his neck. He didn't need to say anything as he held her.

"I'm fine for days, weeks," she said. "I don't have nightmares as much anymore, or flashbacks. And then, suddenly, it all hits me, out of nowhere. That song. Lisa's story. I was fine through it all. But then the way Irena looked at Daniel. It made me remember us, in Manila, and right afterward. How you saved me. And I just...I lost it."

Stone kissed the top of her head. "You did something amazing today, sweetheart."

"Not just today. This is what I'm going to do with my life. I didn't know before. I was just going to college, figuring I'd end up doing...whatever. Teaching, maybe. That was the idea, I guess. I don't really even remember a lot about who I was before, what I liked, what I wanted. This...organizing these events, getting people to tell their stories. Helping people who have been through what I went through, and so much worse...it's who I am now."

Stone nodded, then took a deep breath. "I spoke to Senator Johnson the other day. In all the craziness of getting ready for this event, I forgot to tell you. He came to me with an idea. It's kind of...risky, but I think it's worth it. Part of what Alan wants to do with the Coalition is get a taskforce going. A quasi-military group that goes in and shuts down people like Cervantes. He has several countries on board to help us, or at least look the other way when we go in and use any necessary force to shut them down. We'd be sanctioned by the US government, and Johnson wants me to lead it."

Wren sat up, snatched a tissue from a box on the desk and dabbed her eyes with it. "So you'd be a soldier again?"

Stone shrugged. "Sort of. Not an official soldier, but I'd be doing what I did when I rescued you, except targeted and planned missions with current intel and backup, and proper gear."

"Are you going to do it?"

He nodded. "I think so. It's what I'm best at. I'm at loose ends in the civilian world." He took her hand. "I'd have armor protecting me, and guys as good as or better than me as my team."

Wren stood up, and Stone followed her to his feet, wrapping his arms around her waist. "I'll be afraid for you," she said, gazing up at him. "I'll worry every moment you're gone. I'm not sure how well I'll deal with it, honestly."

"I know. But here's the other part. Johnson thinks there needs to be a female face waiting for them when we get them to safety, someone who knows how to talk to them. They'll be traumatized, and they won't trust men. Johnson is working on getting together a group of doctors and nurses, all women, to be the first-contact medical team. He wants you as the liaison."

Wren just smiled and nodded, curling her arms around Stone's neck. "I think that's brilliant. We'd be together, that way too."

"Always."

She kissed him, her lips soft and warm. "Now, I've been gone too long. We should go back out. I'll have to have Alyssa fix my makeup."

Stone pulled back to examine her face. "Yeah, you've got some smears under your eyes."

Wren frowned and smacked his shoulder. "You're not supposed to tell me that, dummy. You're supposed to tell me I look fine, so I can roll my eyes at how men don't know anything about makeup." Stone just snorted and nuzzled a kiss to her throat, which prompted a soft whimper from her. She pulled away, pushing him out the door in front of her. "Don't get me started, George."

Stone growled. "Don't call me George, dammit."

Wren just laughed and tangled her fingers with his as they made their way back toward the ballroom. Stone watched as Wren waved her makeup artist over, and he waited outside the bathroom while she had her makeup tended to. He fingered the small box in his pocket, worrying at the velvet with his thumb. He had a plan, a buddy from the SEALs and his girlfriend preparing a little private dinner on the roof of an apartment building, with a view of the capitol building lit up in the darkness. There would be roses, and champagne, and a proposal. And, hopefully, a tearful yes.

THE END

EPILOGUE
—*Six months later*—

THE GIRL SHUDDERED IN THE DARKNESS. She heard the footsteps approaching, and knew what it meant. She cowered in the farthest corner, scrunching down to make herself as small as possible.

Then, something unusual happened. There were loud bangs, explosions, rapid gunfire. She didn't know what it meant, but she knew it scared her. The footsteps stopped, went the other way, and the girl sobbed in relief, grateful that she'd been given a reprieve, no matter how brief.

It was only a moment, it turned out. Loud boot-steps clomped beyond the door. A voice growling in a language the girl didn't understand, a response in the same language. Then a deafening crash, and the door burst open, splintering, kicked apart by a huge black-booted foot.

The girl screamed, huddled in her corner and covered her naked, frail body with her arms.

No blows came. No hands forced her to the ground. She peered between her shaking arms, eyes wide, wet. A man knelt in front of her, clad head-to-toe in black body armor. He had an assault rifle in his hands, the barrel pointed down. His face was painted, and he had goggles of some kind on his face. He pushed the goggles up, revealing his eyes. Light spilled from the open door, and the girl could see that his eyes were brown, and kind.

He said something, waved at her, pointed to the door. She glanced at the open doorway, the splintered wood. She knew what would happen if she left. She'd tried, and bore the scars of her punishment. She shook her head and huddled deeper. The man seemed to understand her fear. He shouted something to someone she couldn't see, someone outside her room. There was a scraping noise, like something being dragged. The light was obscured, and a man entered walking backward, dragging something heavy. He dropped whatever it was, and the girl stared in awe and horror.

It was *him*. Dead. Eyes wide, staring, a hole in the center of his head.

She looked up at the man, then back at her dead captor. Hope flooded through her.

Someone else came, another man in body armor, and he handed her a thick, soft blanket, wrapped it around her shoulders without touching her. The girl hesitantly stood up, circling far around the corpse of her tormenter, watching him, making sure he didn't rise up and hit her, force himself on her. He stayed dead, and then she was out in the light, the humid heat. It wasn't light, really. It was nighttime, but she'd spent so long locked in that windowless room that even the relative darkness of city at night was bright.

The girl found herself in the back of a van with more than twenty other girls just like her, all of them wrapped in identical blankets, dark blue wool with a white insignia stamped on it. The girl's English was poor, but she could read it better than she could speak it. *International Abolition Coalition*, it read, the words printed in a circle, with a globe in the center ringed by stylized doves, their wings interlocking.

The door of the van closed, but there was light, and tinted windows to the outside. The van rumbled away, turning and stopping and starting. Lights flashed, circling blue police car lights, following the van, which entered an underground garage. The van doors were opened, and a woman stood in front them, dressed simply in a fitted, floor length yellow dress. Her hair was black, tied back in a ponytail. She was short, curvy, and her belly was rounded slightly with new pregnancy.

She held her hand to the girl, and said in halting Thai, "Hello. My name is Wren. You're free now. No one will hurt you, or touch you unless you let them. Will you come with me?"

The girl watched the woman's eyes, saw genuine compassion, and something else. Understanding. The girl took the outstretched hand and stepped down, keeping the blue blanket wrapped tight around her body. The woman repeated her message to each girl as they stepped out of the van. The concrete was cold on bare feet, and the air smelled of old diesel exhaust, but it was welcome change from where they'd been.

The girls were led into an open room. There were benches, and chairs, paintings on the wall, abstracts and landscapes. The light was soft and yellow, coming from lamps in corners. The girls all sat down, and other women passed out bottles of water, little packets of food.

One wall had a window, showing a doctor's table. Another woman appeared, this one wearing the white coat of a doctor. She was tall and blond, and had kind blue eyes. She spoke in Thai that was so halting as to be nearly incomprehensible: "You coming with me? I look you, make better. Only me."

Over the next few days, the girl, and the others like her, were checked out by doctors, fed, clothed, and asked a million questions by authorities. No one in the entire building was male, however. Even the guards at the doors were women. A Thai woman explained to the girl that she could stay in this shelter for as long as she wanted, and people would help her learn to reenter society beyond the shelter, if she wanted. She would be given the opportunity to learn new skills, if she wanted. She could learn English. She could stay and help others, others who had been through the same thing as the girl had experienced.

So the girl stayed. She learned to go out into the city, always with another person, and though she was afraid, she eventually learned that not everyone would hurt her. Men frightened her, but no one touched her. The girl was there when another van came, another van full of girls like herself, naked and terrified and abused. The girl spoke their language, and knew what they'd been through, and she helped them, like others had helped her.

A Note From the Author

FIRST, A FEW FACTS ON HUMAN TRAFFICKING, according to abolitioninternational.org: over 21 million people are enslaved around the world, which means there are more slaves today than at any other point in history. Just to put that into perspective, during the entire slave trade of Colonial and post-Revolution America, historians claim a total of 12 million people were transported from Africa to America; this covers a time span of almost a century. Sex trafficking is estimated to gross $35 billion dollars annually, and American tourists comprise over 25% of the global sex trade. The average age of girls trafficked into prostitution *in the United States* is 12-14 years old. It's estimated that over 100,00 children have been forced into the sex trade in United

States; and 1 in 3 runaways is approached by a sex trafficker within 48 hours of being on the street.

A portion of the proceeds from the sale of this book will be donated to charities that fight sex trafficking.

The story I've told here is based in reality. What happened to Lisa and Wren has happened far too often. I've taken some liberties and artistic license, since I'm a writer telling a story, but the essence is true. The biggest liberty I took is inventing the idea of interconnected shanties out of which Cervantes ran his operation. I've never heard of this happening, nor do I know for sure whether it's even possible, but it seemed to work out in my head, so I used it.

But the way Wren was kidnapped, that was real, based on many different stories I came across while researching. The forced drugs, being locked in dark rooms and raped unendingly, like Lisa Johnson… that's real. Sexual slavery exists. Human trafficking exists. It happens in every country in the world.

Irena Bulova's story is real too, as is the story told by Senator Johnson about the depressed teenager who ends up addicted to heroin and forced into sexual slavery in LA. Horrors like theirs really happen; I didn't invent that. It happens in your city. In your town. To girls and boys, men and women.

The International Abolition Coalition, unfortunately, is fictional. I wish it were real.

There are real organizations, however, that are dedicated to fighting trafficking. Manila is cracking down on trafficking, using task forces to hunt down the slavers and prosecute them. There are charitable organizations dedicated to helping victims of trafficking. You can help, you can get involved, donate your time and money.

Do something selfless. Leave the world a better place than when you entered it.

Be the difference.

JACK WILDER

JACK WILDER—aka Mr. Wilder—is one half of the writing team "The Wilders." You might know his wife, Jasinda Wilder, as the author of bestselling books such as *Falling Into You*, *Falling Into Us*, *Stripped*, and *Wounded*, among many others. *The Missionary* is Jack's first solo work, but you can bet it won't be the last. The Wilders live in the suburbs outside of Detroit, Michigan, with their five kids, a dog that vaguely resembles a coyote, and a manny.

You'll often find Jack drinking beer and eating Cheez-Its.

Coming Soon From Bestselling Author
(and my wife)
Jasinda Wilder

—THE EVER TRILOGY—

Read on for a teaser from
Forever & Always

Dear Ever,

It's hard to write this letter. I'm not sure what to even say, but I feel like I can tell you things, because we're friends, and somehow these letters are almost like a journal. I know you read them, and I read yours.

My mom has cancer. I just found out today. Breast cancer. I guess she's had it for about two months and they never told me. They wanted to wait and see if the chemotherapy would help before telling me, or something. I don't know. But I guess it's not helping, and they don't think anything will.

My dad told me. He used the same kinds of words I'm guessing the doctors used with him, big words, medical terms. All it means, once you cut through all the bullshit, is that Mom is going to die.

Shit. Seeing that in writing is so much different than thinking it.

What do I do?

She's afraid, and my dad is afraid. I'm afraid. But we're not talking about it. They talk about keeping up spirits and thinking positive and fighting to the end, and all that moral-raising shit. They don't believe it. I don't. No one does.

How can you, when each day passes and I can see her getting skinny, like the skeleton inside her is coming out through her skin? Am I supposed to tell myself it'll be okay, when it won't?

Shit. I'm not a very good pen-pal, I guess. I shouldn't be telling you this stuff. It's depressing.

I'm not even going to bother writing anymore. You don't have to write back, if you don't want to.

I hope you're okay.

Sincerely,

Your friend,

Caden

Dear Caden,

Of course I'd write you back. I'll always write you back. This is what pen pals are for, after all, right? I'm okay. I learned a lot at the arts camp, and I'm using it all in my photography. Maybe next letter I send you I'll include a print of one of my photos. Daddy is thinking of making me a darkroom in the basement, so I can do my own developing.

I guess I'm not sure how to talk about your news about your mom. I'm so sorry that's happening. I know "I'm sorry" or "that sucks" doesn't really help, but I don't know what else to write. I wouldn't try to tell you it'll be okay. When someone you love is hurt, or dying, or dies, it's not okay. I know how you feel. I lost my mom too. She was in a car accident. I think we talked about this at camp. I told you, and I don't tell many people. But I feel like I can trust you. Maybe we understand each other, or something. Like, in some kind of way that words don't really explain. I feel that way. And I know what you mean about these pen-pal letters being like a journal. I write them and send them knowing you're going to read them, but I never feel embarrassed to write things that I wouldn't tell anyone else.

So I'll tell you this: write me as much as you want. I'll write you back every time. I promise. I'm your friend.

I'm sorry you're going through this. No one should have to go through it, but you are, and you have a friend in me. You can talk to me about what you feel.

Be strong, Caden.

Your friend for always,

Ever

I read Ever's letter ten times before I finally folded it back up, slid it carefully into the envelope, and tucked the envelope—which smelled ever so slightly of perfume, like her—in the front of the shoe box which contained the others from her. There were twelve letters so far, one for every week that had passed since the end of the Interlochen summer arts camp. I picked up the lid to the box, which had once contained the very shoes I was wearing, a pair of Reebok cross-trainers. They were a year old, now, and getting too small. I wasn't sure why I had kept the box, but I had. It sat in the bottom of my closet, buried on the left side beneath an old hoodie and a ripped pair of jeans, until I had gotten the first letter from Ever Eliot and needed somewhere safe and private to keep the letter.

Now, the blue box with the red Union Jack flag had twelve letters in it, and it sat under my bed.

I slid the box back under the frame of my bed and moved to my desk. Even though I had a laptop and there was a printer in the living room, I still wrote the letters by hand. I took a long time for each letter, because my handwriting is almost illegibly sloppy most of the time.

I stared down at the spiral-bound notebook for a long, long time, the pencil in my fingers, unable to summon the words. I blinked, took a deep breath, clicked the top of the mechanical pencil and started writing.

Ever,

It feels stupid to write "dear" all the time. So I'll leave that part off, I guess, unless I think of something else to put there.

I'm writing, but I'm not really sure how long this letter will be. Mom is in the hospital full-time now. She stopped the chemo, said no to surgeries. I guess they said they could do a surgery and it had a 20% chance of working, and it was really dangerous. She said no. They already removed her breasts. She has no hair. She's like a stick covered in paper, now. She's my mom, in her eyes, but she's not. I don't know how to put it.

Ever, I'm scared. I'm afraid of losing her, yeah, but I'm afraid for my dad. He's losing his mind. I don't mean that in an exaggeration. I mean it for real. He doesn't leave her side, not even to eat. No can, or even tries to make him leave.

Will it make me sound selfish if I say I'm afraid of losing him too? It's like as sick as Mom gets, he's there with her. Going with her. But I'm only 15, and

I need my parents. I know Mom is going to die, but does Dad have to go too? He loves her so much, but what about me?

I hate how whiny that sounds.

Please send me one of your pictures.

Your always friend,

Caden.

P.S. I tried something besides "sincerely" because that sounds stupid too. But I'm not sure if what I put is more stupid.

P.S.S. Is there a difference between saying "photo" and "picture"?

I thought about signing it again, but didn't. Before I could chicken out, I folded the letter carefully and put into an envelope, stuck a stamp to it, and put it in the mailbox. I was home, and Dad was at the hospital. He always made me come home and do my homework before coming to the hospital. Something about "normalcy."

Like any such thing existed anymore.